Dracula's Match

Dracula's Match

by

Amaya Tenshi

www.penmorepress.com

Dracula's Match by Amaya Tenshi
Copyright 2023© Amanda Thoss
Published by Penmore Press LLC

All rights reserved. No part of this book may be used or reproduced by any means without the written permission of the publisher except in the case of brief quotation embodied in critical articles and reviews.

This is a work of fiction. The characters and events in this book are fictitious and any resemblance to persons living or dead is purely coincidental, with the exception of historical personages as described in the Author's Note.

ISBN-13:978-1-957851-14-3 (Paperback)
ISBN-13:978-1-957851-13-6 (e-book)

BISAC Subject Headings:
FIC009060 FICTION / Fantasy / Urban
FIC010000 FICTION / Fairy Tales, Folk Tales, Legends & Mythology
FIC051000 FICTION / Cultural Heritage

Fremont Troll Image used with artist's permission: Steve Badanes

Edited by Chris Wozney
Cover Art by Neutronboar

Address all correspondence to:

Dracula's Match

Penmore Press LLC
920 N Javelina Pl
Tucson AZ 85748 USA

Dedication

With thanks to my family and many friends for their constant support and encouragement. To Ileana and Mike in particular for their help. I would also like to thank the Oro Valley Police Department for answering my ridiculous questions about ridiculous situations involving cops and supernatural creatures, as that will matter more as the series progresses.

Dracula's Match

PROLOGUE

One October day at noon, in the year 1451, two young men arrived at Hunedoara Castle in Transylvania. They announced their business and were led inside for a private meeting with the Royal Governor and decorated crusader, John Hunyadi.

Once they stood before him, Royal Governor Hunyadi carefully considered the two refugees who had come to him seeking aid. The two young men had traveled from Moldavia, on foot it seemed, for their garments were muddy and the worse for wear. He could only be dubious. Both young men were heirs to thrones of neighboring countries; as such they were potential allies, or potential threats.

The elder was the "Son of the Dragon"; unusually gaunt in the face, but with a frame of body that could be physically imposing, when he wasn't three-fourths starved, as he was now. If anyone was likely to become an enemy, it was this man.

The younger was Ștefan, golden-haired son of Bogdan, the recently assassinated ruler of Moldavia. Hunyadi had been on friendly relations with Bogdan. Not so with "the Dragon"—Dracul. On the contrary, Dracul had died in battle

Dracula's Match

when Hunyadi had fought to depose him, after the humiliation of the Varna Crusade and its aftermath. Ştefan's family had taken in young Drăculea—after Hunyadi had driven him off the throne of Wallachia three years ago and appointed Vladislav II as *voivode* to rule the land. Until now, he had not known what had become of the Son of the Dragon.

Now that Bogdan had been assassinated, the two had come to him. Without a powerful ally, neither of them could hope to regain their thrones; they would be doomed to live in perpetual exile while the rulers of surrounding countries placed puppets on those thrones. Short-lived puppets. *Voivodes* did not usually reign for long. Even so, there was never a shortage of ambitious candidates willing to make a bid for those precarious seats. Men always wanted a chance at a throne, no matter how perilous. Hunyadi had made use of such men himself in recent history, once to oppose Dracul, and again to oust his son Mircea while Dracul was a prisoner of the Turks.

That Bogdan's son would come to Hunyadi was not so peculiar. Poland's king would have been a powerful ally, except that young Ştefan had fought against him the year prior. What Hunyadi could not understand was why Drăculea would be here.

He addressed Drăculea directly.

"Boy, before we continue, I must be clear. It confounds me that you would appear on my doorstep, as if you were unaware of the conflicts between myself and your father and brother Mircea."

"Yes, your Excellency," replied the young man, "I am aware."

Amaya Tenshi

Hunyadi did not care for the response, nor how it was phrased. No emotion; no anger, no pride, no love, no wound.

"You know that I deposed your family, nine years ago."

"How could I forget, your Excellency? As a result, my brother Radu and I were made prisoners of the Turks."

The Ottomans could be ruthless to their political prisoners, Hunyadi knew. How had young Drăculea's childhood unfolded in their custody? Eventually, the Turks had released him from captivity, keeping his younger brother as a hostage. Not only had they let Drăculea go, they had supplied him with support. Drăculea had promptly took advantage of the confusion of Hunyadi's Kosovo campaign to retake the throne from Hunyadi's voivode.

"Your father opposed my plans for the Varna Crusade. He undermined my authority. You know the result. The King of Poland defied me, and his disobedience lost us the campaign. Surely you heard of all this."

What had actually happened was that the Dragon had tried to dissuade Hunyadi from starting a war, warning him that the Sultan went out hunting for sport with a larger retinue than the army Hunyadi fielded. The Dragon had also argued against a winter campaign, urging Hunyadi to at least wait for the spring thaw. His counsel had been ignored. But Drăculea was in no position to correct his host. "Your Excellency. I was in Turkey, not in Ethiopia. Of course I heard."

Hunyadi did not care for that little barb, either. Less, in fact, than the earlier, unreadable tone. Far less.

"Your brother Mircea blamed me for the Polish king's foolishness. He and your father tried to kill me."

Dracula's Match

"I am aware. You were demoted as well, so I understand. Thanks be to God that you were ultimately restored to your position."

Hunyadi eyed the young man coldly. He received a cool, even stare in return.

"And you are aware that your father died in battle against Vladislav II, whom I supported?"

Young Drăculea nodded.

"That your brother, Mircea, also perished in that fight? With his eyes put out?"

"He was buried alive after being blinded, to be exact," Drăculea pointed out. "And then your chosen contender deposed me from the throne of Wallachia, three years ago in 1448. Yes. All this I know."

"Do you see then, boy, why I am... perplexed that you came to ask me for help regaining the throne I myself deprived you of? You, the son of a man whose loyalty to Christendom weakened under Ottoman persuasions? You, the brother of a man who tried to have me killed? You, who relied upon *Ottoman aid* to seize that throne once already? How, then, am I supposed to trust you?"

The Son of the Dragon met his gaze and, without blinking, answered, "Because I could have fled to the Sultan and the Sublime Porte to offer myself as an instrument of the Ottomans. Instead, I chose to traverse dangerous territory to seek your support. Your *Christian* support."

That was as clear an answer as could be given, and not something Hunyadi could argue. But young Drăculea was asking the man who had arranged the violent deaths of nearly all of what remained of his family. Was he expected to believe that the Son of the Dragon had no intention of avenging his family? What sort of ally would a man make who was willing to tolerate such violence against his own blood? Moreover, what of his younger brother, Radu, still a prisoner in Turkish hands? Was the son of the Dragon implying that he would abandon his brother to the Ottomans?

If what he had answered was true, then clearly Drăculea viewed the Ottomans as a greater enemy even than one who had fought against his own blood.

An idealist, Hunyadi mused. He was not at all convinced an idealist would make a good ally, yet there was something promising there. *Voivodes* of Wallachia had traditionally played the two superpowers on either side of their country, allying with one or the other as suited their needs. Even the man Hunyadi had installed on that throne had begun to play that game, to his great annoyance. The young Drăculea might not do so. Hunyadi touched his mustache, pondering risks.

No, not possible, he decided at last. An idealist on a throne was a liability, not an asset, and he could not afford to trust anyone in this young man's position. Not while he had his eyes on other prizes.

"It seems you are not aware of the peace treaty I recently signed with the Turks. Should His Majesty, Vladislav II of the Dănești, die, neither we nor they shall interfere with the Wallachian throne. The boyars themselves shall decide who shall reign. So no, I will not support your claim. I'll give you the time you need to depart," Hunyadi said, "but I shall write to all the counselors of Brașov with the warrant for your arrest. If you should show your face or seek help, they are to arrest you. I suggest you make good time to travel elsewhere."

Dracula's Match

Bogdan's son was visibly appalled by this answer. The Dragon's son took a moment to consider this refusal. *Try me*, Hunyadi thought. *Do something stupid.*

He did not. He turned to his cousin Stefan and spoke softly to him. Then he faced Hunyadi, paid some stiff respects, and let himself be escorted out.

*Now reveal where your loyalties **truly** lie*, Hunyadi thought. The odds were remote, but if this young man proved resourceful, and was willing to support Christendom against the warring Ottomans, perhaps one day he would be a useful ally. But for now, Hunyadi could not take the risk.

As Vlad crossed the bridge from Hunedoara Castle to head back into the city, his cousin came hurrying after him.

"I'll speak to Hunyadi on your behalf," Ștefan promised.

Vlad considered the offer. He'd done what he could, but there was too much bad blood between his family and Hunyadi to have expected support. His cousin was in a better position; Ștefan might now have a chance of regaining his family's throne. Vlad's own position seemed hopeless. If he could find no help from Christendom, he had no help, for he refused to return to the Sultan for Ottoman help. The Sultan would only use him as a wedge to make his conquests of the west easier. All he could hope was that his fervor might be acceptable to God and that He might look kindly on the prince who intended to make a firm stand against the Ottoman Empire before all was lost. He prayed it might be so. To that end, he must be ready to endure whatever hardships came.

He hardened his resolve.

Amaya Tenshi

"Here." Vlad removed the pin his father had won years ago, and his rings. He passed them to his cousin. Ștefan accepted them.

"But... you'll need these," Ștefan said, proffering them back.

"Not now. Hold on to them. Pray to God for me. Perhaps He shall show me favor and restore us both. If so, I will need them from you."

"But you need them so men will be able to identify you—"

"Not now. Now I must disappear, or else the Royal Governor will find me."

Ștefan eyed Vlad's clothes. Though dirty from travel, their quality was unmistakable.

"Pray for me, and speak on my behalf."

Ștefan nodded. They embraced, and Vlad set out on the road, with nothing to his name save what he carried on his back, and a few coins. He had no particular scheme in mind, nor any clear idea how he might survive until such time as God made a path for him.

He cursed that decorated Crusader who had thrown him out, despite his obvious loyalty to Christendom. He cursed his fate and his circumstances, that he he should find himself once again in Transylvania, rather than his own country. Well, he would survive, somehow.

Vlad was well versed in many languages; he could speak them with such correct intonations and eloquence that he could pass for an educated man of that tongue's homeland. So he could make his way as a Hungarian, or as some other nationality. Furthermore, he was literate; he could read and write. It occurred to him that these skills were certain to be in high demand. Rulers always needed translators and scribes.

Dracula's Match

No, he could not make his way as a scribe. Hunyadi would surely find him if he worked at any court. Moreover, amongst nobility he was likely to be recognized by other, even more implacable enemies. To get by without being noticed, he must not be found anywhere a young nobleman might make his way.

He must be a freeman, or even a peasant.

This was where his path had led him. From exile, to court, to captivity, to a throne, to exile, and now to this, with neither family nor friend for help.

So bet it. If it be his lot to bear up under such hostile circumstances, then so be it.

Having set his resolve, he set about solving his first difficulty: his clothing. It should be easy enough to sell them for more money, though finding the proper clothing to replace his finery, within a single day, was a challenge he did not yet know how to surmount. He must trust in God's Providence and his own cunning.

There was always a need for laborers. That seemed the quickest and easiest path to take. He could hide his money for a time and rely on it only in direst need. The Sultan Murad, the man who had ordered Vlad taken prisoner and held in Turkey, had disguised himself and gone about to learn the state of his country. Why shouldn't Vlad do the same? It was a marvelous skill, and if Vlad could master it, he ought to be able to use it to his advantage should he ever take back his throne. There were other methods which he could emulate from the Mussulmen. Methods of maintaining power. His enemies had taught him a great deal—though not the lessons they had intended. One day, God willing, he would be able to reward them for their tutelage.

Amaya Tenshi

Ştefan might eventually succeed in turning Hunyadi's ear, though Vlad did not place large hopes on that. For today, it would be enough to solve the problem of his attire and find a place to sleep. Tomorrow, he would be a common laborer, indistinguishable from the others. Or else he's be arrested. Beyond that, who could say?

Amaya Tenshi

CHAPTER 1
STRANGER IN A STRANGE LAND

The Seattle mist had let up a bit, but the day was still gray. The mist had been insufficient to wash away the stench of human urine and waste as one passed the array of tents strewn here and there on sidewalks like grotesque bread crumbs. Dracula took periodic excursions into the city to stay on top of things, though without much purpose. It was now merely a habit and a way to spend his seemingly infinite time.

He had parked his corvette on the side of the street under the monorail so he could take in what Seattle had to offer. For a lark, he had even ridden the Link light rail that morning. Given how far away from the city he stayed, it was not his chosen method of transport, but he supposed that for folk who lived in the area, it was a marvelous way to get around. The worst part of the ride was the view of the city as one rode: the never-ending construction, the ugly train yards, the mismatched architecture—a hodgepodge of glass monstrosities and aging brick buildings as disparate as oil and water. The oldest brick structures had character, but little in the way of art or beauty except the occasional cornice. He supposed most modern cities must be aesthetically disjointed, but it did irritate him to see it. Modern designs lacked substantiality; at best they were characterless but functional; at worst they were utterly soulless eyesores. The gray and the mist hid the farther buildings from view. He ought to have taken this ride earlier when the visibility was poorer.

He hadn't been to Pike Place in a while and decided, on a whim, to visit. It was time to take note of anything that had changed, find something to eat, and possibly something to bring back to the house for his guest. Not precisely a princely task, but he was a man without a country or a throne now—a stranger in a strange land indeed. He found a cozy little steakhouse and ordered lunch from a seat which afforded him a view of the passersby and the street. Fashions certainly changed, but he couldn't say that the mass-produced, cheap-looking, ill-fitting modern style was any improvement on what had come before. In his day, it may have have taken a tailor or peasant seamstress a week or longer to produce a hand-embroidered shirt of linen or closely woven cotton, but it would have had beautifully accented details and lasted for ages.

After lunch he wandered in search of a market. Local farmers often had better-tasting merchandise than anything he could find in stores. He spotted a certain red-headed young man behind the counter of a shop, and went in.

"Andrew, isn't it? One of Miss Lilly's friends?" he said, stepping to the counter.

They had been introduced back in May at Cammy's birthday, and a memorable night that had proven to be. Of all the company, Andrew had spoken the least—in fact, Dracula could not recall that he had said anything at all after being introduced. As a result, it was unclear whether this youth was as tedious as the others with whom Cammy kept company. The young man glanced up from a small, wooden carton of eggs he had just set down on the display case. The sign in front of the case read "peacock eggs." Dracula took a moment to read the other signs: "chicken eggs," "emu eggs," "goose eggs," and "duck eggs." On one wall were eggs lovingly decorated in various colors and styles and designs. Against another wall were vegetables in wooden crates or plastic bins.

"Hello," Andrew mumbled.

"I recall that your family runs a farm. Are these all from your farm?"

Andrew nodded at the wooden sign with the name "Egger's" burnt into it, hanging above the sleek, white plastic register.

"That was mom's last name," Andrew explained. "They thought that one would be more marketable."

"What is your father's name?"

"Swindlehurst."

Swine herd. They would have to specialize in pork. Assuming that Seattleites even knew what the name meant. Dracula took some time to peruse the merchandise on sale. The young man shared information when asked, though the only tone he employed was mumbling. The decorated eggs, he explained, were painted by a neighbor whom the family paid in food and other barter. The eggs were decorated with fine, swirling lines, dots, and other flourishes in a rainbow of colors, but haphazardly, not with purpose of design. Dracula bought a sampling of the eggs and a small wooden crate in which to transport them, and shortly thereafter left the shop.

Dracula's Match

Andrew seemed to be the best of Cammy's companions. Quiet, polite, hard-working, unassuming, modest. The model peasant. Not a find Dracula had expected to stumble across in the modern wasteland of lost souls. Perhaps Cammy would help him find other such people, though it was a wonder that Cammy was friends with the young man in the first place.

On the way back to his vehicle, he spotted a chain store which sold cheap, mass-produced clothes and other wares. He could purchase some items that he would need in order to dust off a skill he hadn't used in years.

Soon he had in hand what he needed, and discovered that, inexplicably, the shop had numerous registers but only two employees to man them, and both were clearly overburdened. For a culture obsessed with buying incessantly and cheaply, he thought the staffing arrangement quite odd. While he stood trying to puzzle out the reason why a nationally-owned chain store with a highly recognizable brand would only employ two people to man their tills, another employee approached him.

"If you're in a hurry, the self-checkouts are available."

"The what?"

The young woman gestured behind her to an aisle of machines where more customers were lined up. After a few moments, he grasped that the machines were also registers. He supposed that explained why there were few employees. He had missed this shift in so-called progress. No one had mentioned that mankind had finally begun making servile robots, as the visionaries of the early decades of the 20th century had dreamt and described and depicted. For a moment, he thought of *Metropolis* and the concerns Fritz Lang had had about the future of humanity. Morbidly curious to see what manner of robot mankind had conceived, he approached the row of machines.

Dracula spotted his first trouble.

"These contraptions use touchscreens?" he called out towards the employee who had directed him here. She glanced back—having started for the shoes—and nodded.

"Yeah."

Dracula had a stylus he used for his phone, so he decided to try it on the screen in front of him. It did not work. As expected, neither did his fingers.

"You may press the start button and scan an item," the machine spoke to him, in a pleasant, but cold, woman's voice. He did not like it. Corporate employees were generally surly, in his experience, but this mechanized version was utterly impersonal. A disembodied voice speaking to all comers, and therefore to no one in particular. He decided to abandon the attempt. He would find out more some other time.

"Did you need some help?" another young woman with eyelashes large enough for a vaudeville act asked him. She had come from a standalone machine at the far end of the aisle of mechanical cashiers.

"This machine is unusable," he told her. "Good day."

"It's not hard. Here, press 'Start.'"

"I have no intention of wasting more time with this machine."

The young woman made a sound like popping chewing gum in her mouth and tapped the screen. Her plastic nails were nearly an inch long. The screen changed.

"Please scan an item."

Perhaps, if this employee was going to remain and operate the machine for him, it would be worth his time to watch.

Dracula's Match

She looked to him, and he could definitely see she was chewing gum, though she tried to hide it. After a very pregnant pause, she said, "You need to scan what you have."

He took a moment to process what this impolite adjuration meant.

"You mean that I... should perform *your* duties?" he checked.

"You have to scan your things."

He boggled at the very idea. Once, store clerks would go to fetch you what you required, knew who you were, held pleasant conversations with you. Later, they remained polite at least, and often friendly. But after he had been released from his prolonged captivity by Boese, he'd found them all indifferent, surly, and uneducated, but *this*.... How was it that a culture of people who loved shopping so much would do away with customer service altogether? Now they paid for the chance to do a clerk's work.

"Why would anyone do that?" he demanded. The clerk blinked indifferently.

"Some people like it. It's faster, and sometimes you don't want to talk to anyone, you know?"

He glanced at the other customers and tried to gauge whether they were truly leaving the store faster. Perhaps. But in exchange for paying to be an employee? And for the chance to *avoid* other people?

Had mankind lost its mind? Its very heart and soul seemed in peril.

"Who implemented this monstrosity?" he demanded.

"Corporate. It's more convenient—"

"More convenient than what?" He pointed at the lines behind the two cashiers.

"I don't make the decisions. Everyone's putting these in."
He doubted it.
"That is preposterous. Who decided to put these here? I would speak with them."
"You wanna speak to a manager?"
"Immediately."

The young woman clomped off, leaving Dracula to gaze about, studying the lines of customers who ignored each other, and to brood over how mankind had become the hideous, shambling thing of the most recent era—where every man was a stranger, and a mildly detested one at that.

A woman who looked as though life had trampled her underfoot more than once approached him, while the young woman with far too long eyelashes sauntered behind.

"You were having some trouble with the self-checkouts?" the older woman asked.

"I wish to know whose decision it was to install these."

"Corporate decided—"

"Someone at your corporate headquarters made the decision. Someone's finger moved to sign the order. Someone made the suggestion, someone put it into action. I want that name."

"I don't know the names of everyone who works up there," the woman told him. "I'm sure it was something they researched. A lot of people like them."

"I don't care what 'a lot of people' like. I want a name."

"What a Karen," the young woman with the eyelashes muttered, and shook her head.

"I'm sorry, but I don't have that information," the tired woman told him.

"*Sir*," he said.

Dracula's Match

"Hmm?" the older woman mumbled.

"I do not have that information, *sir*," he said.

"I am sorry, sir. I didn't want to assume—"

"Common decency demands you address me with modicum of respect."

"I just didn't—"

"Enough. If you do not have a name, give me the name of the person who knows either who made the decision, or who might know who knows. There must be a chain of command, surely? Your corporate office is not located on the *moon*."

"I can give you our corporate number if you like."

He nodded curtly. When she returned with a hastily scribbled number on a piece of receipt paper—*not even a card!*—he snatched it from her hand, and left the things he had thought to buy behind.

He had barely left the store when a man dressed in filthy, unwashed clothes stepped from around a corner directly into his path, blocking the way. He was not permitted to leave the city, so he did not know the extent of the problem of homeless beggars throughout the country; but he had read in what passed for news these days that the problem was on the rise in many states, especially in regions with mild winters. In his experience, such a crisis was the result of serious political or economic upheaval or instability.

"Yo, I haven't eaten since yesterday."

Dracula sidestepped him and started walking.

"I'm hungry, man. Come on, just a few dollars."

Dracula turned around.

"How old are you?" he asked. This took the homeless person off-guard.

"Thirty-seven."

"I see you have both your arms and legs," Dracula observed. "Other than being filthy, I see nothing the matter with you. You are hungry? I have an estate that requires laborers. If you help tend my crops, I will pay you, and you will have a meal at least twice a day."

"Look, man, life is hard all around. Except maybe for you, huh? You wearing Armani or something? You can spare—"

"Nobody wears Armani except those who wish to be seen wearing Armani. What I wear is tailor made for me specifically. I do not disagree that life is difficult, but you asked me for help. I offered help."

"You want me to *slave* for you? What do you *take* me for? What makes you think you're entitled to all your money, huh?"

Dracula smiled at him.

"I understand that the government here provides for those who are unable—or *unwilling*—to work," he said. "Rather than stand here bothering those who *do* work, why don't you take money that way?"

"You gotta be disabled for that," the man explained.

"Oh? Is that all?" Dracula wondered. "Well, it seems I can help you after all."

Cammy found him in his office, or study, or whatever it was. He had a ledger of some kind open beside his elbow and was busily scratching out a letter with a fancy-looking fountain pen. She felt a bit disappointed he didn't use a quill. That would be funnier. He glanced up at her lurking in the doorway.

"I will be out in a moment."

"Whatcha doing?" she asked.

He glanced up, seemingly angry. She hid behind the door, peeking.

"I am currently occupied, as you clearly can see," he said.

"*Sorr*-y," Cammy replied, and scooted from the door. She went to the kitchen to pour a glass of milk while she waited. Lindsey had texted, inviting Cammy to her dance class. Cammy hadn't wanted to go by herself, and had invited Brian along. Having him along would at least mean she'd have a partner to dance with, but it was hard to catch him with an evening free.

Lindsey had been after her to take up dancing for ever, but Cammy had been too busy with work and school, and too poor to pay for lessons even if she'd had the time, or the transportation. And then her roommate Heather had … died, and Cammy hadn't been able to do anything fun since. After thinking that maybe she ought to try to do something new, move on, find other things to do with people, she'd agreed to come at least once to try it out. Especially since Kenzie wanted to go see a movie afterwards, with the whole group. Maybe it would be nice to see everyone and reintroduce Brian to her friends, since he'd only met them once, at her 21st birthday party. Worst birthday *ever*. At least now she had a restraining order against her mother. Small victories…

Every day, she was struck by constant reminders about Heather. On occasion, she'd see a meme on the internet and think, "I should show this to Heather" only to realize she couldn't. Then she'd have to go hide somewhere until she stopped crying.

In some ways, she couldn't be glad enough that she was now living an hour outside of Seattle, despite how bad the commute was. If she were still in their old apartment, still walking all the same streets where she and Heather had walked together, she didn't think she could function. It wasn't as if she could talk to anyone about what had happened. Professors were less sympathetic about your best friend and roommate having died if you couldn't tell them you were the one who'd killed her. But if you did tell them, it would be so much worse.

She wiped at her cheek again, then realized her host was standing in the doorway. The chair scraped against the floor as she jumped back in surprise.

"My apologies," he told her, curtly. "Are you ready to go?"

Cammy tapped her thumbs on her phone. Maybe not. She really felt like moping instead. But she shouldn't just mope forever, right?

"What's that?" she asked, as a means to distract herself. She gestured at the two-page letter he had hand-written. He glanced down.

"The world is insane," he said, and folded the papers neatly and crisply. It was a small thing, but he could do all sorts of things with an eerie efficiency, poise, and swiftness.

"I mean…" Cammy didn't quite know what sort of comeback to try. Snarky? Honest? Jokingly agree? "I guess?" she landed on. "You're writing to a friend?"

"No. I found myself once more unable to understand how you people survive your own oppressive insanity."

"It's not easy," Cammy told him. He looked at her. "I mean, everything's expensive, and you can't earn a living wage, and I have no idea how I'm going to pay off my college loans—"

"You shouldn't take on debts you doubt you can pay," he told her.

Dracula's Match

"But I can't afford college otherwise."

"Not everyone should go to a university," he said, and turned towards his study once more. She glared at his back and shook her head.

Not everyone's royalty and rich, she thought at the back of his head. *I bet **he** went to college.* After a few moments, she wondered if he actually had. Did princes have to get a higher education? Well, he'd gone on to become a doctor. In the Dark Ages or the Renaissance, though. She doubted you had to study much to be a doctor in that time period.

Dracula reemerged from his office with the letter stamped and ready to go. He gestured for the door, so out she went into the misty twilight, across the gravel driveway, to the garage. While he opened the door, she glanced toward the city and for a moment thought to herself how beautiful the horizon looked in the faint, golden light of the setting sun. In the late year weather, visibility wasn't the best; the sun didn't often get a chance to show its face, or even its traces, but she could see the glow, and the view struck her. It was like she was alone atop a hill with a sea of light all around.

Then she thought she ought to take a picture to share with Heather.

She sulked in the car, hoping the growing dark masked how upset she looked as she wiped away the occasional tear while Dracula drove her into the city. Since he refused to let her get rides to his mansion from ride shares or even from friends, he ended up driving her almost everywhere. It felt like being an elementary school kid all over again, needing her parents to drive her, except she didn't need to ask permission or beg for rides. She just mentioned a place she'd like to go or needed to be, and he would simply make time to drive her. It all seemed to be part of what he considered the responsibilities of a host to a guest, which she'd come to realize he took *very* seriously, in a really old-world kind of way she still barely understood. So weird.

Whatever else he used to occupy his time, it sure seemed none of it was on a deadline.

The dance studio was near-ish to one of Seattle's tourist attractions, the Fremont Troll, a huge construction of rebar-reinforced cement and steel, with hubcaps from a VW Beetle for eyes. The Troll had been fashioned by a local artist more than a decade before she was born, commissioned to deter the homeless from camping under the bridge, and had become something of a local tourist attraction. Heather had mentioned once that there were concerns about the area getting over-developed, but Cammy couldn't remember the details or how that related to the weird concrete troll lurking under a bridge.

Cammy hoped she could get Brian to come with her sometime to take a picture of her by the Troll. The only picture she had of herself there had been taken by Heather, back in high school. Heather had snapped a photo of her standing atop the troll's head triumphantly, arms akimbo, ready to fight the world. She needed a new picture so she could replace that one on her profile. She didn't feel like she could fight anything. Not after what had happened. Not after Heather's parents had been killed, and then Heather herself. Cammy had been next to useless. She hated herself for that. She guessed a new pose would just be standing in front of it like a boring basic nobody. Or maybe sitting between its clawing fingers and the Beetle in its other hand.

Dracula's Match

Would she be erasing Heather if she did that? But every time she looked at the photo she thought of Heather. Maybe she should just delete it.

Dracula insisted on walking her to the studio. They had to park about a block away, down an alley. It was pretty dark by then, so she didn't really mind the company. Occasionally, when she saw the shadow of a person in the mist, her first thought was of cold, grasping hands pulling her out of a vehicle to kill her. Having the guy who killed about twenty vampires all by himself and rescued her in the process right there by her side did *wonders* to banish those shadows.

Lindsey and Brian were waiting outside the dance studio, under an awning. Lindsey stood with a plastic to-go cup of what looked like green tea or flavored lemonade in her hand. Her long, sun-bleached, blonde hair hung down from under her hood in waves. Her eyes were glued to her phone, which cast its bluish glow across her face and turned her eyes into specks of light like tiny phone screens themselves. She didn't notice either of them until they had drawn close.

"Oh, hi!" She beamed. Somehow, she seemed to read Cammy's mood, because she came forward and hugged her around the neck and shoulders. "I'm glad you could make it!" Lindsey turned her blue eyes to Dracula.

"Good evening, Miss Van Wassener," he greeted. Cammy wondered when and how he'd learned Lindsey's last name.

"Oh." Lindsey shook all over. "Oh, that's like I'm my mom. You can call me Lindsey."

Dracula bow-nodded. "Good evening, Miss Lindsey."

Her smile was half bemusement, half confusion, but she didn't comment on his use of "Miss".

Amaya Tenshi

"I didn't realize you'd come too," was all she said. "Will you stay? I thought you said you knew how to dance."

Dracula looked at her, then glanced through the glass windows and door at the small studio, the mirrors, and wide expanse of polished wood floors.

"It has been some time since I last danced socially," he said. "Let us see how customs have changed."

Oh no, Cammy thought. She didn't want to be in a dance class with Dracula.

Brian had come up behind Lindsey, seemingly trying to find something to do with his hands. She was still surprised by how he looked since becoming a cop. He wasn't the tall skater kid with the messy hair she'd known in middle school anymore. Now he had muscle which she could see through his hoodie—it was an old one, and a bit small on him—and his brown hair was always cropped short, no-nonsense. She could see in his eyes he didn't want Dracula there. That was something they could agree on, though Cammy doubted he had reservations for the same reasons.

After Cammy had started living in Dracula's mansion, Brian had jumped to conclusions, arrested the man, and then gotten into trouble at the precinct. He couldn't have known Dracula was actually an asset of the US government and not something a local cop should be meddling with. However, Cammy knew that Brian harbored lasting, serious misgivings about him.

The studio had a worn wooden floor, mirrors on one wall, windows for the two facing both sides of the intersection outside, and potted plants placed into industrial-style metal shelving staged against corners. There were tall, bar style tables with seats, pegs for coats and bags, and, in the far corner along the brick wall, a little coffee counter with a glass jug of iced water that also contained lemon and cucumber slices. It was actually pretty cute. She heard Brian murmur into her ear, "You invited him, too?"

She glared at him.

"No, but I don't have a car. He drove me."

"I borrowed Melissa's car," Brian told her.

"He doesn't want people going up to his place," Cammy explained. She checked the back of her host's head. He seemed to be taking in the cozy little dance studio, and she hoped he hadn't overheard. She had learned he wasn't like the vampires in movies—he didn't mind sunlight, and he breathed and ate food—in fact, she sometimes wondered if he really was a vampire at all; she couldn't be certain what abilities he had, other than being *really* good with a sword. It wasn't a subject he liked to discuss. And Stoker's book was no help, since all he would ever say about it or its author was "He wrote of piece of rubbish, entirely fictitious and poorly written."

Even though she'd been living at his mansion for most of a year, she had to admit she didn't really know that much about the man. He would launch into lectures if she asked him about history, but didn't like discussing his personal history, or monsters, or supernatural things. Most of the supernaturals that supposedly lived on his property didn't seem to want to talk to her or be seen by her—and there were some she had no desire whatsoever to see, or be seen by. *Satyrs, ugh!* On occasion, she spotted the tanuki—a kind of badger-fox-racoon—or the shape-changing fox which Dracula had allowed to live on his property, or their daughter, the tanukitsune, Ginko. Cammy had saved the baby creature, but every time she spotted the little vulpine pouncing on butterflies in the grass, the little fox would only stare at her until the fox mother trotted over, and then they would disappear together. The domovoy who lived inside the mansion and kept it clean was invisible, so she had never seen him, and she didn't want to. According to her host, the domovoy looked like a naked, hairy old man. She could *absolutely* do without spotting him.

It was pretty maddening, actually. Less than a year ago she'd found out vampires and werewolves and monsters were real. But for months now she hadn't come across anything new out of the ordinary. Cammy had hoped more creatures might be nice like Ginko, or at least interesting to meet, but so far, nothing.

Brian was busy glaring. She knew her situation looked weird, but she didn't know what to tell him. "I'm staying with the *actual* Dracula because I stalked him to his mansion here in Seattle after he saved my life from murderous vampires" would sound unbelievable, right? The arrangement was supposed to be just until she found a new place, but without a roommate, she couldn't afford to move out, even if she *wasn't* trying to go to college. So far, he hadn't commented on how it was now November, and she'd arrived in April. She hoped he would continue to tolerate her. Now that she knew there might be mass-murdering vampires lurking around any corner, she couldn't get excited about the idea of living on her own.

That was pretty pathetic, when she thought about it. But the truth was she wanted his protection, for as long as he would offer it, and she wanted to find out more about supernaturals, even though the knowledge frightened her.

Dracula's Match

Cammy came back to the present as Lindsey introduced Dracula to her dance teacher, a woman doing really well for her age: still in great shape, wearing a black unitard with a silk scarf tied around her waist and another to keep her bouncing, curly hair out of her face. Lindsey introduced him simply as "Vlad," which was probably for the best, and mentioned that he knew how to dance. Lindsey pronounced his name the way he did, so it rhymed with "blood" or "odd" to Cammy's ears.

"Well, welcome!" the dance teacher, Bianca, greeted him. She extended a hand. Dracula considered it. Cammy watched him. She thought he considered the offered hand longer than usual, then he took the hand in his and kissed Bianca's knuckles, earning a bemused smile and a little giggle.

"What a creep," she heard Brian mutter behind her.

Cammy wished she knew what to say. She thought it was creepy too, but figured telling him so was more trouble than it was worth.

"What dances do you know?" Bianca asked. "You have experience?"

"Some," Dracula told her. "Nothing of the modern era. Waltzes, mazurkas, polkas, quadrilles, folk dances, and some much older."

"My goodness," Bianca observed. "So a little bit of ballroom? No tango, samba?"

He shook his head. Bianca finally turned her attention to the other new students.

"What about you two, do you have any experience?"

"No," Brian said.

"Just Dance," Cammy said, trying to grin for the joke, lame as it was. Bianca blinked, not understanding.

"It's a game," Lindsey explained. "My friends do it at my house. I tried teaching her Freestyle."

That had been far too ambitious for Cammy, and she hadn't tried to learn more since.

"That's all right," Bianca said. "We can start simple." To Dracula, she said, "You said you have some experience. Will you show me?"

"Certainly."

Bianca changed a CD in the stereo in the corner to some classical-sounding piece Cammy recognized but couldn't name. Dracula took Bianca's hand and gripped her around waist, then led her in some fancy-looking old-fashioned dance from a century ago. Lindsey looked very interested, and some of the other students stopped what they were doing to watch. Cammy supposed he must be good at it, but it just looked like stuff she'd seen in movies.

"That's—you certainly know what you're doing," Bianca laughed when they came to a stop.

"I have grown rusty. Thank you for the opportunity to dust off this skill."

"You know," Lindsey cut in, then bit her lip. "There's a contest I was going to be in, but Hector canceled. He has to go out of town. Would you be willing to help? I need a dance partner."

"Perhaps. Though if it is a modern style I cannot say I will be of much help."

"Well, maybe you still can. It's Electro swing. Do you know that?"

He shook his head. Bianca went to her player and put another CD in. She selected a track that Cammy recognized as one Lindsey liked. Her friend bounced a bit to the beat and began demonstrating the dance she had no doubt been working on for the event. Dracula considered her movements for some time. Then he started to imitate Lindsey, and did a pretty good job for someone who had never danced Electro swing, because of *course* he could. Cammy thought to herself, *Come on. Is there anything you **can't do?*** Not only could he do everything, he did it all *well*.

"You want to get a coffee or something?" Brian asked her.

"You have no idea," Cammy told him.

They stepped out into the mist and drizzle. Brian had snatched their hoodies from the peg near the door and handed hers to her, so she put it on and covered her head. He did the same. There was a coffee shop a little ways up the street, and the sound of an open-air bar playing some sort of classic rock filled what space the cars rolling by didn't. The coffee shop was still open, but the one barista was wiping the tables down.

"When do you close?" Brian asked.

"In five minutes. It's fine," the barista grumbled. With a sigh she stomped behind the counter. Cammy felt a pang of guilt.

"We can find somewhere else—"

"No, it's *fine*," the barista told her.

Cammy ordered a coffee black to save the barista time and effort, while Brian got a cappuccino. Cammy left the best tip she could, but it was still only a few dollars. Brian followed her example, but he wasn't much less broke than she was. At least together they left a decent-ish tip for the single barista who would have to stay later now for serving them.

Amaya Tenshi

They sat outside the shop under an umbrella table, and sipped their drinks.

"How are you holding up?" Brian asked. Cammy ran her thumb over the plastic lid.

"Fine," she said.

Brian looked at her, but he didn't press.

"Do you like 'real college'?"

She snorted.

"Yeah, I guess."

"You picked a major yet?"

"Communications."

"Why that?"

Cammy shrugged. "You mean, why not Business? I dunno. It seemed like a good idea." She rested her chin in her hand. "Do you ever regret not going to college?"

Brian shrugged. "I knew I wanted to be a cop."

She didn't get why. He'd been the stereotypical 'anti-establishment' skater kid back when. She still couldn't believe the change, and she hated the idea that he might not come back one day. Maybe he'd get shot, or he'd shoot someone else. It made her skin crawl. But his turnaround also bothered her in other ways. Maybe being a cop was what he *ought* to be, he had embraced the role so thoroughly. But she didn't know what to do. She felt more or less the same as when she and Heather used to wander around far from home just to stay away. Or when they watched Brian at the skate park, or made a point of petting every dog they ran across, or watched movies together. But none of that translated into a career, or life plan, or what to do in adulthood. How did people find out what they were supposed to *do* with their lives?

"What about you and... your friend?" Brian asked.

Dracula's Match

"We're not… we're just friends," Cammy snapped, hearing the insinuation in his voice.

"But you're living with him?"

"Not like *that*," Cammy snapped harder. "I'm a guest."

"K," Brian grumbled, and sipped his coffee. He watched the traffic go by. "But you're doing ok?" he asked at last.

"I dunno," she admitted.

He nodded, pressed his lips together and kept watching the cars. Cammy stared glumly into her coffee. She wiped water from her face and glanced aside. A white cat trotted up the dry sidewalk beneath the shop awnings towards the dance studio and stopped at the window to peer inside.

Wait, she thought, *maybe that's a supernatural thingie?*

She still had the adder stone Dracula had given her. It was a flat river stone with a hole through the middle. He'd told her it could let her see magical creatures as they really were, through any disguise. She pulled the stone out from under her shirt—it hung next to the old-fashioned key Dracula had given her for her room—and raised it to her eye to look through the hole. Then she noticed Brian watching her.

"Oh, um. I found this."

Brian peered at the stone. He held out a hand to take it. She couldn't think of how to explain that it was actually very special and maybe irreplaceable, so she slipped it off and passed it to him. He must have noticed she was planning to look through it, because he held it up to his eye and squinted at her through it, then flipped it back and forth a few times, and passed it back.

"Looks like a natural hole," he said. "I haven't seen a river stone with a hole in the middle like that before."

"Yeah, it's cool, right?" Cammy said, and took it back. Best to be more careful with it in the future. She checked the dance studio again, but the cat was gone. Instead, there was a woman watching the interior. Maybe a prospective student.

"It's getting late," Brian said. "I guess... *he's* going to drive you home."

"Brian!" she snapped. He looked away. They walked back to the dance studio in silence.

The woman was still standing outside, her arms crossed and her fingers playing on one elbow. She wore fine jewelry, very fancy-looking rings, and a long, pearl necklace with a brooch. Her red hair was tied back in a tight, elegant bun. All together, with her posture, Cammy had a sense of the word 'regal,' which she hadn't felt about anyone she'd ever met. For a moment, Cammy had the feeling this was the sort of look her mother *tried* to emulate, but failed. She shook her head to get rid of the thought.

Why think of Mom right now? she chided herself. Then she noticed the woman watched the people inside the dance studio as though she hated every one of them. She wasn't precisely young, but looked very good for her age, and not just because of the blood-red lipstick or the elegantly applied eye shadow and eye liner. Even her clothes were high-end: a neat pant-suit that fit her better than any version Cammy had ever seen on anyone else, even movie stars in magazine photos.

"Everything ok, ma'am?" Brian asked when they came up to her. She flicked her eyes to him, and cast her gaze on Cammy. Some strange, pleasant-but-deeply-unpleasant scent washed over Cammy. She struggled to make sense of it. It was as though some attempt had been made to mask a hideous stink with strong perfume, but both scents mixed together and competed for dominance.

"Everything is fine," the woman answered. She spoke with a slight accent. "I didn't want to interrupt. Just watching at the moment."

"Ok then, have a nice night," Brian said. She smiled and nodded at him, and her eyes scrutinized Cammy's entire figure. It sent a shiver down Cammy's spine.

"Do you both attend classes here often?" the woman inquired.

Cammy shook her head. Not only was that true, she didn't like the way this woman had asked the question. "I just came to try it out. I don't think I'm going to keep it up," she replied.

The woman lifted her chin in a sort of nod. She eyed Cammy again, and cast her gaze to the window once more.

"She's darling," the woman commented. It took Cammy a moment to realize the woman meant Lindsey. Cammy *definitely* didn't like that.

"Bye," she told the woman, and went inside, Brian two steps behind her.

They spotted Dracula standing beside the little table in the back corner by the coffee counter, while Lindsey and several of the other students practiced some sort of zouk routine—Cammy only recognized it as such from Lindsey's demonstrations and the videos she liked to share. He was watching the scene with the same sort of muted disgust and hatred the woman outside had worn, but there was also something like hunger in his eyes that Cammy did not like. Neither did Brian, when she checked his reaction.

Amaya Tenshi

She left Brian near the door to quietly sulk and scooted along the wall to Dracula.

"You got a second?" she asked him.

He glanced at her, and she realized the glow in his eyes wasn't light reflecting, they were glowing red. Meaning he was pretty mad.

"Whoa, sorry," she said. It just came out. The last time he'd looked at her like that, he'd been threatening to kill her. He took a moment to consider her reaction.

"Something amiss?"

"You… your eyes…" she gestured vaguely. He checked his reflection in the window—he had a reflection—glared at it, sighed, and rubbed his eyes.

"You can't feel it when that happens?" she asked.

"No. And it's only a recent phenomenon, the result of that damned book and the Lugosi film."

"You mean that didn't used to happen?"

He shook his head. She wanted to ask what else had stuck to him over the years, but it occurred to her that if he was angry enough for his eyes to be glowing, she ought to leave it be. He let out another irritated sigh and glanced at Brian.

"I must apologize," he told Cammy, "but would you have your friend drive you back to my place? Warn him to be careful, and don't let him wander about."

"Uh… but you don't want people to drive up there."

"At the moment, it would be best if your friend takes you —so long as you make certain he does not explore the grounds. For his own safety."

She didn't need a glare to warn her that something bad would happen if Brian ran into one of Dracula's vampire-ghost-ladies.

Dracula's Match

"But you're ok with him driving me—"

"For the moment. Go on."

Weird, she thought. "There was this woman outside being really creepy."

Dracula looked at her, the glow somewhat reduced, but still visible if you looked for it.

"She... she was acting strange."

He glanced over her shoulder out the front window. When Cammy turned, she saw no one there.

"And there was a cat."

"Are you saying you think you saw something? A witch, or some sort of shapeshifter?" he asked.

"Maybe. I didn't have a chance to use the adder stone."

"What color was it?"

"What? The cat?"

He nodded.

"White. Does that matter?"

"If it was something we ought beware," he said. "Be very careful on your way. Use the stone if you see anything suspicious, and call Malcolm or me if you notice anything."

She nodded, left him there, and headed for Brian.

"He said you can drive me back if you want," she told him, "after the movie." Brian frowned in puzzlement, annoyance, and suspicion.

"Good thing I was able to borrow Melissa's car then," he grumbled. "Where's *he* going?"

"Dunno," she said. Brian sent one last glower over his shoulder as they walked out into the drizzle. The well-dressed lady was not there anymore. When Cammy checked over her shoulder, she spotted Dracula chatting up Bianca.

Amaya Tenshi

Weird, she thought again.

She and Brian arrived at the movie theater. Lindsey had stayed behind to wrap up at the class. When Cammy met her friends outside, beneath the neon-lit posters of coming attractions, she let them know.

"And you all remember Brian, right?"

It was just Kenzie and Aslan waiting. Kenzie had her hair newly dyed to radioactive green, her fingernails ended in chipping off black polish, and her lipstick was an uncharacteristic electric lavender color. Maybe she was tired of black. Her rings and studs reflected the neon poster lights as she nodded greeting to Brian.

"S'up, my dude," she said, and fist bumped him. "Long time, huh?"

"I work all the time," he told her.

"You remember Aslan?" Cammy prompted. Brian shook the hand of the tall, lanky young man with the sad mustache and the long hair. Cammy supposed Aslan looked like what Brian might have turned into if he hadn't become a cop.

"Where's Andrew?" Cammy asked.

"He's helping his parents. Couldn't make it," Kenzie answered. "Shame. You got tickets? We can head inside. I want some soda."

"What about Lindsey?" Brian asked.

"She's always late to everything except her dance stuff," Kenzie said. "She's always been like that. Plus, she's not really an action-comedy kind of gal; she'll be on her phone the whole time anyway. Come on."

Kenzie turned to go inside, with Aslan following suit. Cammy looked to Brian.

Dracula's Match

"We don't have to if you don't want to."

"We haven't had a chance to hang out since high school," Brian said. "Of course I want to."

It was too bad Brian's half-sister Melissa couldn't be with them. Cammy hadn't hung out with her in so long. Growing up was awful, apparently. You never had time for anyone or anything. Brian had a real job, and so did Melissa, as a nurse in Shoreline. Not a job Cammy thought she'd have been able to do—blood made her queasy. But Cammy didn't know *what* she wanted to do with her life. There didn't seem to be much point to anything.

They went in after Kenzie.

Lindsey did show up late, and she did spend a lot of the runtime on her phone. The movie was a not-great adaptation of an indie comic book, so Cammy and her friends griped about what was wrong with it on the way out. Kenzie complained that it was just like Hollywood to take a great indie creator's work and turn it into a movie "by committee."

"Corporate is the worst flavor on *anything*," she grumped. "They take all the heart and soul and uniqueness out of everything and make it so… so… factory-grade."

"Makes it less human," Aslan added.

Lindsey asked how the movie was different from the comic book, so Kenzie and Aslan started telling her about the trilogy the movie was based on. The conversation was getting animated, but Brian had to go to work in the morning, so Cammy had to bow out so he could take her home. It'd be about an hour's drive to Dracula's mansion. She bid everyone goodbye, and Lindsey hugged her, while Kenzie flashed a peace sign.

Amaya Tenshi

She and Brian listened to the radio without talking. It was the loneliest ride she'd ever taken. They rode nearly the entire hour in silence. She wanted to say something, but she couldn't think of anything. What did *he* think of her being so quiet? It wasn't like her. But the longer they went, the harder it seemed to even start a conversation. She could sense the suspicion he tried to hide by keeping his eyes on the road and nowhere else. At last she gave up trying to find the right words to soothe his suspicions and resigned herself to the dark and the quiet, except for the radio tuned to a classic rock station. She directed Brian up the correct way to the front door.

"Thanks," she told him. "I appreciate it."

He was taking in the dimensions of the darkened mansion.

"*Thanks*," she repeated.

"Uh. Yeah," he said. He nodded at the mansion. "Big place."

"Yeah."

"And it's just… the two of you?"

She crossed her arms. He gritted his teeth.

"Lots of wasted space," he observed.

Maybe. It was definitely quiet when he wasn't home. Even when he was, it was quiet. Occasionally he'd play a record, but mostly he kept to himself, and she just hid in her room.

"Yeah," she agreed.

"And… he just lets you live here?"

"He knew I needed someplace safe. And I guess maybe he was just… lonely?"

"Lonely?"

She wasn't sure. That explanation hardly made sense, given how he largely ignored her. Sure, she'd helped him learn how to handle a laptop, but that had been months ago. He'd said something about *obligations* that she couldn't remember. He claimed he had other guests, but over the months he hadn't had anyone else over but Malcolm, and Malcolm never stayed long.

"He's got vineyards out there," Brian said, and nodded his head in the direction they lay, though it was nearly impossible to see them in the dark. How did he know where they were?

He was spying using his cop equipment or something, Cammy realized.

"See you later," she told him. He took the hint, sullenly.

"Fine, fine," he said, and put the car in gear. Just as he lifted his foot off the brakes, he put it back down. "If we go to something again, let's not let him along, ok?"

"Yeah," she agreed.

She watched his headlights disappear into the trees until she was left standing in the dark. Probably he wouldn't park down the road somewhere and explore the woods, right? He had graduated to a real cop, so he wouldn't trespass, surely? She waited, watching his taillights disappearing down the drive. It was pitch black out here, no streetlights, so at night cars were like moving lighthouses in the dark. Once she had lost sight of those twinkling red dots, she turned to go inside.

Without thinking, she pulled out her phone to text Heather about how bad a night it had been. Her hand froze on the first word. She slammed the door shut and went to go cry by herself.

CHAPTER 2
UNEXPECTED

    Brian stewed the whole next day about Cammy and her "friend" or whatever he was. Fake doctor-FBI-Russian spy guy with the weird garlic allergy. Brian didn't know much more now than he had a few months ago, when whatever had happened to Cammy and Heather had happened. Seeing that mansion hadn't helped allay his suspicions. It wasn't even that the man himself was so suspicious, but that Cammy was lying to him. She had to be. Something had happened to Heather, and to Heather's parents and Cammy's parents. But he had no idea how to explain any of it. He didn't work homicide, and he wasn't hearing any scuttlebutt about the cases at work. Which meant something *really* bad or *really* weird had happened. Even that city councilman who'd turned up exsanguinated in April only got mentioned here and there in a sort "how crazy *is* this town?" sort of way. It just didn't make sense. Brian hated that.
    Besides confirming that Cammy's "friend" couldn't eat garlic, he hadn't had much opportunity to learn anything

else, no matter where he went digging. He'd need a chance to talk to the guy alone. But he'd also found out that if his stupid suspicions were right, there were about a thousand different descriptions of vampires, and he wasn't sure which ones might be of use.

And just how idiotic was he for not being able to let *that* go?

So he wasn't in the best of moods when he was getting ready to leave work in the evening and Akerman texted him with a request.

Hey man, need help. Plz get my wallet?

Brian stared at the message.

You left it at the station? he texted back.

I got kicked out of bar its on teh bar

That was a new one. Akerman didn't strike Brian as the kind of guy to cause a problem. But also, a cop getting kicked out of a bar? That didn't bode well. He got the name of the place from Akerman and resigned himself to go check what was going on.

Several electric bike share rides and a trip on the Link light rail later, he picked up the wallet and then left to track Akerman down at another bar just down the street. His buddy was pretty far gone when he found him. The baby-faced officer was sitting at a table rather than the bar, with his head resting on his arms.

"Here you go," Brian told him, and slapped the wallet on the greasy, wooden table. Akerman blearily raised his head and cast his eyes on the wallet. He mumbled thanks and pocketed it, fumbling.

"The bartender told me you got into an argument with some woman?" Brian prompted. Akerman rubbed his red eyes. They looked pretty watery, not just red from drinking. Hoo, boy.

"You ok?" Brian asked, dreading that Akerman might be drunk enough to answer honestly.

"I just thought... I thought she was the one."

Oh no, Brian thought. *Not this again.* He should have kept his mouth shut.

"She just... we want all of the same things. I thought..."

"Hey, don't worry about it," Brian told him.

"I just... I just want a nice girl, you know?" Akerman said, sitting straight up and holding out his hands to petition some ghost across from him at the table. "Is that too much to ask? Just... the two of us... we can live by the sea..."

"Akerman, you need to go home."

"I wanted to be a fisherman..." Akerman grumbled. "Bring home fish every day."

"Come on, time to go," Brian told him.

"Just... be a provider, you know? Just... I don't want to be alone..."

"Come on..." Brian tried not to plead. He grabbed Akerman's wrist, but his buddy pulled free.

"I didn't want... she seemed like the right one. She wanted to get married. We talked..." Akerman slapped a palm down on the table. He shook his head. "She was gorgeous. I should have figured out... she wasn't..."

"Wait, you were that serious? Who was she? How long have you known her? You never mentioned anything."

"Just met," Akerman mumbled.

"What, *tonight?* Akerman, you need to go home and sleep this off. You're drunk. It's no big deal." Akerman must be *way* gone to propose to some woman he'd just met. No wonder things had gone south.

"Gorgeous. I should have *known*," Akerman grumbled. "*Too* gorgeous. You should've seen her, Warren. Long dark hair, eyes like… like lightning. Tall, exotic. Real feminine in that long skirt. Like… old times, you know? Long skirts… with petticoats… Dangerous… gonna report her…"

"Report her for what? Saying no? Listen: you're drunk. You need to go home. Forget about her."

"Have to stop her… before she latches onto someone else. Gotta call her in… she's dangerous…" Akerman reached for his phone but Brian stopped him.

"Listen: *you need to go home*, ok? Don't call anyone. Just sleep it off. Everything is fine."

"Hey, if you two could quiet down your pity party? Some of us are trying to have fun over here."

Brian glared over his shoulder at the guy sitting at the bar. Some douche wearing way too much product sitting next to two young women who clearly didn't mind that he smelled like he'd showered with body spray instead of water. Probably because the guy was tall, well-built, and had a face like a movie star. Figured. Some guys had all the luck.

"Mind your own business, friend," Brian told him.

"Tryin' to," the stranger snarked back.

Let it go, Brian thought to himself. *No need to escalate things. Just some douche.*

"Yeah, mind your own business!" Akerman added. The douche swiveled his head back around and stared them both down. He squinted his gold eyes for a moment, studying Brian, then Akerman, and then inexplicably pulled on the band of his wristwatch to expose a small tattoo of some sort on his wrist. Having done that, he returned his attention to the young women.

"What was *that?*" Brian grumbled. He turned back to Akerman to see his buddy looking down at the table.

"I should go," he said in a subdued voice.

Finally, Brian thought.

Unsteadily, Akerman got to his feet. Brian kept an eye on him to make sure he didn't face-plant into the table.

"Wait a minute, turn that up!"

It was the douche again. Brian swiveled his head, keeping one hand on Ackerman's arm. The douche was half-standing up from his stool and leaning over the bar to get the bartender's attention. His gaze was riveted to the wall mounted flat screen TV, set to a local news report. Brian's cop training kicked into high gear and he listened to find out what had this guy so interested.

"... unfolding story: the strange exhumation of local celebrity and former Double-U star, Roar Thorirsson, better known as 'The Viking'. No one can explain the strange act of vandalism. One eye witness claims a pack of dogs are responsible."

The report displayed images of a graveyard, and footage of a particular grave in what looked like Lake View Cemetery entirely dug up, with unnaturally long claw marks scarring the fresh soil. The coffin at the bottom of the grave was exposed, and the skewed lid was also scored by claw marks in long lines of four. Brian thought they looked like fingernail marks for a moment, but they looked way too deep for that. The coffin was wide open, and empty. Brian had never heard of dogs digging down six feet to get at a recently interred corpse. It must be some sort of weird, elaborate hoax perpe-

Dracula's Match

trated in bad taste. Maybe by the wrestler's agent to generate posthumous popularity? The local reporter was at the gravesite. A picture of some muscled guy with long blond hair popped into the top corner of the screen. If that was the wrestler, he'd been a big guy. The T-shirt he wore struggled to keep his shoulders from ripping it wide open.

"… to add to the mystery surrounding the grisly death of a beloved Seattle figure, amid rumors of pagan rituals, Roar's body has been *stolen!* This development is rocking fans of wrestling and the city as a whole…"

"Oh *no*," the douche said. He pulled out his phone.

"What's the matter?" one of the young women with him asked. He shushed her. As soon as his call connected, he started speaking some foreign language that Brian didn't recognize into his phone in an awful hurry. He abandoned the two young women without a second glance and hurried for the door.

"What's all that?" Akerman blearily asked, looking at the news report with red, glassy eyes.

"Don't worry about it. I'm going to get you an Uber."

Akerman mumbled and squinted at the news report. Brian pulled his phone and ordered a ride, then nudged Akerman along and made his way for the door. It was dark outside, and there was the douche, standing on the corner, still speaking whatever language into his phone. All Brian could pick up was that he sounded agitated. He decided the night air was probably best for Akerman at this point, and that he might as well try to figure out the mystery douche. What had him so agitated? There wasn't much in that report to trigger what looked like an emergency phone call in a foreign language and ditching his two hot dates. So maybe there was some connection between him and the cemetery vandalism.

"Do you think there are any good women anymore?" Akerman wondered.

"Sure," Brian answered, distractedly.

"Why can't I find one?"

Brian pinched the bridge of his nose.

"Everyone's got that problem. My sister has been through, like, eight relationships." He declined to talk about his own history. Or lack of any. At least Akerman'd *had* a few relationships, even if they hadn't worked out. Brian tried to listen in on the douche, but he was still speaking whatever language. Now he sounded angry.

"That's a shame," Akerman mumbled. "Your sister. She's nice, right?"

"Yeah," Brian said, absently.

"She's single now?"

"Yeah. Wait." He returned his attention to Akerman. "Don't you dare."

"Well." Akerman rubbed his eyes. "But she's nice, right? She's a nurse, she has to be nice."

"Akerman, don't make me have to tell you not to go there."

"Did you two seriously bring your pathetic pity party out *here*?" the douche demanded, holding one hand over his phone.

"Hey, you're the one who ran out here after finding out a crime was committed," Brian pointed out. Maybe the guy would reveal something. The way Brian phrased the retort obviously put the guy on his guard, because he straightened up, looked Brian up and down, and turned away.

Dracula's Match

Brian debated walking over to see if the guy knew anything else about the vandalism, when movement from up the street caught his eye. He couldn't distinctly make out what it was what with all the pedestrians and cars, the darkness and fog lit by headlights and streetlights. Something pale and seemingly fluid and large was rising like a mound of smoke.

A pair of labradors started barking loudly and snarling, and snapped at their owner. The woman tried to calm them, until one bit her on the hand. She yelped, dropped the leash ends, and the two dogs bolted down the street. She chased after them, calling their names.

All of a sudden, the pale, fluid shape snapped into focus, and Brian saw a tall guy with long pale hair. As he tried to figure out how his eyes had played such a weird trick on him, the pale guy let out a scream such as Brian had never heard. Like a roar, really. Nothing human-sounding. The tall guy started storming down the street towards them.

The douche gasped out something into his phone in a rush. Clearly, whoever he was talking to hadn't understood something, because he practically shouted out a phrase into his phone, and Brian heard something like "*Sanguisuga*" in the muddle.

The douche turned and pushed between Brian and Akerman, practically sprinting past them, away from the roaring stranger. Akerman fell to the sidewalk, one hand cartwheeling haphazardly for balance. Brian cursed, then grabbed Akerman's other flailing hand to help him up. Akerman glanced past Brian, and—drunk as he was—his eyes widened and he kicked himself backwards, trying to get up. Brian turned to see the big, pale guy storming through the press of pedestrians—anyone who didn't clear out of the way fast enough got knocked aside like a pinball. The pale blond guy looked bigger. Much bigger.

He's on something, Brian thought. He was off-duty, and pretty much out-massed by this guy, who was wearing a torn suit, the sleeves detached from the torso and the dress shirt beneath popped open to reveal a set of pecs that Brian wouldn't be able to match even with all the protein powder on earth. But he had to do something.

The pale, walking mountain of muscle stepped straight into the intersection separating him from Brian and Akerman. A car screeched to a stop just in time to avoid crashing into the guy, and Brian breathed a sigh of relief. The car's horn blared angrily and the pale giant turned.

The pale guy raised both fists and slammed them down on the car hood, smashing the entire front of the car. As Brian gaped, the pale guy reached under the chassis and *lifted the front of the vehicle right off the street*. With a shout of what sounded more like rage than exertion, the guy then *flipped* the car over backwards.

"What the—!!"

Brian felt a tug at his wrist, and realized Akerman had managed to get back to his feet and was trying to pull him away.

"Did you see that?!" Brian asked.

"Run!" Akerman suggested, and tugged again.

Brian pulled out his phone as they retreated. He glanced back to see the maniac literally *ripping* a car wheel free from the axle and then hurling it through the window of a nearby shop. Brian dialed 911 and did his best to report what he was seeing.

Dracula's Match

"I'm sorry, you said this man flipped a car?" the dispatcher demanded. This wasn't his precinct, so he didn't recognize the dispatcher's voice, but it also occurred to him how that sounded now that he'd said it out loud.

"That's right," he told her.

"And where are you?"

"I'm going into Pike Place right now. He's coming right behind me! Send *someone*. This guy is insane!"

"Sir, calm down, I will send a patrol car—"

"THIS GUY JUST FLIPPED A CAR! WERE YOU LISTENING TO ME?" Brian demanded.

"Please remain calm, sir. Help is on the way."

Now Brian had a sense why people didn't like police sometimes. But at the same time, who would believe anyone screaming into a phone that they had just seen some guy casually flip a car over?

The pale guy abandoned the car and started sprinting towards Pike Place. Brian checked Akerman. Adrenaline was overriding some of the booze in his friend's system, and he was managing to stumble along fairly quickly. They had almost reached Pike Place and Brian was trying to direct people out of the way when he heard a scream from behind. He turned to see the pale guy had grabbed some pedestrian and picked him up. The man was about fifty, balding, and was kicking as best he could to get away. The pale guy sank his teeth into the middle-aged man's throat and—

Brian almost threw up. No way. No way he'd just seen some giant of a man high on who knew *what* almost decapitate another man with his teeth. No way. Some of the other people who hadn't moved clear got splattered by blood and a few started screaming. The rest started running.

"Sir? Are you all right? What is happening?" the dispatcher on the phone asked. Brian had forgotten he was still holding it to his ear.

"He just… he just a killed man…" Brian told her.

"Does he have a weapon?"

The pale giant dropped his victim to the ground and let out another roar. People started sprinting.

Brian realized he and Akerman were the only ones not running as this monster came towards them. And after the giant caught up with them and did whatever he was going to do to them, this maniac was going to keep right on going until he ran out of steam or someone stopped him.

There was still time for Brian to be that someone. There was a walkway that cut around between Pike Place and the drop to the Sound. If Brian could direct this pyscho toward it, there would be fewer pedestrians. It wasn't ideal, but he had nothing else he could do.

"Hey!" He jumped up and down, and the pale guy's equally pale eyes settled on him. Red teeth appeared behind the red lips. Brian ran towards the grass, shouting and waving his arms.

"Warren!" he heard Akerman shout. A young couple tried to clear a path, but the girl tripped over her dog's leash and almost dragged her boyfriend to the ground with her as she went down. Their Papillion-mix snapped at the air, foam dropping from its tiny teeth. It ran for its life, the leash whipping behind it.

Brian smelled something awful. Like a corpse left out in the sun for days; putrescence, rot. His stomach churned. He turned to see how close the monster was.

Dracula's Match

Four feet away, with both hands out to grab him. Brian dodged to the right, yelling to make sure the monster didn't notice the other targets.

Glass shattered into a rain of crystals off the back of the pale guy's head. He froze, snarled, and slowly turned. Standing this close, Brian could clearly see his bluish, almost translucent complexion, his sunken, milky eyes, pale blond hair nearly white.

The pale-blue guy set his eyes on Akerman, who had thrown the beer bottle. Akerman gulped. He darted past the pale-blue monster towards the path Brian had chosen. The pale-blue guy lumbered after him. Brian tried to intercept. He got a punch to the gut that practically pile-drove him into the grass. He felt something go *crack*. When he hit the grass there was no air. Just sharp, *sharp* pain in his chest, and the blue guy lurching after Akerman, who was almost actually running.

The smell faded away. Brian tried sitting up, only to feel like his chest was ripping wide open. He collapsed back to the earth. Akerman kept sprinting—as much as he was able—while the psycho behemoth came after him. Brian forced himself to his feet, grimacing against the agony in his chest, and hobbled after them. Akerman managed to cross the catwalk to the stairs leading down to the pier. The monster was hot on his heels. Akerman tripped down the last few stairs and rolled out onto the little street beside the Sound.

Brian realized that he was never going to catch up, even if he used the elevator so he wouldn't have to hobble down the stairs himself. Helpless, he made his way to the rail and peered over to watch Akerman weave through traffic. The monster kept after him, knocking a car aside that didn't brake in time to avoid him.

Of all things, Akerman tried hopping the rail into the Sound. He'd only just gotten both hands on the rail and was trying to negotiate the climb when the psycho caught up with him. Psycho-dude grabbed Akerman with both hands, hoisted him into the air, and then hurled him into the water. Once this was done, the psycho turned back to the road, scanned the raised street, and roared in frustration. He stormed back onto the road, overturning another vehicle in his rage. Brian hopped into the elevator, hoping the psycho would be too angry to notice him as he made his way back up. Fortunately, that worked, and Brian was able to hobble to the pier and peer out at the dark water. He saw no one and nothing.

Shouting Akerman's name hurt like getting torn open, but he tried a few more times. No response. He couldn't possibly swim in his condition, so he reached for his phone, only to realize it had been in his hand when he was knocked to the ground, and he had no idea what had happened to it. Probably he'd dropped it in the grass. And now he had no idea where the psycho had gone, or where the douche from the bar was. Douche guy had booked as soon as he'd gotten a good luck at the pale psycho.

Thinking of the douche and the news report that had gotten him so agitated, Brian realized he actually recognized the pale-blue-skinned psycho. After all, he had been almost close enough to head butt the guy. Psycho was the dead wrestler from the report. The famous guy whose coffin had been raided.

CHAPTER 3
PASSIONS

Bianca made it clear that, once her duties as an instructor were ended, she wanted solitude. So after bidding Lindsey and the other students goodbye, Dracula headed to Wallingford in search of female companionship; whether he wished to or not, it was time to feed the demon to which he was unwillingly subject. This was one of the difficulties he was forced to contend with since waking up all those centuries ago. He was in the grip of vices—passions—which made demands. They had to be fed, no matter what he willed. All he could decide was *when*, not if, but the when could not be put off indefinitely. The *when* was a window within which he could operate. There was no true freedom.

He found a tavern he hadn't visited for some time and located a pair of women who seemed to be visiting. He managed to isolate one, but things went sour almost immediately, as she could not stop checking her phone every twenty seconds, chuckling at whatever it was she saw on it.

He was going to abandon her altogether when his own phone rang. The woman—whose name he had already forgotten—took the opportunity to return her attention to her own phone screen.

"What is it?" he asked.

"Something happened at Pike Place. Get down there," said the Special Services agent on the other end.

"'Something' is vague. And at a public venue? That's most unfortunate for your organization, isn't it?"

"Get down there. Now. You're armed, correct?"

"Naturally. What sort of monster is it?"

"Not certain. Lots of eyewitness accounts make us think it's an undead of some sort. We don't know yet what kind."

"I'm on my way."

He didn't particularly wish to deal with anything for Special Services—at any time, much less when the hunger to which he was now enslaved was gnawing at him—but he was making no progress on this front. After he hung up his phone, he reached out and grabbed the woman's drink from in front of her and downed it in one gulp.

"Hey!" she snapped. "That was mine!"

"I paid for it," he told her, then rose from the bar and left her there, bewildered and offended.

The distance would take less than ten minutes to cover, and he did not intend to worry about parking legally. However, he encountered a police line blocking the road.

He wasn't supposed to speak about the things Boese wished to keep secret—himself being one of those things—so he had no protocol to follow, just a fake FBI badge he was supposed to use only if the need arose to hide behind it. But that had not worked out well last time he'd used it, and he was reluctant to risk another arrest. Such things strained Bose's resources, and he resented that the burden subsequently fell on him.

So far as he knew, a supernatural breach like this, in a city full of people who all carried phones with cameras in them, was unprecedented. In the past, it had been relatively easy to sweep events under the proverbial rug.

One of the officers approached his car as he pulled out his phone. The policeman tapped on the corvette's window with one knuckle.

"Sir, you can't come through this way," the officer told him once he had lowered the glass.

"I've reached a police blockade," Dracula said into his phone. "How should I proceed?"

"Which cross streets?"

Dracula gave them.

"Sir, please back your vehicle up. This area is off limits," the officer told him.

"Wait there," said the agent over the phone.

Dracula hung up and waited.

"Sir, this is a crime scene. You have to go around. Everything is closed."

Just then, the officer's partner answered a call on his radio. He walked over to the officer at Dracula's car and they exchanged a hurried conversation, before they both waved him through, lifting the police tape so his corvette could just slide beneath. Dracula continued along deserted streets.

One of Boese's agents was standing near the tourist information kiosk just beside Pike Place, the market's large, neon sign uncharacteristically black against the night sky. The whole street was dark, every window dim. The scene struck him as curiously bleak and morose. Like a pillaged village or town from which all the townspeople had fled.

The agent awaiting him was of medium height, dressed in street clothing. He wore a baseball cap over his short hair and watched the street furtively. When he spotted Dracula coming, he waved him over.

"Took you long enough."

"What happened here?"

The agent glowered at him before answering. "Some huge humanoid monster appeared about two blocks north"—the agent pointed in the direction—"and came storming this way. It disabled a car; the driver and passenger have been sent to the hospital. Killed one guy who got too close, chased some off-duty officers to the waterfront, then came back up here."

"Came back? It had some purpose in this area in particular?"

"Yeah, this way." The agent led him around the tourist kiosk and down, to pass through the so-called Gum Wall.

Dracula had heard of the bizarre oddity, a place where people came to stick their chewing gum as a memento of their existence, or perhaps their arrival in this city. He could not understand how the municipal custodians tolerated such an unsanitary "tourist attraction", yet it persisted. He had never, ever intended to see it in person. Yet here he was. It was a little alley tucked down out of sight, the brick walls on either side smothered beneath wads and strings of gum. In the dim light most were shades of grey, but here and there were pink blobs or blue strands. Some colored pieces had been arrayed into attempts at artistic vision. Some lumps were pressed onto to the beams that crossed the ceiling, and the ground clutched at the bottoms of his shoes. It was dis-

Dracula's Match

gusting. He paused a moment, taking in the absurd eyesore, marveling that people traveled from afar to see this—and to contribute. What sane human being could see any sense in glorifying wads of chewed gum stuck to a public space?

Two people had been brutalized by whatever monstrosity had passed through. One, a young man, had been crushed up into the wall of the gum alley, dragged along it, and flung down onto the cement. Gum that had stuck to his clothes, skin, and hair was stretched off the wall; he appeared to have rainbow-colored tendrils coating one side of his body. The young woman was easier to read. She had been seized by her hoodie and thrown directly up into the ceiling. Her skull had cracked and her body had fallen to the ground. The couple's phones lay smashed on the ground.

This carnage was quite the display of strength. Whatever this creature was, each revelation ratcheted up Dracula's estimation of its formidable nature. However, despite the ferocity and viciousness of the attacks, the monster had murdered only a small number of people, considering how crowded the area usually was. Had the horror come here with a purpose other than murder? Could it reason?

If so, that bode its own particular kind of ill.

He stepped forward onto the exposed walkway beyond, continuing on about two hundred feet beyond the gum wall to climb the stairs to his left. This led to a place called a Selfie Museum. Dracula was barely aware of what "selfies" were. Cammy had done her best to explain their purpose to him, and shown him her social media profiles. So far as he could tell, selfies were simply vanity gone viral, as if the modern phones were technological parasites redirecting their hosts' energies with ever increasing demands for attention. Cammy had asked how selfies were different from having a portrait painted, and shown him images of his own portrait that she'd conjured up on her phone. Somewhat tersely, he'd answered that portraits were part of family history, or were commissioned to commemorate one's accomplishments. "It's the same thing today," Cammy had insisted. "Selfies are our histories. We share them with friends. We show each other where we are and what we're doing."

Without replying, he had studied the tiny image of himself. The portrait he had sat for, which had been commissioned. The others of him drifting about in the collective consciousness of the wider world had *not* been commissioned, and he had not been the model for them. They were to made to show him as a tyrant, a madman, a man of evil. To the extent that they were executed skillfully, portraits commemorated an artist's talent. They were made to serve a *purpose*, not simply to *do it*, and certainly not to do it *all the time*. He had heard of a merchant in Western Europe who had painted the outside of his home with scenes of his own life. In his opinion, the penchant for selfies was that same narcissism taken to some ludicrous extreme by technological convenience. And there was a *museum* dedicated to the practice!

But now that museum was demolished. Looking around, Dracula saw it had been something like a photography studio, with props and lights and colorfully painted walls. Now the walls had great holes punched through them, and several employees had been slaughtered. Either they were the targets, or they had been trapped inside and unable to escape before the monster completed its rampage. They had been killed brutally, but with such dispatch that he could not help thinking that they had been collateral damage, not the true targets of the monster's wrath. The young woman near the entrance had been slammed face-first into the floor, but only once, so far as he could tell. However, one of the other employees, another young woman, he found partly devoured, so the monster also had some desire or need to satiate a terrible hunger.

After he ascertained that no one still alive and in need of medical attention was present, he rejoined the agent by the gum wall.

"Your department has no idea what this thing is?" Dracula demanded.

"It doesn't correspond to anything in our profiles."

"You've reached out to Ophois?" He expected that the occult mercenaries would have some knowledge, or even some hand in this event. Besides their practice of magic, they were infamous for selling their goods to *any* bidder who had the money: human or supernatural was of no concern to them.

"They've gone to ground, but we think they had something to do with this thing."

"Oh?"

"Yeah. The walking dead guy is the one who got dug up. One of our techs was a wrestling fan back in the day and recognized him. Turns out his friends had reached out to Ophois before he died. We were looking into the grave vandalism, so we already had pictures of him when this happened. From some of the phone camera footage we got, we realized he's our animal. Our intel is that he and his buddies had been in contact with Ophois for several months, maybe a year. Then he does a little murder-suicide and comes back as… whatever he is. Something tough."

"I've seen more of his handiwork," Dracula said, "and I concur. Is there any sign of the monster now?"

"No. After this rampage he farted off somewhere. No one saw how he did it. Just disappeared."

"If he, or it, became incorporeal, he could be some sort of spirit," Dracula suggested. "Perhaps summoned for the purpose of sowing chaos? Or calling attention to the supernatural?"

"For a spirit, it sure seems solid. Stands to reason it's corporeal when it's flipping cars and taking bites out of people."

"This could have all been relayed to me over the phone."

"It was still rampaging when we called. Disappeared just a little while ago."

Dracula grunted. A waste of his time. All that remained now was cleanup, and that was in the hands of Special Services. He had no way of managing news crews or a horde of eye witnesses with camera phones.

"Well, if you don't need me, I'll be on my way," he said.

"The director wants you to call him."

Dracula grunted again. He'd do that in the morning. If the director had something to say, he could call himself or he could wait.

Once back in his vehicle, he did call Malcolm. The phone rang and finally went to voicemail. That was unusual, so Dracula dialed again. No answer once more. That did *not* bode well at all. Perhaps Ophois *was* involved. If so, then it was no mere happenstance that created that monster. Furthermore, it could mean that he and Malcolm might wind up in opposition as their rival masters—he sneered inwardly—pursued their very different objectives. It had always been only a matter of time before Malcolm's relationship with one of Special Services' "assets" put him in between the two organizations.

However, all of that was a problem for later. Right now, if he did not placate the vice to which he was subject, he would become dangerous. So he returned to his earlier activity, intending to find out more about the strange monster, and Malcolm's possible involvement, in the morning.

Malcolm listened to the sounds of panic behind him. He'd gotten a pretty good look at whatever it was. It was able to form itself out of mist. Should be a short list of things that could do that, but he was pretty sure he already knew what it was. The real problem was that Ophois was probably behind the appearance of the monster. That meant that people would be going to come asking questions—or *more* than ask questions.

Whatever Roar "Thor" Thorirsson had turned into, it was the meanest thing Malcolm had ever been near. Undead Roar radiated some sort of malice so strong that the screaming noise that dwelt inside Malcolm had reacted immediately. Some kind of resonance. If he had stayed any longer....

Well, he wasn't out of the woods yet. That energy had gotten him badly riled up. He was barely keeping it together, and listening to the screaming behind him wasn't helping.

If Roar had turned into what Malcolm figured he had—one of the strongest undead out there, and not seen for hundreds of years—then the best plan was to make tracks. He couldn't face down something that strong. He wasn't sure there was anyone in the North American continent who could.

Vlad, maybe?

Maybe. Vlad was the only thing which might be comparable, but strigoi were in a whole different weight class—a lighter weight class. Roar looked to be in one of the heaviest.

Malcolm felt that push to drop to all fours and run after the nearest person he could find and rip out their throat. Sometimes it hummed, sometimes it screamed, but it was never silent. Now it was screaming, and if he didn't give in, it would overtake him eventually. Extremely soon, by the feel of the intensity. He balled his hands into fists and purposefully walked away. He dared not run. Get too excited, he might lose it. He had to get home, and *fast*. Capitol Hill wasn't too far away. The problem was he hadn't bothered to drive. A half hour walk wasn't usually a problem for him, but he was running out of time.

It was a risk to get a ride, but he didn't have a choice. He wasn't going to last half an hour. Someone had probably called the police by now, so he ordered a ride for a location a block away.

He made it there by glaring at the ground and ignoring everyone he walked past. All the happy couples and people with normal lives. People with real jobs, with benefits, with friends, leading happy little lives while completely asleep. They weren't going to be called up to take on a demon monster.

Bunch of happy, ignorant, munching sheep is what they all were, and he really, *really* wanted to bash all their faces in. Knock their teeth straight down their happy little throats. Bludgeon them all into bloody pulp and his knuckles were torn wide open showing tendon and bone.

He found the sedan he'd called for, and got in.

"You ok, buddy?" the driver asked.

Dracula's Match

"How about you drive like I hired you to and I won't rip your heart straight outta your chest Kali Ma style, huh?"

"Listen: I've had a bad day. If you can't be civil for ten minutes I'll cancel this ride and you can find someone else or walk, got it?"

Malcolm let his breath out between his teeth and sank back into his seat. The driver eyed him in the rearview mirror for a moment before he pulled away from the curb. Malcolm gripped his knees and tried very hard to keep his breathing even. The two beers he'd had tonight weren't helping. He squeezed his eyes shut. He could smell the driver. The guy hadn't showered since yesterday. Stressed. Nervous.

Humans smelled bad. Well, most things did. The overwhelming cacophony of scents was something Malcolm couldn't escape. He could tell when someone used the bathroom in the next apartment. He could tell when they had bathed last, whether they were diseased or not. He couldn't prove it, but he suspected he could tell what the pH of their bodies was based on the smell. It drove him crazy. Everyone's dogs and everything each stupid mutt had rolled in lately. On the occasions he'd gone out to the forests, things were better. There were fewer smells. Mostly plants, some wild animal tracks. The air was clearer.

All he could think was how *easy* it would be to kill the guy sitting in front of him. Once they parked, he could reach around the seat and strangle the guy one-handed. Let that demon out and stop fighting it. Just kill the stupid mother right in front of him. Right there.

The car rolled to a stop. The driver made eye contact with him through the rearview mirror again. This time, he could tell something was wrong, because he whipped his head around to get a better look at Malcolm.

"Right here," he prompted.

Malcolm considered him. It would be *so* very easy…

"Take care of yourself," he told the guy, and got out. He walked towards his apartment building along the semi-dark sidewalk, pulled out his phone and called his handler, who was a mid-level guy in Ophois. High enough that he oversaw the goings on in Seattle and some parts of the Pacific Northwest. Malcolm spoke Latin to him. If some educated-looking Catholic was walking by, he could switch to Greek or Egyptian or some other obscure language he knew.

"I'm gonna lose it," he told his handler. "That guy, the one who got back up. There's some *serious* dark juju with him. I can't… send someone to get me tomorrow."

"Where are you now?"

"Just outside my apartment."

Malcolm hung up and stumbled inside. He slammed the elevator button as rapidly as he could, and when some college kid came up beside him he turned, glared, and snarled directly in the kid's face. The kid backed off.

He rode the elevator up alone, made it past the door where some stupid college morons were having a loud party, to the end of the hall to his own door. There were extra locks on it. Black magic written all over it in weeping black paint. The landlord had said something about it *once*. Ophois had made it clear to the guy that minding his own business was in his best interests, and he had ever since.

Malcolm got all the locks open, slipped inside, and shook the beaded sweat from his forehead. Getting real bad.

Dracula's Match

Inside, the place smelled of his cologne and shampoos and other soaps. Besides that, there were the plants he burned for spells. Some takeout he had left on the counter. Candles. Smoke. Burning sulphur.

Beside his bed was a harness built by hand out of steel pipes and heavy chains. Lots of them. He threw his phone on his bed and hurriedly knelt down beside the harness anchored directly into the wall and the floor. He wrapped one wrist with a towel and slapped one of the heavy-duty manacles over it. Some sort of antique from some real-life dungeon, nothing modern. Lots of misery imprinted deep in the metal. He clapped the big one around his neck, another on his ankle, and wrapped his other wrist.

Then he realized he'd forgotten to play something on the stereo. Something with enough screaming and creepy stuff no one would think much of what else they might hear. Whatever. No time left. He kicked the lever that pulled all the chains taut and dragged him to the floor.

The murder-rage-haze exploded in his mind. All hate, envy, rage. He wanted to kill absolutely every single person on the planet. But especially his handler and all that pack of monsters who had done this to him. Send them and him all straight to hell together.

The faint, white glow of sun through clouds pulled him out of his deep haze. His wrists and ankle ached. His shirt was stained by sweat and he was lying in a puddle of his own drying urine.

He hated everything.

About a half an hour later he heard the footsteps in the hall and that *smell*, that stench, which announced the arrival of his handler in person. He didn't know the guy's real name, the guy just wanted to be called "Master" whenever he showed up. No one in Ophois was going to share names with underlings.

The locks all popped open and the door to the studio apartment swung open. In walked a guy dressed in a long black trench coat like some kind of stereotype. He had his graying hair slicked back and wore gloves. He spotted Malcolm.

"Nothing broken?"

"Get me out of this, willya?"

The harness was designed so once sprung it would be impossible for Malcolm to unlock himself. If he broke the chains—which wasn't entirely beyond possibility, though he hadn't done it yet—then all bets were off.

"So you saw Mr. Thorirsson last night?" his handler said, crossing the room to unlock the manacles.

"Yeah. Got a good look at him." They were speaking in English now. Malcolm was always weak as a kitten after transforming. It was worse than berserking. "I think he's a draugr."

"Given what we've found, we think so too," his handler said. He opened the clasp to the manacle around Malcolm's neck, then both wrists. He let Malcolm open the ankle one. Malcolm swayed; he lacked the strength to do almost anything yet. He used the wall to keep nearly upright. It would take him a while to work up the energy to sit up under his own power. He needed sleep. Days of sleep, a week of sleep—but with a draugr running around, he probably wasn't going to get it. There were bottles of sports drinks and jars of

Dracula's Match

bone broth in his pantry, plus coffee. He'd have to down huge quantities as soon as he could stand.

"And that's something you morons helped cause?" Malcolm snarled.

The handler withdrew beyond arm's reach. Not that Malcolm could have killed him at the moment.

"He and some of his friends wanted our help," the handler said. "Which we provided. They paid us very well."

"Yeah, well, we're going to get blamed for turning a freaking celebrity into one of the strongest undead ever," Malcolm snapped.

"We've been in contact with the US government since this morning," his handler replied slowly. "Don't get worked up about it. We'll turn this around. They'll probably need us to deal with the late Mr. Thorirsson's friends."

"Given that 'dogs' dug him up, I figure you guys taught him and his buddies how to be werewolves."

"Naturally. Mr. Thorirsson and his friends had interest in such things, and we are experts on how to transform into werewolves or other creatures."

"Perfect," Malcolm hissed. "But while you were chasing a profit, you caused a problem that Special Services will go ballistic over. This guy showed up in *public*. When Uncle Sam finds out you taught a bunch of amateurs how to turn into people-eating berserkers—"

The handler raised a hand to silence Malcom.

"We are handling it. Uncle Sam has skeletons in his closet, too. We didn't get rich teaching *peasants* how to sell their souls for a chance to indulge their taste for human flesh. Uncle Sam knows how we operate, and that we pledge allegiance to no government, only to money. That's why they like us so much. All people in power like playing with fire. They always get burned by it, but return like moths unable to resist that sweet flame."

"Speak for yourselves, huh?"

The handler's face wrinkled in an off-putting way. Despite his weariness, Malcolm wondered how satisfying it would be to sink his teeth into the throat under that condescending smirk and rip it open.

"Careful there," his handler said. "If you go off and do anything to me, I needn't remind you what will befall you."

"Yeah, well, one day maybe I won't care if you guys kill me afterward," Malcolm told him.

"Of course you will," the handler countered. "Because you know that, as bad as I am, what awaits you beyond that crossing will be far, far worse. On a *related* note," he grinned nastily, "you're count is up to five now. It's confirmed."

Malcolm looked down at his hands. He only had the strength to form one fist, and a weak one at that.

"Get cleaned up. I imagine we'll have work for you soon."

Malcolm summoned the strength for two fists.

"Good dog," the handler told him, then let himself out.

CHAPTER 4
HIDDEN PEOPLE

Classes had started again, and Cammy had transferred to a "real university" as her mother would have put it. Given all the credits she'd amassed from years of community college, she'd been forced to select a major. She'd only landed on "Communications" because it sounded like something she could do. She had to catch the bus to get from the Mindful Bean to campus on days when she had classes before or after her shift, but not having to pay rent was helping Cammy's finances *enormously*.

Dracula did not explain why he'd sent her back with Brian, or where he'd been. He greeted her in the morning with the same cool cordiality as always, and drove her to the Mindful Bean. It had been months, and it was still weird. She had the feeling he'd treat anyone under his roof with the same degree of detached, distant politeness—so long as they didn't break anything, or steal something, or go wandering around where they weren't supposed to. For the most part, he left her alone and she stayed out of his way. There'd been that one time she'd taught him how to use a laptop and surf the internet; since then she'd seen him spending hours reading newsfeeds in languages she didn't even know the names of on his laptop. Occasionally he listened to music, usually old, vinyl records—he had records that no one had ever bothered to convert to e-files—and sometimes when he did she'd quietly slip into the music room. She found that doing homework to music without words, or words she didn't understand, or operas she didn't recognize, was oddly soothing. As weeks and then months had passed, she was no longer having nightmares every night. If he ever heard her crying alone in her room, he never mentioned it.

He bid her goodbye and she went to work her morning shift.

Kenzie was working in the afternoon that day. The first words out of her mouth when she breezed in were, "So, did you ask Draaaagulah whether the real-life Vlad's first wife's death by suicide is what made him such a bad guy?"

Cammy looked up from the floor. She'd been sweeping crumbs from under a table by the front windows. She liked cleaning things. It was better than talking to people. Seeing everyone else happy made her think of how she'd never talk to Heather ever again.

Kenzie liked to pester Cammy with questions about the historical Dracula, since she was positive that Cammy's host was a direct descendant, proud of the name and inclined to mimic the mannerisms. So far as Cammy could tell, Kenzie didn't suspect that the man in whose mansion she was living *was* the historical Dracula. Fan or not, it didn't seem that Kenzie could believe that vampires might actually be real.

"What?" Cammy asked.

Dracula's Match

"You know! That story about Dracula's wife committing suicide because she thought he'd been killed in a battle against the Ottoman Empire!"

Cammy hadn't been paying much attention to Kenzie's bubbly ramblings lately. Vampire movie trivia wasn't as interesting now that Cammy'd not only been kidnapped by real ones, but killed one. Heather. She could still *feel* that piece of wood punching through Heather's chest. It made Cammy queasy to remember.

"I don't know," Cammy said. If Kenzie had asked her to pass that question on, she'd forgotten. She also felt pretty sure he wouldn't want to talk about it.

"Well… could you ask?"

"*You* could ask," Cammy told her. Kenzie puffed an errant strand of her bright green hair out of her eye.

"I dunno. I think he doesn't like me asking him questions."

Probably not, Cammy thought. Kenzie made a face, but went to clock in. When she reemerged after putting away her fuzzy spider purse, she said, "Hey, next time you see Lindsey, can you ask her to do a Halloween party at her parents' place next year? I tried it at my apartment and it just doesn't have enough space. I think she'll be more willing if you ask than if I bug her."

"What? Why?"

"Her mom thinks I'm a bad influence, so I can't ask."

"But why there? And you're really thinking of next year already?"

"Yeah, because it didn't work this year, and Halloween is supposed to be amazing. Besides, you've seen her house. Her family is *loaded*. I want to do a *real* party, especially now that

63

we're over twenty-one. I already told her that I'd go with a whole themed group."

"What?"

"She wants to do a Monster High theme party. You should come. There are still some characters that haven't been picked. Pink is just not my color, but if I don't go as a vampire, I'll never live it down."

"Uh, ok," Cammy agreed. She'd declined going to Kenzie's party last month. She hadn't felt up to do anything social yet. Aside from last night, she hadn't hung out with her friends since May, and she really should go out and meet with people instead of just going to work, school, and Dracula's mansion. And by next year, she ought to be feeling better, right? The idea of *not* being miserable because Heather was dead bothered her. That would be like forgetting her, wouldn't it? Then she realized that probably all the guests would be dressing up as vampires and ghouls and zombies and all sorts of monsters. People let their kids dress up as monsters. Her mind conjured up the image of Kenzie's little sister dressed up as Heather in a scraggly, blood-stained shirt, her face unnaturally gray, her eyes wide and black and dead. Cammy turned her head to the window so Kenzie couldn't see her shudder.

"Have you heard what happened at Pike Place last night?"

Cammy took a deep breath and turned back to Kenzie.

"No, what?"

"There was this crazy guy who ran through and destroyed stuff. He killed some people," Kenzie explained. "And he totally wrecked the Selfie Museum. Lindsey texted me about it last night. It was on the news."

"I don't watch the... I didn't hear anything," Cammy said. In her mind, she pictured Brian going to catch some madman armed with a bloody machete and her stomach tied into knots. She didn't like him being a cop. It was way too dangerous. Especially now that she knew there were creatures out there *far* deadlier than madmen with machetes. "Who was it? Did they catch him?"

Kenzie shook her head.

"The weirdest part is the news just stopped talking about it completely. They aren't even covering the story of that wrestling dude whose corpse got dug up yesterday. It's just business as usual. Weather and drug busts. Some of the videos I saw online are gone, too."

"Gone?"

"Yeah, YEETed right out of existence. Billie posted something she found and it was pulled today." Kenzie played with her lip ring and grinned. "You want to hear the weird part?"

"What?" Cammy asked.

"Some people were saying the crazy guy down there looked *exactly* like the dead wrestler dude."

Cammy felt her stomach roll over. She wanted to call Dracula, or Malcolm at least. They might know if the situation was supernatural. She felt sick.

"Wait a minute," she said slowly. "Doesn't Andrew work down there?"

Kenzie's mouth hung slack as the realization struck her, then she started tapping furiously on her phone.

Luna, the Mindful Bean's owner, came out of the office and spotted what Kenzie was doing.

"Get your apron on. Cammy, isn't your shift over? Talk after you've clocked out."

"I gotta check something…" Kenzie mumbled.

"*Now*," Luna told her. Kenzie shot Cammy a look, and pocketed her phone.

"I'll check on Andrew," Cammy mouthed to her while untying her own apron.

On the ride to campus Cammy texted Andrew and checked his social media profiles. Of the group of friends Kenzie had introduced her to, she knew Andrew the least well. He didn't talk much, almost never posted anything, and rarely replied to messages. The only person who might know where he was was Aslan, since the two of them played games online. She texted Aslan, asking if he knew anything.

Cammy made it to campus a little early. She checked her phone. No messages from Andrew or Aslan. Dracula didn't answer texts, but Malcolm did, so she shot him a message about what happened, then decided to call Dracula. She didn't want her conversation overheard, so she stood on the corner outside a coffee shop across the street from campus.

"Is there something the matter?" Dracula asked.

"Did something supernatural happen at Pike Place?"

"Yes. Special Services still isn't certain what the creature was."

Cammy's stomach tightened more.

"My friend Andrew works down there. I don't know if he's all right."

"As it happens, I spoke with him two days ago. Since Special Services is investigating, I can assist them by visiting his family business to see if I learn any details."

Her heart thumped with relief.

"Thanks," she said. "I really appreciate it."

Dracula's Match

"I will let you know what I find when I pick you up after your class."

Hearing that he would look into what had happened made her feel much better, even though that made no logical sense. If something had happened to Andrew, it wasn't like Dracula could change past events. But if there was anything to be done, he could do it. He'd stopped all those vampires in April. Surely he could stop whatever was running around now.

She decided to get some food now rather than wait until her classes were over to eat. After ordering a croissant sandwich and a coffee from the shop, she sat at an outside table and pulled out her phone. She tried looking for information on this dead wrestling person Kenzie had referenced. She might as well; ruminating about life was unbearable, and having something to do was a welcome distraction. Maybe this time she could help one of her friends *before* something supernatural got them killed.

It didn't take long to find reposts of local reports of vandalism at Lake View Cemetery by "dogs." But nothing on official channels, just as Kenzie had said. The only official report she found was a morning show discussion of a sudden increase in dog attacks in Downtown. There were also a few confusing reports that there had been a disturbance at Pike Place that had required police to evacuate the area.

Dogs digging up graves? Maybe it was werewolves. Cammy had seen that Malcolm, like Dracula, didn't conform to modern ideas of what supernatural creatures were supposed to be. Maybe someone going berserk could explain why no one was really sure what had happened at Pike Place. As far as the news not reporting it, that had to be Boese and his minions trying to cover the whole thing up. Just like Heather's death, and the deaths of Heather's parents. Boese, the director of the branch of Special Services headquartered in Seattle, wasn't very interested in helping, just sweeping everything under the rug.

Even though this search was going nowhere, it was definitely better than moping, so she called the other person who might know something. He hadn't texted back, but he might answer if she called.

"What?" Malcolm half-growled and half-mumbled when he picked up.

"Did a bunch of werewolves dig up some dead guy at Lake View Cemetery yesterday?"

Malcolm sigh-growled.

A small murder of crows descended on the corner of the shop and started cawing at passersby beneath.

"Yeah. Probably. I don't know why. The dead guy in question also got back up."

Got back up? So he must be undead. "Was he old-school, or something new?" Cammy asked.

"So far as I can tell, old-school. *Real* old school. And *bad* news. I don't know what he's up to. If you see *anything*, run as fast as you can."

"Why? Is he an old-school vampire? Like Vlad?"

"Not like him. More like a zombie on steroids. A more technical term might be *revenant*. Did you call me just to ask about that?"

"Yeah," she admitted. She wondered if there was any chance the cat she'd seen last night was related. "Can witches turn into cats?"

Dracula's Match

The crows descended on a student with a backpack who was leaving the shop with a sandwich in hand. They pecked at the sandwich and he dropped it with a shout of surprise. The crows swarmed the sandwich, beating each other with their wings for the chance to snatch a piece. She pulled out the adder stone to see if there was something to this unusual behavior. They just looked like crows.

"Why? Did you see one acting strangely?"

"Um, sort of," Cammy said. She heard Malcolm grumble-growling something to himself. She scanned the street through the adder stone. On the one hand, she didn't want to see this thing if it was around; on the other hand, she'd never seen anything supernatural through the stone, and she wanted to. Did that mean there was something wrong with her? Of course she didn't want to see a murderous zombie on steroids, but weren't there supposed to be talking animals and gnomes or whatever? Still, Dracula had told her that most of the supernatural world was pretty shy.

"Some witches can transform," Malcolm mumbled. "Some things just change shape by their nature."

"What about werewolves?" she asked. She scanned the street and store fronts through the adder stone. Was she ever going to see anything with it? What would she even do if she *did*?

"What about them?" Malcolm growled.

"Well, is it a power, or something else? Genetic?"

"You asking about me or the modern stuff?" His voice had an edge like that battle axe he'd used to protect her from vampires when she'd first moved into Dracula's mansion. Something eerie, brutal, and angry about it.

"What about the ones that vandalized that guy's grave?" Cammy knew Malcolm didn't like to talk about himself either.

"I don't know!" he snapped.

"Um, is everything ok?" she asked. This wasn't like him. He liked to snark and smile, not seethe like this.

"*No*, as a matter of fact, everything is *not* ok!" he snapped. "I had a very bad night and you called me up out of the blue for no reason!"

"I was curious!" Cammy protested. Just then, she spotted a young girl, maybe ten, wearing a little black cap and some kind of old-fashioned folk-costume dress come darting out of a store with two paper sacks in hand. She sprinted into traffic, weaving dangerously around the cars that never even slowed down or honked. Cammy gasped and jumped to her feet—to do something. Anything. Run out there and push the girl out of a car's path maybe.

But there was no girl. Just cars and students and pedestrians. Cammy blinked, scanned the crowd. She couldn't possibly have lost the girl in all that. Her clothes stood out *way* too much. A long, red skirt, an apron, some sort of vest, and that funny-looking little black hat. And she had been running. She ought to stand out.

"What just happened?" Malcolm demanded.

"I..."

The adder stone! Dracula had told her it could reveal invisible things. Cammy held it up to her eye again. Sure enough, there was the girl, running towards campus, though with less speed. She didn't even turn around to check if she was being followed.

Because she's invisible and she knows it! Cammy realized. That's why the cars never stopped or honked.

Dracula's Match

"There's an invisible girl!" Cammy blurted into the phone.

"What?" Malcolm demanded.

"This little girl! She ran into traffic! I think she took something from—" Cammy checked the storefront where the girl in the funny skirt had come running—"a sandwich place. She almost got run over."

"She can't be invisible if you can see her."

"Vlad gave me his adder stone to hold onto for a while." Cammy hastily snatched up her drink, holding it awkwardly in one hand. Fortunately, she had used her headphones for the call so she could stuff her phone in her purse and hurry after the girl. If she sprinted, she could make the light.

"Are you running?" Malcolm asked. "Wait, are you *chasing* some invisible person? Vlad gave you that? That thing is *priceless. Are you running with that?!*"

"Yeah, I'm going to lose her if I don't hurry," Cammy said.

"Don't chase invisible people!" Malcolm shouted. "Are you stupid or something? Nothing that spends its time invisible is good news!"

"But it's a girl," Cammy said. "A kid. And she had to avoid cars. She might get hurt."

"Who cares?!" Malcolm roared. "Who cares if some invisible bugbear gets hit by a car? Stop chasing her right now! Where are you?"

"I'm on campus," Cammy said. The girl was crossing the parking lot, so Cammy had a clear view of her. "I have classes today."

"I can hear you still running," Malcolm snarled. "Stop it. For your own good. That thing is bad news."

"Well, what is she?" Cammy asked.

Amaya Tenshi

"I can't tell without seeing it," Malcolm said. "Now stop. Running. After her. You have a death wish?"

Death wish? Cammy wondered. There wasn't much reason to do things. College? It wouldn't get her a job, and the loans... Talk about movies with Kenzie? Or go to dance classes with Lindsey? For how long? To do what? Heather was dead. Cammy couldn't help anybody, and she couldn't fight vampires either.

Maybe she did have one.

The girl rounded a building and Cammy struggled to close the distance. If she lost sight of her, even the adder stone wasn't going to help.

"Stop!" Malcolm shouted.

Cammy rounded the corner.

She spotted the girl breathlessly leaning against the building. A boy, maybe twelve, stood before her. He was also dressed funny, wearing a little cap with a tassel on it, and stockings. He gestured angrily at the paper bags in her hands and was shouting in some language Cammy didn't understand or recognize at all. The girl feebly protested as he continued to berate her. Though she couldn't understand the language, Cammy guessed he was angry at her for stealing, since Cammy doubted the girl could have paid for anything if no one could see her without a magic stone. Cammy lowered the stone, and the boy's voice vanished with her ability to see him. Weird. Apparently adder stones could reveal sound as well. She lifted the stone again.

The boy had spotted her. He squinted suspiciously. The girl followed his eyes and the two of them regarded Cammy. Now Cammy wondered what to do. If she dropped the stone, she wouldn't be able to see them, and if they *were* dangerous like Malcolm insisted they were, then she needed to keep track of them. Did they recognize the adder stone?

Maybe they're fairies? Cammy wondered to herself. Dracula said there weren't any any around anymore, but fairies would recognize the stone, right? He said he'd gotten it from them, right? Although these children were awfully big for fairies, and they didn't have wings or anything.

The boy spoke softly to the girl, and they started moving away, keeping an eye on Cammy as they went. She figured she shouldn't follow too closely. They'd realize for sure she could see them if they hadn't figured it out already. But she didn't want to lose them either. Following people while holding a stone ring to your eye was pretty suspicious-looking, though. They could probably recognize her from just from that.

She stepped forward, her mind still spinning on the problem when she felt a hand on her shoulder and jumped straight up with a little squeak of alarm.

"What do you think you're doing?!" Malcolm hissed into her ear.

"Ow! What are you doing here?"

"I only live a few minutes away," Malcolm growled. "Put that down!" He slapped the adder stone out of her hands, and it fell against her chest. Angrily, she hid it from sight.

"I was just—"

"Shut up. Stop. Whatever you were going to say, *don't*. You're unbelievable."

"I think they were fairies," Cammy told him. "They noticed me watching—"

"You let them *spot* you?" Malcolm demanded, and one of his huge hands went to his head. "Vlad should put you on a *leash*! You're going to get yourself killed!"

"Vlad should… is that why you're here? Did he hire you to babysit again?" Cammy asked, growing angry. How dare he keep treating her like a *child* all the time! It wasn't like she was going to go try to kill a top vampire by herself. Again.

"I'm on standing orders to keep you out of trouble if I think you're up to something stupid," Malcolm growled.

He looked like he hadn't slept in three days; he had bags under his dull and tired gold eyes. She also realized he didn't smell of cologne as usual. Just shampoo and body wash. In fact, his hair was damp, now that she looked again.

"Did you just get up?" she asked.

"None of your business," he snarled.

"What is with you?" Cammy demanded. "Woke up on the wrong side of the bed or—"

"I just had to run downstairs and drive over here in a hurry to make sure you didn't get kidnapped by some kind of monster because you're acting like an idiot. I had a real bad night. I'm not in a great mood, ok? There's some sort of top-tier super undead on the loose, and who knows what else. The *last* thing I need is to have to drop everything and come running over here to make sure you don't—"

He glared past her, narrowed his eyes at something, and then pushed her aside to walk past. Cammy scowled at him, but he totally ignored her and headed towards a young woman sitting under the shade of a tree. Reclined, actually, like a figure in a classical painting. She was dressed in a "bohemian" style, in retro blouse and a long, flowing skirt. Her dark hair hung in long, curling, wild strands.

Dracula's Match

Some kind of fluffy little yellow dog moved by her leg. A Yorkshire Terrier? No, wait, Cammy couldn't see its head.

Another thingamajig! she realized. Malcolm had spotted the headless... whatever it was and was going to take care of whatever the problem might be. She hurried after him to get a better look at whatever it was before he spooked it off. When she was about ten feet off, she could see better that whatever it was didn't look like an animal. She couldn't tell what it was. A duster? A tiny mop?

"Excuse me, miss," Malcolm addressed the lady. "I'm sorry to bother you, but your petticoat is showing."

The young woman focused her electric eyes on him and sat bolt upright. She straightened her skirt, hiding the moving duster. She huffed.

"Thank you," she said, and smiled *very* invitingly at him. "Who might you be, who knows how to talk to me?"

Huh? Cammy thought. The woman wasn't dressed like the invisible kids, and she spoke English, but with a real thick accent. Cammy edged closer.

Malcolm lifted his hand and pulled his watch from his wrist, revealing a small tattoo that looked like the outline of Anubis' head. The woman's eyes flashed like lightning when she saw that, and she jumped to her feet, pressing herself against the tree.

"Yeah. I'm with Ophois," he told her. "You're a long way from home, to listen to you. And we've got some weirdness going on."

"Seattle is always veird," the woman pointed out, and shook her mane of hair. An errant leaf fluttered out. Cammy could see mud and grass stains on the skirt. She wasn't sure the woman's clothes had ever been washed. Given the state of her clothing, Cammy expected her to stink, but she couldn't pick up anything except maybe grass or sod.

"That's Portland," Cammy pointed out.

"Seattle's pretty weird, too," Malcolm told her.

"Do you mean the draugr?" the woman asked, ignoring Cammy and speaking to Malcolm. She played with a lock of her long, long hair. "That has nothing to do vith me."

"So you know about it?" Malcolm asked.

Draugr. Cammy had heard that word. From a video game Andrew and Aslan had talked about a few years ago. Some kind of dangerous undead thingie.

"I saw it," the woman said. "And I ran avay. I did not expect such a thing here. I have heard this place is guarded by someone very *great*."

Vlad? Cammy wondered. "Do you mean Vlad?" She asked aloud. The woman's eyes lit like sparks, and she set them on Cammy. She was lovely, but something about her features seemed unnatural. She had high cheekbones, and it was like they were slightly *too* high, or *too* shapely. Her eyes were bright in a way Cammy hadn't seen before. But it was all subtle. Cammy doubted anyone who didn't know there were supernatural creatures running around would pick up on it.

"You know him?" The woman stepped toward her, very eagerly. Malcolm thrust out an arm to stop her advance.

"You got business with the big guns here?" he asked.

"I came here *especially* for him," the woman said. "But I couldn't reach him. His place is vell guarded and I dared not approach."

"Ok, let's play this by the book," Malcolm said. "I'm Malcolm, with the Order of Ophois. One of their werewolves. Who are you; who do you work for?"

Dracula's Match

The woman tossed her hair and grinned with an alluring gleam in her eye.

"Siri," she said, "I do not vork for anyone. I lived in the forests with my mother and sisters. Ve vere not as vell off as ve vonce vere. So I left. To the cities. I learned many things, and heard of the man who lives *here*. I thought I should learn of the world, as it is now, and vonce I have learned, to return and help my people. Or else…"

"You're from Norway?" Malcolm asked. Cammy wondered how he knew. Siri nodded.

"Yes. I took boats to reach this land, and traveled by foot."

By boat and by foot? Siri must have been traveling a long time. Maybe that didn't bother supernatural beings.

"Well, if you're here for info, then keep your head down," Malcolm advised her. "The US government's got a branch out here, because of how much weird is here. And they're going to be combing the area for anything they can find now that there's a draugr on the loose."

Siri shrugged one shoulder and pulled free one lock of her hair. "I dyed it dark. They wouldn't recognize me now." She turned to Cammy. "You know him? The vun called Dracula?"

"Yeah, I know Vlad," Cammy answered. Malcolm turned to face her, wrapped one arm around her shoulder and leaned down to look her in the eye.

"Hey, don't talk to the *huldra*, huh?" he told her. "Especially not about our mutual friend."

"But—"

"*Listen*," Malcolm snarled, his gold eyes blazing. "I am in no mood for your stupid questions. Don't. Talk. To her. She's not something you can befriend, ok? *Hulders* can be dangerous—"

"You say that about *everything*," Cammy pointed out.

"Because it's true!" Malcolm snapped. "*Hulders* kill people. That's a fact. They kill them for all kinds of whacky reasons, but they do it."

"What do you mean 'whacky'?" Cammy asked.

Siri tapped Malcolm on the shoulder. He whirled on her; she stepped lightly back, just out of arm's reach, and smiled her alluring smile.

"Good sir," she said, "there is no need for such caution. I like humans. I intend to become vun."

"Good for you," Malcolm said. He pointed at Cammy. "This one's off-limits. Leave her alone."

"I have no intention of harming her," Siri told him, still smiling. Cammy stared. The smile wasn't one of her mother's cold, fake smiles, but there was something a little off about it. Cammy couldn't put her finger on what.

"Keep it that way," Malcolm told her. He tightened his arm around Cammy's shoulders and marched her back towards the parking lot.

"Hey, I've got class," she said.

"Not right now, you don't. That thing is *awfully* interested in Vlad and I bet she's going to follow you." He looked over his shoulder. Cammy snuck a peek as well. Siri hadn't moved, but she stood playing with a lock of her dark hair, watching the two of them walk away. She still wore her smile, more eager than before.

"Is she related to the invisible kids?"

Malcolm shoved her against his Camaro, yanked open the door, then breathed out an angry sigh and patted the roof, before pushing her down into the seat and closing the door carefully. Cammy crossed her arms as he came around and dropped into his own seat and locked the doors. He checked the rearview mirror for Siri. Cammy turned to look. Sure enough, the huldra had come within eyesight of the parking lot to watch them.

Malcolm pulled out of the parking lot. "Ok," he told her. "Here's the short version: *hulders* are a type of forest nymph, kind of. They have tails."

"Oh *that's* what I saw under her skirt," Cammy realized.

"Right. Some have fox tails, some have cow tails. That one had option b. The fluffy end was showing. Anyway, if you *mention* the tail, they will kill you."

Cammy stared at him.

"I'm dead serious," he told her. "You have to be careful what you say. That's why I went the old-fashioned route."

"Yeah, I wondered," Cammy said. "She wasn't wearing a petticoat."

"Right. Saying 'Your petticoat is showing' is one of the safe ways of warning a *huldra* that her tail is showing. Anyway, they take men as lovers, but kill them if the men don't measure up," Malcolm said.

"What?" None of this sounded anything like a nymph.

"They live in forests, usually," Malcolm went on. "They like to lure young men to be their lovers. And they exchange their weird babies for healthy human babies. Changelings. The way fairies do."

"Vlad said there aren't fairies anymore."

Malcolm made a face.

"Maybe not the Irish ones," he said. "But you could argue that any 'hidden people' group could qualify."

"Hidden people?"

"A blanket category I have," Malcolm said. "'Hidden people' is actually sort of what the word *hulder* means, but in Icelandic they also have the word *huldufólk*, which means the ones considered to be elves. The term covers the Little People, Hill People—basically any sort of humanoid that hides in nature, sometimes invisibly, with various magic talents. Dwarves, elves, fairies, *ludki*, all the *rå* people. Those brownies Vlad has would qualify."

"But they don't live in nature," Cammy said.

"No, sometimes they like to hang out with humans. Even help them. Marry them. Live with them, all that. Doesn't mean they're not still dangerous."

"So those invisible kids are the same sort of thing? Some kind of hidden people?"

"Maybe. Unless they're witches."

"Witches? Really?"

"*Yes*," Malcolm snapped.

"That's a lot of things to show up all at once," Cammy observed. "Invisible kids, and a huldra, and a draugr, and werewolves."

"Welcome to the supernatural," Malcolm said. "Like attracts like. Stuff that's similar tends to congregate, even without meaning to. Essences can strengthen each other and resonate with one the other.

Cammy considered that.

"And they come here to Seattle because... ?"

"Do you live under a rock? With all the weirdoes living here going back to Doc Maynard and before? All the messed up graves and the cults? This place is *attractive* to the supernatural. It's nicer to live here than somewhere more sane. Monsters like to live on the fringe or beyond. Well, we live *in* the fringe. Plus, I bet the homeless population is nice fodder for a lot of them."

"What?"

"Yeah, you know, people no one knows about or no one would miss. No record of them anywhere. If you're one of those things that go bump in the night and likes eating *human,* homeless populations look mighty tasty. Preying on the homeless is easier than maintaining an exclusive diet of children."

"There are things that eat *only children?*"

"Of course there are! Why do you think people hated supernaturals so much?"

Cammy let that sit for a minute. She'd heard Grimm's Fairytales were grimmer before Disney got a hold of them, but were they *that* much grimmer? With human-eating monsters running wild, she could see how something like Boese's department got founded.

She hated the idea that the homeless were prey for the supernatural. If Boese was serious about wiping the monsters out and protecting people, he ought to do more to help those people out, like maybe provide housing arrangements. But he'd never do that. He would rather rant and rave and blame everyone but himself.

If children went missing, someone would notice. As much as she thought Boese was horrible, he'd have to do something about that. People noticed kids disappearing.

Sheriff Carl Schulz was awoken from a deep sleep by a curiously loud and strident throat-clearing sound. He sat up to gaze in bewildered astonishment at the tableau in his room. A sweet but sickening scent was pervading his bedroom and somehow muddled his thinking.

Ambient city light filtered in through the curtains, but the sun wasn't up yet, so it took him a moment to make out what was before him in the gloom. A female stranger stood at the foot of his bed; beside her stood his six-year-old daughter, Cate, who was knuckling sleep out of her eyes. The stranger's beautifully manicured, red nails clutched the child's shoulders. Behind her, near the door, stood a man with black hair, dark beard, and black eyes. His hair and eyes were so dark they seemed to cancel out the feeble light, but that was't what riveted Carl's attention. One of the man's large hand was gripping Carl's wife's neck. She trembled quietly, her eyes on Carl's.

"Sheriff Schulz, I apologize for meeting with you in this manner, but I crave a moment of your time," said the elegant woman with her hands on his daughter. Gems glittered on her fingers.

He had a nine millimeter in a safe in the drawer in the night table, but he couldn't possibly get to it in time if either of the two were armed. Even if they weren't, he couldn't be certain he wouldn't hit his family if things got chaotic. He sat still, trying to think of a solution. Then he realized the family collie was lying at the foot of the bed, unmoving. He didn't see any wounds, but the dog was *awful* still to be asleep. He couldn't feel any warmth through the sheets with his foot.

"Thank you for taking the time to speak with me," the strange woman said. Her red hair was neatly tied back, revealing a long necklace of pearls. She looked and sounded like some wealthy Eastern European tourist. "Have no fear,

Dracula's Match

Sheriff Schulz, I won't take up much of your time. But what I have to say is important."

Schulz's eyes strayed back to the strange man holding his wife's throat. He was wearing ordinary-looking clothes, not all put together like the woman. He wore his hair fairly long, and a trimmed beard. Everything about his face made Schulz's skin crawl and his teeth hurt. He didn't like looking at him. It was like he wasn't even human. He had never seen eyes so black and soulless. Shark-like.

"It is likely that you'll soon be receiving reports of missing children," the woman told him. "The fact is, it would suit me very well if you did not try very hard to find them."

"Who are you?" he demanded.

"We are not at a point where I will divulge my identity," she responded. "Though if you prove useful and loyal, perhaps I will tell you at some future date."

"What do you want?"

"As I said, I want you to look the other way with regards to missing young people," she said. "If you like, I am willing to reward you quite handsomely for such a service."

"You want me to *not* look for missing kids?" Schulz said. His mind was spinning. The guy holding his wife hadn't moved a muscle. Had he even blinked?

"I do. The fact is, I expect quite a number to go missing over the coming... weeks? Months, even."

"You... you're traffickers then? You'll get feds up here for that."

"Oh no, nothing like that, Sheriff. There will be no illegal transportations. But even if law enforcement from a federal level should come, I believe you still have a great deal of authority to direct them. The locals here are merely nightwatchmen of various sorts. Only you hold a legitimate office, no? In any event, I presume you want some sort of proof of our ability to reward or punish you for your cooperation or resistance?"

"Wait, no—"

"Have no fear. I know that if I do any harm now you will have no incentive to hear me out." She tapped her finger on his daughter's shoulder. "Thank you, my dear. Have a sweet. Go now, and thank you very much for your help." The woman elegantly pulled a lollipop from her exquisite purse lined with pearls and handed it to Cate.

"What about Lady?" the girl asked, pointing to the cold dog.

"She's very tired. Let her sleep a bit more. Your father will bring her downstairs later," the woman assured, and sent the girl off with a friendly pat on the back, then took a seat on the foot of the bed. Schulz had taught Cate to be careful around strangers. Why would she trust this woman?

"Know this: I can do her harm when I wish," the woman said in a voice like steel.

He glared at her.

"To demonstrate." The woman gestured elegantly to her silent companion, and Schulz felt his heart beat against his ribs in anticipation of whatever he was about to do. But he did nothing. Schulz looked to the woman again, but she was not there.

"I can reach her when I please," the strange woman whispered in his left ear. He jumped straight off the bed. She now stood by the window. How had she managed that? The man with the creepy black eyes stood between the edge of the bed where she had been, and the window. She couldn't have gotten there without Schulz seeing her. And her weight hadn't shifted the bed at all, he realized. He hadn't felt it when she sat, nor when she rose. He stared at her.

"And don't get any ideas about defending yourself against me. You'll find I am quite difficult to harm, much less to kill," she told him.

"What the... this is a trick..."

"You have a knife here, I believe," the woman said, gesturing to the night table. "You could try that. It's quieter. If you try to shoot, I will stop you. I don't wish for this meeting to fall apart if the local police are called. Go ahead." She pulled open the drawer and gestured to it. He took a moment to consider the silent creep with one hand around his wife's throat, and the woman retaking her seat on his bed. "Go ahead, my companion won't harm your wife if you try. I want you to see that you have no choice at all."

He could certainly try to stab her to death. Maybe she was just crazy, and her boyfriend over there was just her enabler. Schulz couldn't be sure what the hulking brute near the door would do if the crazy woman died, though. *She* might think she was immortal or impervious, but what did he think?

The woman huffed angrily, reached into the drawer to retrieve the knife, and stood. She turned to Schulz and grabbed his wrist. Her fingers burned like ice. She slapped the knife into his hand, closed her cold fingers over his, and thrust the blade into her stomach.

He tried to pull away but she held him fast. She had a grip like he couldn't believe. He was still pretty fit, and he didn't often get overpowered by anyone, even when he practiced boxing. But he couldn't pull out of her freezing grip. The cold around his wrist seeped into his arm and crawled through his body. The sickening sweet smell washed over him, hazing his thoughts. She dragged the knife back and forth, which would cut her wide open like a game animal, but he felt the knife meeting no resistance. He was cutting air. At last, she released his hand to reveal that she was unharmed.

"Weapons don't concern me," she told him. "Bear that in mind if you choose to ignore my request."

His mind ground through the situation. Who was she? How had she done that trick? Had she snuck in while no one was home and replaced the knife with some trick prop? He touched the edge with his thumb. Sharp. He carefully gripped the blade with his thumb and forefinger and pressed inwards. It was solid. He had been the one holding the handle. He made a brief attempt at finding a trick switch that would cause the blade would slide into the sheath; there wasn't one. It looked like his own knife, felt like it. There was the wear on the metal. This was the bowie knife his grandfather had given him. It was old. Hard to fake that. But how had she survived? No blood, no wound.

Her cold eyes regarded him, and she breathed a little heavily with satisfaction. Her breath was so cold, he could feel it in the air, falling around him, chilling the room. Then he detected a stink, like a corpse left out in the sun for a week. His stomach heaved at the smell. He was more used to the scent of rot than most, but this made him physically ill. As though there was something more to the stink than just molecules in the air.

"If you like, I can offer you a chance to be like me." She gestured at herself. "I've made the offer to others. Some have found it appealing." She walked to the door. She waved for her friend to release Schulz's wife. He did so without a word and pushed her away. She ran to her husband, and Schulz did his best to comfort and shield her from them.

"Something for you to think on," the woman said, pulling a small collection of photographs from her purse. They looked like polaroids, of all things. She scattered them across the floor and his bed, considered the last one in her hand, and then breathed fire on it. He could only stare. It looked like real fire. But she *breathed* it. He'd seen the glow behind her teeth, at the back of her throat before the flames burst out. Some sort of chemical could fake the fire, but all those should be too toxic for a person to have in their mouths, and even if she was crazy enough to try, she didn't seem burned at all.

The woman flicked the flaming photograph onto the bed, where it blazed with cold flame. The baleful light caught in the collie's glassy, dead eyes. Schulz took a glance at the photos, wondering why she had dropped them, to see that they were a series of snapshots of his daughter at school, shopping with her mother, waiting to be picked up.

"In the end, I do not particularly care whether you accept or not. If not, you can be killed easily enough and I will try again with your replacement. I am far more patient than you realize, and quite indifferent to you or your health. I offer a carrot and a stick, you see. It matters not to me which you choose."

"Lady, I have no idea what you're talking about."

"What I am saying is that you could be like me: immune to weapons, undying, everlasting. A bit more than that. Or, you can be dead, cold in a ditch somewhere, with your family alongside. Like Councilman Wright."

"You still don't make any sense. You're talking crazy here. Wright? Dean Wright? The one they fished out of the Sound in April?"

"Him, yes. Though that wasn't my doing. I don't like getting blood"—she made a *moue*–"rather, I don't want a man's blood on me." She looked chagrined, then nodded at the photos she had scattered. "Your daughter is a bit young for me, but I could make an exception." Her deep-set eyes settled on his and seemed to paralyze him. "And I will, if you don't cooperate with me. Is that plain enough? Or still too crazy?"

She pointed at the scattered photos and the one sputtering out on the bedsheets. When Schulz looked up again, the woman was gone. Her black-eyed companion still stood by the door, which was shut. There was no way the woman had opened the door, slid out, and shut it. Not in half a second. The black-eyed man let himself out the bedroom door. Schulz could hear his heavy footsteps on the stair, descending. Schulz reached for the safe to fetch his gun. He had to make sure his daughter was still safe.

When he got downstairs, he found Cate at the table doodling and no sign of the two intruders anywhere.

CHAPTER 5
ENERGIES

Brian sat at his computer. He'd given his statement and been taken to the hospital where he had been informed that he had two cracked ribs and a third which was bruised. He was now on Paid Time Off for the next few weeks. He had struggled to get a ride home, since he hadn't been able to find his phone. A kindly nurse had overheard his trouble and arranged an Uber for him. His sister Melissa was working overnight; it would be hours before she came home.

He'd been searching for all the information he could about the late Mr. Thorirsson. He dimly recalled hearing some scuttlebutt at the station.

Mr. Thorirsson had been struggling with marital issues, but no calls to the police about domestic abuse, thankfully. His career had come after the steroid scandals that racked the whole industry, so his size was likely all him. Brian feared to think what steroids would do to a man that size, and what would happen if he lost it.

He had also been openly speaking about the religious practices of the Vikings. He'd always talked proudly of his heritage, but it seemed he'd gone farther. Fan forums talked about how he worshipped Thor, saying the people of the past *really* lived. He'd befriended the guy from Britain who wrote and performed the song for that movie he'd starred in; the Brit made a big deal about how some distant ancestor of Mr. Thorirsson must have been a Viking invader. Brian thought that was a dumb thing to be proud of—Viking invaders were the bad guys, if you'd lived in the villages they sacked and burned—but whatever. The musician had OD'ed and died about a year ago, but Roar continued to hang out with his brother: a big, blond guy who Brian could find out next to nothing about except his name was Erik. Roar's band of weirdos included another wrestler guy, taller than Roar, who'd been injured early in his career. His handle in wrestling had been "Wild Wolf" Shaw. In recent photos, Shaw had a salt and pepper goatee, and though he wasn't as ripped as he'd been while in the industry, he clearly hit the gym a lot. He was a pretty imposing guy. Not someone Brian would want to tangle with, either.

Roar had murdered his wife—all signs indicated that she was carrying on an affair with his manager—and then committed suicide. There were suspicious items found at his home. Bones that fans speculated were human, though no official statement had been released as to whether they were. The thing that caught Brian's attention was a picture that the news had released, taken of a seemingly innocuous pile of letters in Roar's apartment. Poking out of the stack was a piece of paper or an envelope with a symbol on it. It looked like the outline of the head of Anubis, but Brian recognized it as the symbol the douche at the bar had revealed under his wristwatch.

So whoever he was, the douche was involved. That certainly explained why he'd been so interested in the news report about the grave. That didn't leave Brian with a lot to go on, though. And then there was the *final* problem.

The guy he'd seen punching cars and *eating* part of a man was a dead—what an unfortunate joke—ringer for Thorirsson. Who was categorically *very* dead. Dead and buried. With the investigation into the guy's murder-suicide, there was no way that an autopsy hadn't been performed. No one was going to survive that. Not even someone who could slow their breathing and lower their body temperature.

Brian didn't know of anyone living who could perform the feats of strength he'd seen. And he wasn't an expert on makeup effects, but he'd gotten a *real* good look at the guy's skin. He didn't know of any makeup that could give that kind of hue, like a real corpse, and make it *translucent*.

Brian couldn't tell his brain to shut up. So far as he'd been able to find, Mr. Thorirsson didn't have a twin brother that anyone knew about. It was impossible, but the only conclusion his brain could come up with was that the guy had somehow come back as a weird rage-zombie.

He grinned for a moment at the idea of 'roid rage affecting a zombie, but laughing hurt and killed his mood.

Someone knocked at the door, startling him and sending a bolt of pain ripping through him when he jumped. He winced, gripped his side, and rose from his chair. Who would be bothering him at this hour?

Brian made his way slowly towards the door and peeked through the peephole. He spotted a familiar baby-face on the other side. As quickly as he could, he swung the door open.

"Akerman! You're ok!"

Akerman's hoodie looked damp, and he smelled like sea water. In greeting, Akerman held up Brian's phone.

"You dropped this," he said.

"Get in here!"

Akerman stepped into the small apartment, taking a few glances at the interior. Brian accepted his phone back and squeezed Akerman as firmly as he could, but still with a wince.

"I told the officers and the emergency service people what happened. How did they find you?"

"They didn't. I can swim really well," Akerman said.

"No injuries?"

Akerman shook his head. "He just tossed me. Didn't hit anything on the way in."

Brian considered his phone. No cracks, and it didn't feel wet. It turned on no problem, though the battery was low. He hefted its weight.

"How 'bout you? I saw you took a hit." Akerman said.

"Cracked ribs."

Akerman nodded, commiserating.

"The perp," Brian said. Akerman looked at him. "What... what did you think?"

"Who knows." Akerman hugged himself. "Some lunatic high on something. "

"You *saw* him. You saw what he did. You're trying to tell me that there's *any* drug on the market that can get you to a point to casually upend a *car*? Come on."

Dracula's Match

Akerman looked down at the floor.

"Look, you don't know what you saw," Akerman said. "You know how people can think they saw something, but they didn't really—"

"Don't," Brian snapped. "Don't you do that. This *thing* picked you up and tossed you thirty feet. You *saw* him *pick up* cars. With *ease*."

Akerman glanced at the door.

"It's just"—Akerman licked his lips—"think about how that sounds. What are you even saying? That some kind of monster smashed up downtown—"

Brian grabbed his hoodie—and winced. "You and I know we both saw something we can't easily explain, and that it sure *looks* like some famous dead man *crawled out of his grave* and *he's* the one who rampaged through Pike Place."

Akerman looked at him. He fidgeted.

Brian studied him. "You... you *know* it. You *know it*. You know it and you're standing here telling me, 'Oh, who can really say what happened?' Right here, right now, in my living room?!"

"Warren," Akerman said. Brian glared at him. "Warren, listen. This is a weird town. Weird stuff happens. Don't throw your whole career away over this—"

"This psycho zombie guy *murdered* a man right in front of my eyes, Akerman! I can't just turn aside and—"

"You don't have to sweep it all under the rug. Just... you know, dial it down."

"I told them what I saw," Brian said.

Akerman sighed and rubbed his eyes with his fingers.

Brian considered his behavior. The weird cult stuff with Anubis, Roar being interested in Norse culture, Dr. Weird-

Calling-Himself-Dracula living way out in Snoqualmie with Cammy, and a city councilman turning up *exsanguinated* a few months ago... right around the time Cammy started living up there.

This is a weird town. Weird stuff happens.

"You know this is all real," Brian asserted. "You *know*. You've seen something like this before. You've seen feds come out of nowhere and jump all over..." *Feds. Someone got Dr. Acula out of jail when I brought him in.*

Was that possible? But *why*? And it still begged the question of *who* had reported that Brian had arrested the creep. Him and his vintage cars. Brian gritted his teeth.

"Warren, just... just keep your head down, all right?"

"I can't believe this," Brian said. "So how long have you known that there was stuff like... like this going on?"

Akerman looked at him, and rubbed his mouth.

Wait a minute. "What about Dr. High-Profile-Name in his fancy mansion bought by Romanian royalty out in the Cascades? What about *him*?"

"Warren," Akerman said, "you don't want to tug on this. Trust me. Just leave it lie."

Brian couldn't get his head around this. How long had Akerman known? Were there other cops who knew?

*Wait, does **Cammy** know?* She had never told him exactly what happened that night back in April, or why she was living up there instead of with her parents—although after that scene in the restaurant her psycho mother had pitched, no one was going to wonder why Cammy would rather live anywhere but home. He'd been trying to untangle theories about Dr. Russian Spy and why Cammy might not be willing to talk about whatever had happened—international intrigue, homeland security, who could say. And he'd tried *so* hard not to jump to the conclusion that vampires were real. Even though everything pointed to it. Dr. McCreep was "allergic" to garlic, he claimed. Allergic. Right.

Was *that* why Dr. Russian Creep was so ready to jump to the defense of that particular historical psychopath with the penchant for impaling? *Could* he actually be the same guy? To hear him talk about the man, anyone would conclude he had some serious fixation.

Brian was going to press Akerman more when he heard keys in the lock, then the door popped open.

"BB, you forgot to lock the—oh, hello." Melissa carefully nudged open the door. She carried a bag of groceries on one arm. "Hey there," she greeted Akerman. "Are you one of BB's friends?"

"Felix Akerman," he answered, and offered a hand. "Brian and I work together."

"Well, nice to meet you," she said, and took his proffered hand. "Excuse me." She ducked between them and scooted to the kitchen to put things away. "Can I get you anything? We've got a few beers left."

"No, thank you. I was just leaving, actually."

Brian glared at him.

"Well, it was nice meeting you. You a new recruit, or something?"

Akerman pressed his lips together. His baby face was getting the usual interpretation.

"Akerman's been with the department for about ten years," Brian explained.

Melissa's head shot up from behind the fridge door. She smiled, bemusedly.

"Oh, I'm sorry. I didn't realize… sorry about that."

Akerman shook his head. "Don't worry. Lots of people make that mistake." He glanced at the door. "Guess that's part of the reason I'm still single."

Just let it go, man, Brian thought. To think Akerman'd still be on that after all the craziness that had happened.

"Boy, tell me about it," Melissa said. "Dating is such a nightmare these days. Every guy you meet is a creep. And *definitely* don't date coworkers. Then there's two of you bringing work home. There's just no way to meet anyone."

"Yeah," Akerman agreed. He looked at Brian, silently admonishing him not to do what he intended to do.

*I know **exactly** what I'm going to do, pretty boy*, Brian thought. Akerman ducked his head and let himself out with another muted "Good bye."

"Glad to see you've got friends from work," Melissa said. "You ok? Something wrong?"

Brian shook his head. "I'll tell you later."

"Ok, then." Melissa had a box with a pre-made sandwich inside, which she popped open. "You know where I am." She went to the TV and turned it on. Brian held up his phone and carefully made his way back to his room and computer.

Malcolm played the radio at full blast on the way up to the mansion, and glared at the road. Cammy decided it was better not to talk. She didn't really want to talk anyway. Nothing good had come from finding out about all this weirdness. Just Malcolm and Dracula telling her to "stay out of it" because it was "dangerous."

And Heather was dead. That was always going to be true.

Dracula's Match

She couldn't talk to Brian about it. She couldn't talk to Kenzie or Lindsey about it. She didn't want to talk about it, either. She didn't *want* to think about Heather's wide, dead eyes in a face that still moved, her mouth covered in blood, the feeling of that shaft of wood punching through her friend's chest, and the cold weight dropping down on her afterwards. Heather not moving ever again.

Cammy wiped a tear from her eye and watched the glistening rain drops haphazardly slide across the window.

The mansion looked dead and dark when they arrived. Under the cloud cover, it always looked dull and dark, even the ivy crawling up the side looked gray. She stared at the patch of vampire watermelons under the tree that brushed its branches against one side of the edifice. They didn't move much in the day—or even at night. Just occasionally. Or she'd find one in the morning had rolled half-way across the driveway with no way it could have gotten there by natural forces. But they didn't seem to do much. Boring.

None of the vampire-ghost-women were out—not that Cammy had ever seen one—and there was no sign of the fox or the tanuki or their child. The weather must have driven them to hide.

Malcolm opened the car door for her when Cammy didn't move to get out. She didn't think it was politeness; he just wanted her out of his car. They crunched over the damp pebbles, dark from the drizzle, and they came inside the back door, to find the place dark.

"Yo!" Malcolm called into the foyer.

Dracula opened his study and peered out.

"I was about to call you." He spotted Cammy and regarded her. "What happened?" he asked.

"Found her chasing some invisible people around and trying to talk to a huldra."

"She wants to know more about you," Cammy explained.

"Who does?" Dracula asked.

"The huldra," Malcolm answered. "Seems she came all the way from Norway especially to talk to you."

One of Dracula's eyebrows lifted.

"Then I thank you for bringing Cammy back. Now, I have questions for you regarding what happened at Pike Place."

"Draugr. Almost undoubtedly," Malcolm replied.

"How does one defeat such a monster?"

Malcolm heaved a sigh and thrust his hands in his pockets. "You have to wrestle a draugr into their graves, set the body on fire, let it burn, and scatter the ashes. Even that doesn't always work. They're rage zombies. *Strong* zombies. *Really* strong, and *really* ragey. One of the most powerful undead there is. And their rage can be... contagious."

"That might prove problematic."

"Oh, you picked up on that, did you? Yeah, you could call it problematic." Malcolm grimaced. "Even their remains can cause animals to go mad, so scattering the ashes has to be done *carefully*."

Dracula considered that. "Do they have any other abilities I should know about?"

"They can change their size at will, turn into mist, sink straight into the ground and pop back out somewhere else; they have the strength of *many* men, change shape into animals, loads of stuff. They can't cross running water, to my knowledge." Malcolm grunted and said, "His presence sets animals off, and it might affect other supernaturals, even the

Dracula's Match

ones who are normally quiet; so if your, um, tenants start acting up, he's nearby."

Dracula frowned. "That is most concerning. And a very… odd set of abilities."

"Why?" Cammy asked.

Dracula considered her a moment. "They are not unlike the abilities Stoker imagined."

Whoa, Cammy thought. *This guy is basically a match for* **Dracula?**

"Did Uncle Sam sic you on it?" Malcolm asked.

Dracula nodded.

"Best of luck to you. At least he shouldn't be able to mash *you* into pulp. Or if he can, it shouldn't bother you. But hey, just in case you thought this would be easy, I have another piece of good news for you. Before he died, he got Ophois to teach his friends how to become werewolves."

"The draugr?"

"Yeah. The dead guy. Thorrisson. Former wrestling star. He banked on this whole Viking persona. He's a local celebrity, you know."

Dracula raised another questioning eyebrow. Cammy supposed he wouldn't know about a spectator sport that had more or less died out after the 90s or whenever. She wasn't a fan either. Malcolm pulled up a video on his phone and walked it over to show Dracula. She approached so she could catch a glimpse of whatever he was going to share. On the little screen, lights flashed like brilliant, fiery sparks, a crowd of people screamed and roared and waved signs in the dark all around a wrestling ring. Four men were in the ring, and Cammy could hear the phone speakers peaking as an announcer shouted out names like "Viking!" and "Wild Wolf!"

and "Lance Bryant!" some of which she recognized from regular pop-culture. That Lance guy had been in a few movies, given that he was known for being the prettiest 'bad boy' in wrestling, and he used it to his advantage.

"This was Madison Square Garden," Malcolm explained, almost gleefully. "2009. Tag team between Roar—the Viking—and his rival, Lance. This is the fight that ended Wild Wolf's career."

Cammy watched the group of muscle-bound men pretending to punch each other. Even on the small screen, Cammy could see they were playing around. The crowd cheered with each staged strike. Malcolm even pumped a fist when one of the wrestlers—the wolf guy—climbed on the ropes and then dove *smack* down on another guy. The crowd went wild. Dracula's face soured more and more as the video played on.

"What is this?" he demanded.

"Worldwide Wrestling, or Double-U as we like to call it. It's actually pretty fun. Hang on." Malcolm grinned, and found another video. The logo, three 'w's in different colors overlayed over each other, played first. Cammy didn't recognize these wrestlers, but Malcolm grinned when pyrotechnic sparks flew into the air as one wrestler came jumping up from apparently underground. He howled and stuck out his tongue in an open-mouthed howl. Now Cammy recognized him as the wolf wrestler guy from before, only much younger, in a much older video. The crowd seemed to love it as the lights flickered overhead and he leaped up into the ring to clothesline another wrestler wearing red tights. Dracula's frown deepened as he watched more, though Malcolm seemed to cheer up.

"I think I understand," Dracula said.

Dracula's Match

"Roar wasn't the biggest in the industry," Malcolm explained. "But I saw a few of his matches when he toured here."

Dracula pointed at Malcolm's phone. "Those are what they call 'matches?'"

"Yeah."

Dracula managed not to roll his eyes, but Cammy could see the disgust in them.

"What about the huldra?" she asked.

Dracula looked to Malcolm.

"This one has a cow's tail. May or may not have a hollow back; that detail more or less got dropped from the folklore. And now it may be the case that if you marry one, she might not turn ugly afterwards, which is how it used to be."

"They marry humans?" Cammy asked.

"The women, yeah. Well, *hulder* is the female form. *Huldrekall* are the men. They're hideous. The women try to marry men to get souls."

To get souls? "Wait, that's like the original *Little Mermaid*, right? Not the Disney version?"

Dracula clearly had no idea what she was talking about, but Malcolm nodded.

"Yeah. Denmark and Norway aren't too far apart geographically. Some of the folklore and beliefs bleed over. Lots of different countries share similar fairy tales. George MacDonald—famous writer—described a tree spirit with a hollow back. That was the warning sign." Malcolm inclined his head towards Dracula, "You met him, right?"

Lindsey had told Cammy the original Hans Christian Andersen story; she had a collection of fairytale books from when she was a child that she still kept. When Kenzie had heard about the mermaid's choice, she'd rolled her eyes and said that she'd take an expanded lifespan and magic powers over a soul any day. "Not like I'm even using mine," Kenzie had chuckled, and winked.

"What does this one want with me?" Dracula asked.

"Well, most of the supernatural seems to know you're here," Malcolm said. "Maybe the world over. Those funny talking animals from Japan heard about you, right?"

Dracula considered that. Cammy had wondered about that, too. The tanuki and fox had arrived because they'd heard Dracula presided over a monster sanctuary. If monsters all over the world knew that, then maybe they showed up in Seattle for that reason?

Maybe those invisible kids had come for that reason, too. They seemed like children, no matter what Malcolm said. They had to steal food. Maybe they were homeless. When they thought she could see them, they hadn't attacked her or anything, just tried to move off.

Cammy resolved to find them again. But…

"Do you think you can fight that draugr?" Cammy asked timidly.

"I've no idea. I've never encountered one before."

"Could it kill you?"

"I doubt it," he said. Then to Malcolm, "Do you know what motivates him?"

"Usually they guard treasure."

"It seems to me he moved with purpose. There is a great deal of city between Lake View Cemetery and Pike Place. But he traveled without being seen, and what I saw of his handiwork seems as though he traveled with intent. To destroy the Selfie Museum."

Dracula's Match

"But why would any angry zombie want to destroy that?" Cammy asked.

"Don't know why a revenant would, but *I* sure didn't like it," Malcolm said. "Two different chicks wanted me to go with them to get photos for their feeds. Got all bent out of shape when I said no."

"What do people usually do there?" Dracula asked.

"You go there to pose with their sets, so you can post slightly better looking pictures of yourself to social media," Malcolm explained.

"Hmm," said Dracula.

Cammy realized that even though he'd updated his laptop, he probably didn't have any social media profiles set up. She wondered if she should show him how, then thought it would probably be worse than teaching your grandma how to use Twitter. He already didn't like selfies, and she doubted he would have anything to post.

"There must be some reason the monster went that far for that target," Dracula said. "Do you think he will return a second time?"

"I don't know what he's after," Malcolm told him. "Like I said, these things usually hoard treasure. They don't go on rampages unless someone disturbs them, or tries to steal from them. But it's not like he has a tomb to guard, and he wasn't buried with anything valuable. I don't know what his friends want, although it's pretty obvious they dug him up."

"To raise him as this monster?"

Malcolm made a face. "That demonic frenzy energy might have latched onto some lasting frustration of his. Something that enraged him in life. He probably had some serious grudge or resentment, *and* the magic he was already playing with, so he was probably going to get back up even without their help."

"But not everyone who dies angry comes back as a draugr," Cammy pointed out. "Why did he?"

"The supernatural isn't predictable. Nothing is 100%. *Sometimes* people who die angry or who were berserkers in life come back. Not *all* of them. But he was always talking about his Nordic heritage. After his failed attempt at Hollywood, he took it *way* more seriously. So odds are good he was already aligning with the sort of energy he needed to get back up, combined with the fact that he was obviously upset—most guys don't murder-suicide themselves and their soon-to-be-ex-wives, right?"

"So people need to... align themselves with something supernatural to... 'get back up?'"

"More or less," Malcolm said. "Thoughts have energy, right? When you obsess over an idea or decide to engage in a certain behavior, you start aligning with that energy. That's how I figure it works, anyway. Traditionally, people would only encounter the ideas of their own cultures, but these days a person can look up anything to work with, so you could get Americans turning themselves into anything from around the world, for example."

Cammy supposed that made sense.

"Given that there is likely a pack of werewolves on the loose, to say nothing of the other threats at the moment, I would have you escort Cammy until this situation with the draugr is resolved," Dracula said to Malcolm. Malcolm furiously shook his head.

Dracula's Match

"Bad idea. That draugr's aura sets me off. As I said, that rage is contagious. If I hadn't been able to lock myself up last night, let's just say things would have gotten *real* ugly."

"And the other werewolves your organization helped make? Are they likely to be similarly affected?" Dracula checked.

"Probably. Ophois tends to make the old school flavor and I bet Roar and his buddies would have preferred to be berserker-wolves rather than full-moon wolves, even though my flavor's pretty out of fashion. Sounds like Roar liked tradition, though. But I bet his werewolf buddies aren't gonna turn human anytime soon if they keep hanging out with him."

"So are they're like you?" Dracula asked.

"More like me than the modern ones, I bet," Malcolm said. "Meaning they're a *loup garou* variety, or maybe berserker."

"What's a loo garoh?" Cammy asked.

"The kind of werewolf that caused a panic in the 1500s. You need to make a real evil pact to get a belt made of wolf skin that will let you transform into a wolf so you can indulge in all your deepest, darkest desires. Like cannibalism."

"What?!"

"Nothing about being a werewolf *doesn't* imply you're not interested in killing people at minimum, and eating people at most," Malcolm told her. "The berserking kind mostly just kill people, but most varieties of werewolves eat them too."

She stared at him. The last time she'd asked him what sort of things he'd killed he'd gotten snarly. Did that mean that *he…*?

"But... I mean..." Cammy said. "Why would anyone *choose* to become that?"

"You got loads of frustration and resentment and anger boiling at the base of your skull, then someone come along and says, 'Hey, I can help you can let all that out, all you have to do is *let it all out*,'" Malcolm told her. His eyes were dark. "You give into that little devil on your shoulder. Only when you do, it's not like being drunk and all your inhibitions are just gone. That little devil's got a megaphone and he's shouting in your ear about how much *fun* it'd be to do to everyone else what you've been wanting to do all along."

Cammy's fingers felt cold.

"I see," Dracula said. "Let me think on that problem, then. If you should run into them, let me know."

"Sure," Malcolm growled. He pushed past Cammy and left without saying goodbye. Once he had gone, Dracula gave her his attention.

"I thought you had a class today?"

"Malcolm didn't want me to stay because of that huldra. She wanted to meet you and she knows I know you."

"I see," he said. "Very well. Is there enough time left to head back to the university for your class?"

"Not for that class. But I have two today."

"Very well, let us be off."

CHAPTER 6
UNFAIR FIGHTS

"I found no information about your friend, Andrew," Dracula told Cammy as they drove to the city. She looked at him. "His family shop was untouched, and I found no evidence of violence there. Nothing amiss."

"So he's ok?"

"It is possible that he and his family were gone by the time the monster arrived. Or that the monster did not enter the shop."

She considered that. "What will Boese do about all these people who saw Roar running around?"

"This is an unprecedented problem. While it has happened in the past that dozens or even hundreds of people witnessed a supernatural outbreak, I imagine it was easier to prevent others from believing before cameras in portable phones became commonplace."

"Would he… kill people to keep this quiet?"

"He has in the past. However, it is usually easier to blackmail or threaten people into silence than explain away deaths. And all he needs is to cast enough doubt on their stories that they will not be believed."

She sure hoped so.

He dropped her off without incident, and she made it to the building only about five minutes late. Cammy sat in her class, fiddling with the adder stone. She peered through it twice, but saw nothing in her classroom that seemed supernatural. The hour and a half passed with her scrolling through her phone for more info on the dead wrestler guy, and what she could look up about draugrs and huldras. She didn't learn much more than what Malcolm had told her, which was disappointing. Except that sometimes people who were killed by a draugr came back as draugrs themselves. That could be a problem, but she bet that Boese's people were already all over it. She wondered how his department would explain to the families that their loved ones might get back up. Or would they just preemptively burn the bodies and scatter the ashes?

Then she thought about Heather and shut off her phone.

When class was over, Dracula was waiting for her in the parking lot, confirming her guess that whatever he did could be put on hold at a moment's notice. She decided to take a quick peek with the adder stone before walking to the parking lot, but spotted nothing. She wondered where the invisible children were.

Dracula did not like to play the radio while driving. The silence on the way back was deafening. She couldn't take it, even though she didn't want to talk.

"Thanks for driving me."

"Not that I should have *had* to," he said. Something he'd said before. "If you hadn't tried to involve yourself in dangerous matters, I wouldn't have to escort you to this extent. It's as though you haven't learned anything since your last encounter."

"If you don't want to save me you don't *have* to," Cammy grumped.

"You are my guest," he said.

"Because I'm your guest you go way out of your way for me?"

"Is that not clear?"

Cammy set her chin in her hand and looked out the window. "Have you ever lost anyone you cared about?"

She was answered by silence, so she turned to look at him. His eyes were on the road.

"Have you ever—"

"Do you honestly expect me to answer such an insulting question? I am more than weary of you asking me such questions."

"I didn't mean—"

"I presume you are asking because you are mourning the death of your friend?" he interrupted, sounding irritated.

"Uh," Cammy said. She didn't want to admit how much she still mourned Heather. It wasn't like here wasn't anything she could do. "Kenzie said your first wife committed suicide because she thought you'd been killed. She jumped from a tower and drowned herself."

His eyes remained on the road.

"She said it's a famous story."

"It is," he said.

"So… how did you deal with that?"

"I never had a wife who committed suicide," he said.

"You didn't?"

"My first wife was very alive when I was killed, and survived me by some time."

Apparently that story was *also* wrong. But it bothered her how he rebutted it. "*I never had a wife who committed suicide.*" Why make a complete sentence like that?

"So lots of stories about you are wrong."

He nodded.

"Kenzie said there's another one where you saw a guy with a shirt that wasn't sewn properly or something, so you asked him if it was his fault or his wife's fault, and he said it was his wife's fault, so you impaled her."

Dracula watched the road.

"You didn't do that, did you?"

"I might have," he said. "I don't remember the particular incident, however."

Cammy stared. "You don't remember walking around with the peasants and seeing a guy with a shirt that wasn't finished and deciding to *impale his wife?*" she demanded. "You'd know if you *hadn't* done it, right?"

"I don't appreciate your tone. I don't remember a specific man or his wife, but it sounds like something I might have done."

"You..." Cammy couldn't believe her ears. "You... *might* have impaled some woman for not making her husband's shirt right?"

"That's correct."

Well, him being a raging psychopath was back on the table. After all his time getting offended at people misunderstanding him, to find out he might have killed someone for something that petty, and he had the *gall* to get offended for being called a psycho.

"Why would you do that? *How* could you do that? What is *wrong* with y—?"

He slammed on the brakes and swerved to the side of road. They'd left the city and were well on the way to his place.

"I will *not* be judged by some ignorant child like you, and I do *not* like your snippy, saucy attitude. I have been *more* than patient with you on account of the fact that you are clearly the most ignorant person I have ever met, but there are *limits to what I am willing to tolerate*. I have opened my home to you, lent you a stone worth more than diamonds, and *saved your life* more than once. You would do well to dwell on all that before you open that smart mouth of yours again."

Cammy shut her mouth and pressed herself against the door. He stared her down for a while longer, before he put the car back in gear and pulled back onto the road. She hugged herself and side-eyed him. He ignored her. Maybe that was for the best.

He pulled into the driveway and parked in front of the mansion. He let himself out quickly, then locked the doors when Cammy tried to get out.

"Hey, what—"

He pulled his magnum and aimed it at the back of his car.

"Show yourself," he said. Cammy could hear him through the glass. She craned her neck to see what he was talking about.

A woman with wild, long, dark hair and flashing eyes rose from behind the trunk. Siri. The huldra. Cammy hadn't noticed her hanging on to the vehicle, or whatever she'd done. Siri held Dracula in her alluring, electric sight. She didn't seem concerned about the gun.

"Greetings, your Majesty," she said, and smiled. "I have come a long way to court you."

What? Cammy had not expected *that* to be the reason Siri had come all the way from Norway.

"If that was the case, you've gone about it in a very inappropriate way," Dracula said. "Come out from behind there. Let me see you."

Siri obeyed, sauntering into the open. She was wearing the same outfit, but there was no sign of her tail. Would Siri kill Dracula if he mentioned it? *Could* she? Cammy didn't know of anything could kill him, although garlic made him violently ill. Supposedly, burying him face-down in his grave might be a way, not that she had any idea where his grave might be.

"Why me in particular?" he asked.

"It is said that if a huldra should marry a good, Christian man, she can acquire an immortal soul, as humans have," Siri answered. In the car, Cammy boggled at the idea of describing Dracula as a 'good Christian.'

"There are numerous Christian men in the world. I asked why *me* in particular."

Siri played with a lock of her hair. "Because you know about us. Because… you vould understand. You vould not fear, or hate. And I have heard that it is nice, vhen vun is human, to have amenities. A house, money. You have a great deal."

"I see," he said. "It has been a long time since last I was married. Still, you've come a long way. We should speak." He nodded to Cammy to step out of the vehicle. Wait, it couldn't be he was seriously taking up the weird tail lady on her offer, was it?

He gestured Cammy stay close to him, and kept himself between her and Siri. So he must still think she was dangerous.

Cammy let herself into the mansion, and Dracula indicated the kitchen. Cammy started for it, but he waved her off and escorted Siri. Cammy decided to lurk in the living room to listen in. She hunkered down and swirled the cold ashes in the fireplace with a poker as the other two walked past. Dracula would be able to see her from the kitchen if he didn't sit down, and he had to know she was intending to eavesdrop, given her pathetic excuse for an activity, but he didn't shoo her away. At long last, she might learn something about the supernatural.

"What do you eat or drink?" Dracula asked Siri. She set herself on the corner of the table and shrugged playfully.

"I like all the things humans like."

"Aki," Dracula called out.

A slim, Asian woman walked past Cammy and she jumped sideways. Cammy hadn't heard this person, and she didn't recognize her. The woman was very slim, very petite, with long, black hair tied conservatively back. Dracula gestured to a chair at the table where Siri should place herself. She moved to it a little sulkily, but remained buoyant enough to put her smile back on. Cammy still couldn't put her finger on what was wrong that smile. Dracula did not sit.

"Milk?" Dracula offered. Siri shrugged, so he nodded to the strange woman, who fetched glasses and set about serving them both. Cammy smirked at the idea of Dracula drinking a glass of milk. "From the beginning," he told Siri once she had her glass. "What do you want, and why, and why should I acquiesce?"

Siri played with the glass, tracing the rim. "The old voods, the vild places, are smaller and smaller. My people are dvindling. Ve cannot go about as ve did. So I thought I ought to seek an immortal soul, become human. Or learn some knowledge vhich might help us and return home. That is vhy they told me to go. To find... something. I came to find you. You know vhat the vorld vas like before. Before men became so-called 'rational.' Vhen they knew of us and our kind and the vay of the vorld. Vhen ve helped them with their coal, and they vere polite and respectful. You... remember. And understand. I thought you might know something that vould help my people. But I vould prefer to become human, and stay here."

He nodded, though Cammy though it was to communicate he understood, not that he agreed.

"And why should I agree to your proposal?" he asked her.

Siri's head jerked back with surprise. It apparently hadn't even occurred to her that he wouldn't simply accept her offer.

"I vould... give you anything I could. Ve have magic—"

"That is of no interest to me. I can see you have not thought of a reason. You claim marrying a Christian man will grant you a soul?"

Cammy couldn't help but agree with the profound doubt she heard in his voice. This had to be the stupidest thing she'd ever heard.

"Yes, that is vhat happens," Siri said.

"Why do you think you don't have a soul at this very moment?"

Dracula's Match

Siri shifted uncomfortably. "It... it is vell-known. Humans have... something vhich ve do not have, vhich persists after they die. And it seems humans think ve do things vhich are wrong."

"If you were not already bestowed with the image of God, which mankind has, marrying someone will not grant it to you, if that is what you are after. That is immutable. Nevertheless, something does occur when your kind marry humans. You already have a soul, else you would not be alive; but the *essence* of your people, which seems distinct from humans, is warped. Perhaps by the practices your long-distant pagan ancestors made a part of their lives, and that reduced your capacity to live as other humans do. Something occurs when you marry, which helps to heal that hurt."

Siri frowned. So did Cammy.

"Ve are the other children of Eve."

"You cannot change the essence of a thing." Dracula was clearly trying to clarify his argument. "You can only warp it, dim it, damage it. It's not that you lack a soul, it's that the eye of your soul is not yet opened, or that they have been injured. I presume you can bear children by human men? Even without marrying them?"

"Of course."

"I have read that your people can—and do—steal human children and replace the stolen child with one of your own. Does the human child you steal become like you?"

"Yes," Siri admitted, after a long pause.

"Because," Dracula told her, "you already *are* human."

What! Cammy stared. That was impossible. They had *tails*! She noticed the woman called Aki was studying him blankly.

"That cannot be right," Siri said. "That cannot—"

"From what I understand of your race's behavior, you have no clear moral compass, which seems to me that the eye of your soul is so dark you cannot tell right from wrong. The fact that lovers and children are utterly interchangeable for you suggests your race lacks the capacity to love."

"Whoa!" Cammy interjected, forgetting her intention to stay quiet. "Love is overrated, really. People are *real* hard to love. Everyone's always angry, or stupid or—"

"I don't recall asking your opinion," Dracula said, glaring at her.

"That's why it's better to try to be kind," Cammy went on. "You can't love everybody. It's exhausting. It's hard enough to love one person—"

"Kindness is a poor substitute for love," he snapped. "Only love would motivate someone to undergo suffering for another."

"Suffering for somevun else?" Siri repeated, confusion radiating from her tone. "Vhy vould you do that?"

"Would you be polite to someone? Even some you don't like?"

"Certainly," Siri said.

"Would you suffer for someone you liked?" Dracula asked her.

"I..." Siri frowned. "Vhy vould I?"

"When you love someone, their pain becomes your pain. Even seeing them suffer is painful to you. So you would do whatever you could to alleviate their suffering, even if it meant taking it on yourself."

Siri looked aghast.

Dracula's Match

"You can't say that's the benchmark," Cammy said. "What if she, like, can't? And kindness is basically the same thing."

"Considering your relationship with your mother I would have thought you would know the difference," Dracula told her. "And once more, I did not ask you for your opinion."

Cammy's mouth dropped open. He did *not* just...

"You talk a big talk about love," she retorted. "Your marriages were all 'political' and 'practical,' right? What do you know of love, or suffering? I mean, you never had a wife who killed herself for you, right?"

He kicked himself from the table and stormed toward her. She stepped back, bumping into a settee. He wasn't slowing down, so she tried rolling around the settee to escape, but he caught up and seized her by her hoodie and nearly yanked her right off her feet as he dragged her towards the back door. He threw it open.

"I told you there are *limits* to what I am willing to tolerate. I am only a man. I can only take so much of your ignorant vitriol." And with that, he threw her out the door, hard, onto the gravel driveway, and slammed the door shut. Cammy got to her knees, wincing, and checked her hands. Gravel was stuck to the palms of her hands, and a few sharp edged stones had punctured the skin. She rubbed them off, then picked out one errant pebble stuck in a shallow wound and dropped it.

He had just thrown her out and slammed the door.

Outside.

Where it was not safe. Lots of the things who lived outside were deadly, apparently, or eager to do her harm, and did not do so only because she was his guest.

Was she not his guest anymore?

Amaya Tenshi

She got to her feet and knocked on the door. No response. She knocked harder. Still nothing. She pounded on it, and refused to stop.

The door swung open and she accidentally pounded on his chest once as he stood in her path.

"Do not test me at the moment," he warned. "I am in no mood, and will not be responsible for my actions if you continue to berate me."

"I can't just sit out—"

"If you harm any of my windows to get back in, you will regret it. For every pane of glass you damage, I will break one of your bones."

She stared, horrified. He slammed the door and she heard the lock click.

Silence. Well, except for the faint wind in the leaves. But mostly silence. She scanned the trees and the grass. No sign of anything. Which was good, right? She was happy not to see anything.

The hairs on the back of her neck and her arms stood up. When she'd first come up the winding back road, she'd felt that eyes were on her, and apparently there *had* been. Just because she couldn't see them didn't mean they weren't there.

She fingered the adder stone. But did she want to see if they *were* there?

She scanned the wilderness and the vineyard past the gate. Visibility wasn't great because of the mist coming down, and the whole world disappeared into a gray nothing about a hundred feet off. No sign of anything. But best not to stay in sight of the vineyard, right? He had satyrs on his property, and she didn't trust them. Neither did her host. She did not want to find out what they might do if they found her out here alone.

She moved around the side of the mansion until she couldn't see the vague form of the vineyards anymore. It occurred to her she ought to call someone. Someone to pick her up. Even if she wasn't evicted, she couldn't hang out in such a dangerous place. Only she didn't have her phone with her. It was in her purse, inside.

She could feel her fingers trembling. In her mind, she could see Heather's dead eyes, her blood-stained mouth and shirt. The pack of vampires who had dragged Cammy screaming out of a car to kill her.

Dracula and Malcolm were always saying the supernatural was dangerous. For some reason, she couldn't believe them until she found herself standing out here, alone, locked out of the only safety she knew. By car, she was more than 40 minutes from the city. Only Brian knew where the mansion was, but unless she could text him, he'd never show up. If something happened to her, Boese would cover it up, the way he'd done with Heather and her parents. Brian would probably never know what happened to her.

She'd made a mistake coming to live up here. She should have just moved in with Brian and his sister, or something. Found *some* other option. Would being homeless be safer? Not with things that *ate* people. Witches and vampires and huldras. But ignorance was sure looking like bliss right about now. But she could not go back to normal. Not after what happened to Heather.

She crouched down and eyed the trees and their trembling leaves. She had no idea what to do. She was starting to shake all over. Where were those vampire-ghost-women Malcolm had told her about? All she could see were leaves fluttering on branches. Shadows, maybe. Her eyes played tricks, telling her that an exceptionally long branch waving slowly in the wind had a human shape, but second glances told her otherwise. The gray mist blurred distant shapes into shadows and silhouettes which could be anything.

A little gray head popped up out of the grass at the edge of the driveway, pointy nose twitching. The tanu-kitsune! Cammy waved to her.

Please don't run off! she thought. *Come on, I saved your life!*

Her brain decided to remind her Dracula had told her the same thing. He had, but he'd also put her out here, in danger.

Ginko, the little fox she'd rescued, stared with yellow, cat-like eyes Cammy couldn't read. At that moment, the little creature was as inscrutable as any wild animal. The little fox kept on staring, and Cammy wondered for a moment if it wasn't Ginko at all, but some actual wild fox that roamed the property. Or maybe Ginko had forgotten her, didn't recognize her.

Her heart practically flew right out of her when the little gray fox came bounding across the gravel towards her. The baby fox's paw pads made a heartwarming little patter on the gravel, and soon Ginko had crossed the distance and stood looking up at Cammy with worried, yellow eyes. Cammy snatched her up, and the fox squeaked in protest, but didn't try to wriggle free when Cammy hugged her. She even tolerated Cammy setting her on her lap and petting her ears.

It was nearly dark when Cammy heard the front door open. She sat bolt upright, and Ginko's little fox ears twitched as she listened to what must be a conversation happening at the door. Cammy rose to her feet and tried to tiptoe around the mansion towards the front door, but it was impossible to walk across the pebbles silently. After crunching close enough to peer around the corner, she saw Siri standing outside, her hands crossed modestly in front of her, looking pensive. She could hear Dracula saying something, but couldn't make it out. Siri turned and walked towards the long road back to the city. Apparently he wasn't going to drive her.

Then he leaned out and angrily waved Cammy inside. She glared at the pebbles and made her way over. Halfway there, she realized she was still carrying Ginko, so she stooped and placed the little fox on the pebbles. No sooner had she done so, then the slim Asian woman she hadn't recognized stepped out the front door and *snap!* turned into a yellow-orange fox, who darted across the gravel towards Ginko.

Oh, that's Aki! Cammy hadn't realized the fox was also doing work inside the mansion. She had assumed they were all living outside in the yard, where their den was. The two foxes darted across the driveway and disappeared into the grass together.

She made her way slowly towards the front door, where Dracula waited, one hand in his pocket. She glared at him, and he leveled a steely-eyed, withering stare back. She looked down, but flashed him a view of the palms of her hands. He said nothing to that at all.

In the bathroom, she washed her wounds with tears in her eyes and ruminated on what had happened. A fight? It didn't feel like a fight. But it wasn't an argument, either.

A knock at the bedroom door made her jump. She glared at the beautiful wood which separated her from her host.

"What?" she demanded.

"Will you open the door?"

No, she thought, but then it occurred to her he might be here to apologize. She opened the door and crossed her arms as dramatically as she could at him. The gesture was not lost on him, from how his eyes narrowed.

"Well?" she prompted.

"Do you understand why I threw you out today?" he asked.

"Oh, so you're *not* here to say you're sorry."

"I am not. Because I am not sorry. But I want to make certain you understand what happened, else it might happen again, and I lack the patience to do this twice."

"Do what? Throw me out again?" She pointed to her wounded palm, but he still looked unfazed.

"I am, as I said, a man. I have limits. Until now, I have been cordial, polite, and tolerated your impertinence with extreme patience."

"What extreme patience? I just asked you a *question*—"

"You asked a very *personal* question of me, as though you have any right," he nearly growled. "And interrupted me while I was trying to have a serious discussion with someone who needed more facts about her fate."

"But I was just—"

"You are my guest," Dracula told her. "But you are not my equal."

"Not your *equal*?" Cammy demanded. "What kind of backwards—"

"I am a prince. You are a peasant. Though my guest, you are not entitled to interrogate me at your whim, neither are you welcome to niggle at me while I am in the middle of business."

"I'm not a peasant," Cammy protested. "I'm an American citizen—"

"A peasant by *definition*," Dracula countered. "Are you a lady? A duchess, perhaps?"

"Well, who knows, right? Maybe I could find out if I try 23andMe—"

"Unless you hold ancestral lands and carry an active title, what distant noble line you may or may not unearth in your bloodline is worth very little, especially since you Americans ascribe no value to titles. I am given to understand most modern people have some noble ancestor or other lurking in their distant past. Sometimes even legitimately. Many are merely by-blows."

"Well, so, that just means that everyone's nobility and—"

"I understand that you are also upset about the fate of your friend," he continued, knocking the protests right out of Cammy all at once, striking right at the heart. "I presume death is not something you're accustomed to?"

"No," Cammy confessed and angrily wiped a tear she hoped he didn't see. "That's why I was asking earlier."

He tilted his head back, seemingly confused.

"In the car," she explained. He gave that some thought.

"Ah," he said. "I misunderstood your intention. I thought you were trying to insinuate that I was unable to love anyone given what the world thinks of me."

"Well," her stupid mouth went before she could stop it, "after all this time? And you said you might have impaled a woman for—"

"I have no need to justify my actions to you," he said, his tone sliding towards anger again. "Nor to speak of personal matters if I don't wish to."

"But I can't understand you if you don't *tell* me," she said. He considered her, as she stood playing with her wounded hands.

"Is your friend the first time you've dealt with death?" he asked.

She nodded. "What about you? How old were you?"

"I don't recall. They used to execute condemned men outside my window when I was a boy."

Well, *that* put things in perspective, she supposed.

"I should be clear: I did nothing cruel for the sake of cruelty. I threw you out earlier because it is very clear to me you do not yet understand what is at stake, nor do you take your safety seriously. You also do not understand the relationship you and I have."

She did *not* like how he phrased that.

"We're not in a—"

"Not a romantic relationship, clearly!" He sighed angrily. "There are other kinds of relationships, despite that you modern people seem to have reduced all the options down to one. You have turned all human interaction into something sexual, and no longer have a means to interact meaningfully in other ways. That is a failing of your modern culture. It is not how it always was. The proper treatment of guests is something you no longer understand. Death is something else you don't understand. Nor consequences. Your friend died—"

"Because some vampires kidnapped her, I know."

He looked down at her.

Dracula's Match

"Your friend died because she fell into desperate circumstances because of her habit. Yet you never noticed, despite living with her?"

"She... she was good at hiding it," Cammy mumbled.

"Moreover, you gave no thought to Robert McKenna."

"Who?"

"The man you hired to drive you into an obvious trap set by the vampire from whom I rescued you," he reminded her.

Robert. *That* Robert. The driver.

"I tried to stop them—"

"You should never have hired him in the *first place*," Dracula snarled. "That man is dead as a direct result of your stupidity and rash behavior."

Cammy blinked at him. "I tried to stop them—"

"He would never have been near that house if not for you. Worse than that, you didn't even so much as send flowers to his widow."

"I didn't know where he lived. I couldn't do that. I couldn't look her in the eye—"

"So you *know* you are responsible. *This* is why I treated you harshly. Despite the fact that you rendered two children orphans, you *still* ran heedlessly into danger. You have learned *nothing*."

Cammy stood, shaking. Tears rolled down her face.

"Have no fear, I sent flowers on your behalf," Dracula told her. She couldn't understand, but he continued. "I have made Robert's widow financially secure, and set aside money for both his children as well. It is the very least I could do."

"You... helped them?" Cammy wondered, bewildered. She tried wiping her face, but her knuckles were wet; she turned her hands over to use the battered heels of her hands. "But why?" *Why would you? You killed someone for not sewing a shirt!*

"Because I am your host, and therefore obliged to protect and provide for you. I am also responsible for you. I cannot do more for his family than I have done, but you did nothing."

"I can't even pay for my own college. How can you ask me —"

"I am not saying you should do what is currently impossible. But at the very least you could pray for his soul."

"... But... I'm not religious."

He looked down at her, and she had never felt so small. Not when her mother stood over her at the breakfast table with a report card in one hand which she took issue with. Not even when Boese had her down at his lab. Sobs overwhelmed her. She remembered that photo on Robert's phone, the whole family all smiling together happily. A portrait of a happy family, now broken. And he was right. It was her fault.

"I just wanted... I wanted to... s-stop Colston, before he did more..."

"But you weren't able, and only made things worse. Malcolm told me he told you to wait."

Cammy sobbed harder. She nodded.

"But I couldn't do *nothing*!" she protested. She heard him sigh.

"If you truly want to help, you must understand what you can and can't do, and not put other people at needless risk. Else you are throwing gasoline on the fire. You not only drew an innocent third party into that trap, you yourself could have died, and that would have done no one any good."

"But I want to *help*—"

Dracula's Match

"Which I understand. If you are serious, you must do what you *can*, not what you *can't*. And you cannot be cavalier with your life or with the lives of others. Have the humility to know your own limitations."

She blinked at him through her tears. Could he even say something like that? The guy who had watched people get executed while he was a child?

"Think on what I said," he admonished; he sounded less angry. "I will fetch something for your hands."

She shook her head and shut the door on him. She made extra, doubly-certain to lock the door to her room, and curled up under the big down comforter. The mattress felt like down too. It was almost always soft, but it needed to be reshaped periodically. It felt like it needed that again to get back to its fluffy norm. She cried herself to sleep.

Once Cammy had locked herself in her room and was unlikely to leave and cause mischief, Dracula drove into the city. On the way, he got a call.

"Where are you?" a voice demanded. He did not recognize it; this was probably one of the newer agents.

"You can track me, you should know," he replied.

"You were supposed to be in the city by dark. That draugr is probably going to show up again."

"I'll be there shortly."

Dimly, he heard a familiar voice in the background demand "Is that him?" He heard shuffling, then Boese snarling.

"Did you put a homeless man in the hospital?" Boese demanded.

"I don't recall putting one into any hospital," Dracula answered.

"Do you recall smashing anyone's kneecaps, crushing his hand, and knocking out every one of his teeth?"

"Oh, you meant to ask whether I had *injured* a homeless man. Yes, I did. He was asking for help."

"Do *not* get cute with me. You know exactly what I was asking. Why aren't you already in the city?"

"I got a late start," he said, "but your monster has to travel as well. It is doubtful he will be out and about immediately after sunset."

"How do *you* know?"

"Because he did not appear immediately after sunset at Pike Place yesterday. I calculated how long it would take to get from Lake View to Pike Place on foot. It seems he took nearly as much time. Moving quite fast for foot travel, but it's clear he did not drive."

Boese was silent a moment, then said, "Don't get clever here. If you aren't useful, I can easily put you back down in that hole. Going off and attacking a man in broad daylight, you monster—"

"He had no place to live, no assets or wealth, and no desire to earn an income. But I understand your government provides assistance to folk who are disabled." Dracula smiled. "I helped to solve his trouble."

"Can it. You crippled a guy with bipolar who was starting to go off his meds."

"It sounds to me as though I did him a favor, then. He will be receiving the medication he needs but cannot afford so long as he is in the hospital?"

Dracula's Match

Boese growled out something unintelligible, then snapped, "If that thing shows its face again, you're up. We need someone with physical strength who knows how to fight. So do your best to actually try, huh?"

"Why, Director, how pleased I am to know that I am your last hope in all the world," Dracula said. "I shall certainly do all in my power."

"You better. I don't have the manpower to cover this whole city. Not even the tourist traps, if that's all this monster's after, and the tech department is stretched thin keeping a lid on this. Get this taken care of."

The line went dead.

Reaching the city, he slowly made his way to Pike Place. If the monster had gone there with intent, it stood to reason it might appear there again if there was some business left unfinished. After Malcolm had informed him of the dead man's identity, Dracula had taken the time to watch some of his so-called "matches." All he could say of them was that they were clearly performances, not actual fights. Mr. Thorirsson had apparently learned to fight, but had become an entertainer for his career. Which meant there was no way to know how well he might be able to *actually* fight, or how difficult he might be to overcome.

Dracula's phone rang.

"It has made an appearance?" he asked.

"The Space Needle! Get there!"

That wasn't too far away. But why there? He supposed he might find out if the draugr proved talkative.

He parked as close as he could—illegally. Boese's people would handle any fees or towing issues that might result. If the creature caused the same sort of trouble as the last time, the whole area would be under lockdown soon and parking violations would not be a primary concern. In fact, it seemed the street was already locked down. He came to a line of police tape, but there were no officers in sight. He ducked under and went on.

When he came within sight of the Space Needle, he realized that defeating the monster would be no trivial undertaking.

The first thing he noticed was the prodigious stench, that of an open grave or a charnel house. The draugr was twenty feet tall, standing atop the entryway of the Space Needle, slamming its fists over and over again into one of the supporting columns. It did not seem that the creature had done any damage, despite its roars of frustration, but its size would be an insurmountable obstacle if Dracula was expected to *wrestle* with the thing.

He stepped forward, then realized what he had thought was a pile of trash beside the gutter was a mangled human corpse. He hadn't recognized it at first due to how *badly* the man was mangled. A balding man, a bit heavyset.

There was no one else around. Any pedestrians who had lacked the good sense to flee must have been directed elsewhere by police.

Given the monster's preoccupation with the monument, Dracula wondered if he ought not leave it be. From what he could tell, it was not strong enough to bring the structure down, and he did not like the size difference at all.

"What are you doing?"

He looked to his left. A man stepped out of hiding and slowly crept through the fog towards him. It was one of Boese's dhampirs. Dhampirs—the offspring of a strigoi father and a living woman, made good vampire hunters. Boese had arranged a little patrol of them for his organization when he had Dracula down at his lab.

This dhampir was a young man, in his thirties; scars cut through the hair on one side of his head, not unlike Boese's own set of scars. Another dhampir, the same age, followed him. Dracula couldn't remember their names.

"Took your time, didn't you?" the first demanded, and gestured at the giant. "Get in there."

Dracula considered both of them, and considered the obstacle.

"Not now," he said.

"We can't keep this whole area locked down. We have a few local officers trying to keep things in order. You need to do something, and *now*."

"Considering you're a glorified lab rat, I take no orders from you," Dracula told him. "At the moment, I am seriously disadvantaged, and if there is no further risk of collateral damage, I say we see what the monster does. It may be that if he cannot destroy this edifice, he will return tomorrow evening, by which time we might all be better prepared."

"We are *not* letting this crisis persist that long. The department wants this thing gone *tonight*."

"How many battles have you been in, boy? How many fights?"

The young man blinked.

"What?"

"How many?"

"None, but lucky for me, I'm not the one who's up to bat."

"And since I am, I am deciding how to swing."

"No, you're not," the agent said. He pulled a gun from inside his hoodie—civilian attire was the norm when Special Services agents were out and about—and fired into the monster's back. Dracula could not tell at that distance whether the bullet had done any damage, but the creature whirled about, its pale eyes settled on the trio of enemies. Dracula let his breath out through his teeth, and glared at the agent.

"You're up," the agent said, and withdrew. His partner went with him.

The monster roared in rage and jumped down off the entrance to storm towards Dracula, who remained planted. He cursed, and drew his magnum. It wasn't likely to inflict any damage, but he wanted to see what it *was* capable of doing.

The answer was "nothing." The monster didn't even seem to have been hit, though Dracula was quite the marksman and could not possibly have missed a target that size. He drew the sword he'd brought. He hadn't encountered many supernatural monsters of size, and had no clear plan for how to deal with this giant. Hand-to-hand seemed unlikely to work.

The monster had closed the distance and raised a fist to slam down. Dracula darted forward and slashed at its knee. Though it was dead, the injury might hamper its movements.

The slash did nothing. It left not so much as a mark.

There could be no fight. Not against something more than three times his size, with arms as long as he was tall. Something that he could not harm. Impossible.

He ducked to one side and then retreated as fast as he could as the monster swung around to catch him. Was there anything at all he could use? The space and stairs before the Space Needle was largely open ground. There were glass sculptures nearer to the structure, but all they *might* do is slow the monster down if Dracula chose to retreat through them. Draugrs could apparently become mist and sink into the ground; Dracula wondered if concrete or asphalt disrupted that ability. From the reports, it had traveled from the cemetery's open ground to Pike Place without being spotted, or at least, no report of its being spotted between the locations had come to his attention.

Malcolm had said draugrs could change size at will; was there an upper limit? Perhaps; otherwise the monster would simply have made itself even larger to tear apart the Space Needle. So he might stand a chance if he could get the thing to shrink. Theoretically, if it pursued him into a space too small for its frame, it might shrink to something more manageable, against which he might stand a chance.

Could he get inside the Space Needle? Boese's agents must surely have cleared the structure by now. It wasn't an ideal solution, however. Once inside, he'd be cornered and have little space to maneuver. Some other location? But where? The Museum of Pop Culture was within sprinting distance, and there was plenty of space inside. Some rooms were quite large, but there were hallways, exits, entrances, stairs, multiple levels, and there were bound to be numerous strange displays he might be able to use to his advantage.

He was retreating up the stairs leading to the Space Needle, dodging ferocious, long-reaching swings from those arms, moving as fast as he was able. If he had not centuries of practice on which to rely, he doubted he could successfully evade the monster at all.

The draugr was coming from a little to his left; the glass sculptures which led around the other side of the Space Needle lay to his right. The glass was unlikely to slow the monster, and that way was a longer route to the Museum of Pop Culture, whereas there was an open space nearer the monorail. He might be able to escape through some narrow opening the monster could not possibly squeeze through at his current size, so Dracula turned to sprint that direction—and saw a pack of five wolves in the fog. Very large wolves. Undoubtedly the dead man's friends who had contacted Ophois and who had tried to exhume him the other day. One was a tawny, nearly yellow color, and a very large gray one stood in the middle.

Wolves were a natural enemy of *strigoi*, but these were not natural wolves, and therefore no more dangerous to him than a particularly vicious human being. However, their numbers were bound to be a problem. If he was forced to fight through them the draugr would catch him. Its strides were enormous.

The draugr was nearly on him. Dracula didn't have time to switch back to a gun to fell the werewolves, so readied his sword. If they didn't cow and retreat, he would be forced to take them down. That would slow *him* down, and he was unlikely to outpace the draugr at its current size. He charged towards the werewolves.

Three of the five leaped up immediately. He beheaded one, slicing off its outstretched paws with the same stroke. A dead man, his severed head, and hands slammed onto the concrete, while the next nearest wolf sank its teeth into Dracula's thigh. As he raised his sword to slash the werewolf, another made an attempt at his throat. No sooner had he dispatched the leaping threat than something wrapped around his chest and hoisted him violently into the air. The other wolf obligingly let go his leg.

Those precious seconds had just cost him very dearly.

One of the werewolves snapped at his foot as he was lifted higher into the air. The draugr glared at its captive. Dracula tested his strength against it, but could not overpower the fingers wrapped around his chest. Then the draugr took hold of his sword arm and wrenched it free. Both the arm and the sword were thrown at the Space Needle. The draugr then drew back its hand and hurled Dracula with all its might.

He collided against one of the buttresses, careened down into the bend near the base, and fell sprawling across the roof of the entrance. The draugr leaped forward and reached for him. Dracula got to his feet to flee, and managed to jump down to the ground in order to force his way into the building. The werewolves were not likely to be sane enough to use tools, elevators, or doors if he could barricade them, and the draugr might shrink, though now that he was short an arm he had no idea how to defeat it, even if it shrank to man-size.

The werewolves snarled and charged his new location. Once again, he lacked the time to deal with all of them while evading the larger threat. He pushed past the security checkpoint while the werewolves seethed after him. They were faster than he had anticipated, and one sank its teeth into his heel and tripped him. He kicked at the creature, smashing its face against the glass, and it slumped to the floor, a dead man.

The draugr caught up with him again, seized him by one ankle, and dragged him back the way they had come. He kicked at the creature's wrist, but could not break its bones.

This was no ordinary undead monster. Dracula had never faced anything this strong before.

It was very possible that before the night was over, he'd be in pieces all over the street.

The draugr lifted him and smashed him down into the concrete with all its might. Over and over and over. Then it pushed him down onto the ground and dragged him along, stripping the flesh from his face. He tried to grab hold of a passing pole he could barely see, but could not get purchase on it. One of the werewolves bit him hard on the wrist; he did his best to smash it down against the concrete. He could not tell if he killed it or stunned it, but his wrist was free. That was of no consequence, because the draugr roared angrily, lifted him again, and hurled him down hard on something which partly broke beneath him, and punched clean through his chest. Then the draugr ripped his other arm free, roared in his face, and began to devour his arm. It turned its attention to the Space Needle again.

By craning his neck, Dracula was able to see that he'd been impaled on a streetlight some distance from the building. He had no way to get off the pole without arms. A werewolf on the ground growled beneath him, but he could do nothing about it, either.

The fight seemed to have gotten the draugr to thinking, because it ceased its useless attack on the building, considered the height, and shrank to man-size. It stormed into the entrance. Two werewolves trotted after the draugr.

Dracula comforted himself with thoughts of what he would do to Boese's little pet the moment he had the chance.

Some minutes later, glass up above shattered, and a distinctive, female scream pierced the night as someone was *thrown* from the top of the building. So it hadn't been cleared of people. Dracula supposed he shouldn't be surprised. Boese's agents wouldn't have had the manpower to evacuate while also trying to secure the area and deal with eyewitnesses.

The sounds of screams and general destruction interspersed with the howls of wolves continued for perhaps twenty minutes. When everything had gone silent, mist came rolling out the entryway—only visible because it was thicker than the ambient fog—spilled down the stairs, and into the street, where it disappeared down a storm drain. The remaining werewolves darted out into the dark. One of the two agents took shots with a nine millimeter at the wolves, but hit neither of them at that distance.

Then the two agents approached him, still stuck on the pole.

"Heh, Vlad the Impaled," the first one joked.

"Impal*ee*," the other corrected.

Dracula kept silent. Let them laugh. This was quite the situation for Boese and his people. They had nothing to field against the draugr, and who could say how many people had been slaughtered? This monster might just be able to rip the lid off everything and reveal the whole of the supernatural to the world. Wouldn't *that* be a pretty little mess for them all?

CHAPTER 7
HIDDEN SECRETS

Cammy poked her head into the hall. She was still nervous about the mood her host might be in. No sounds whatever came to her ears, so she snuck downstairs, her eyes darting around every corner.

She encountered no sign of him. There were no dishes set to dry, which was strange. Since he stayed up all night, he often ate food and drank during the evening, meaning there were cleaned dishes in the morning.

Did he leave? He must have. But he also knew she needed a ride into town for work and classes. He'd always been very careful to make certain her needs were met—until yesterday. Perhaps he was still angry and hadn't bothered. But somehow, she doubted that.

She decided to call. His phone rang and rang and rang. She didn't like that at all. Malcolm had been pretty worried about that draugr, but presumably Boese's people were dealing with it. But that could mean… Boese liked to use Dracula to subdue supernatural menaces. Maybe he'd been sent to deal with it? And then not come home? That didn't bode well. She dialed again.

Ring. Ring. Ring. Ring. Ri—"What?" Boese's voice on the line.

Uh oh. "I was hoping to speak to—"

"Your sugar daddy won't be home for a while. Do you have anything helpful to tell me?"

"He's *not* my—!"

The line went dead. Well, now she knew why Dracula hadn't come home.

She dialed Malcolm.

"What?" he growled into the phone.

"Vlad's down at Boese's lab!"

Malcolm grunted.

"Word on the street is the draugr attacked the Space Needle last night. Lots of dead people."

Cammy's heart felt like it was being crushed.

"Anyway, sounds like it was too beefy for this city's big guns," Malcolm grumbled. "No way the director didn't send Vlad in. That thing's some serious bad news." Malcolm swore until he ran out of breath.

"So… how do we stop this thing?"

"How do *we* stop this thing?" Malcolm shouted. "*We* aren't going to! I have no idea what *anyone* is going to be able to do about it."

"But you can go berserk, right? That's what old-school werewolves can—"

"I am *not* getting roped into fighting a rage-ghost-death-machine, and going berserk just means I would get myself killed *sooner*. I get a boost to strength, but against a transforming murder ghost, I wouldn't be much good. *You* would die in an instant. And if you get yourself killed, let me tell you, I know some *black* magic, and I'll extra ruin your day if you get me in trouble—"

"I wasn't thinking I could fight it," Cammy snipped at him. "If Boese is keeping Vlad down there because he didn't beat this thing, then I was asking *how* we could defeat it."

"Stay. Home."

He hung up. She glared at her phone. Same old Malcolm. No help at all. But then it occurred to her she also had to ask him to drive her. But she didn't want to ride with him, and he sounded angry enough he might refuse. Especially if he thought she might sneak off and get in trouble—since she'd already done that once. Twice. But who else could she call? Brian knew where the mansion was, but he was probably working. Desperate, she called him.

"Everything ok?" he answered. She couldn't believe he'd just picked up. He was always busy since becoming a cop.

"Um, well actually, I need a ride…"

"A ride?"

"I'm sure you can't. If Melissa is working, it's not as though you can borrow her car."

"She's already at work. I can get the car and pick you up. She won't need it until later."

"Oh, well… thank you," Cammy said. She hoped Dracula wouldn't be angry to find out she'd had Brian come to the mansion again when he wasn't there.

"Be there in maybe an hour and a half," Brian said, and hung up.

She'd end up being late for class, but there wasn't anything she could do about that. In the meanwhile, she had over an hour to kill.

Dracula's Match

She didn't know why, but she looked up more about the guy who'd turned into a draugr. She couldn't fight him, and if Malcolm was right, it looked like Dracula couldn't either. She found some comments about the Space Needle attack. Theories flew back and forth, though it seemed a lot of people were settling on "terrorist attack," partly because the Space Needle app wasn't working. Some people said there was a leaked security video, but she couldn't locate it anywhere. The comments from people claiming to have seen it certainly seemed like they had seen the draugr. They described a giant, angry man smashing everything and everybody he stumbled across. Some noticed his mouth seemed to be covered in blood before he entered, and someone mentioned it looked like he was carrying part of a human arm. And there had been wolves with him.

This was a big, *big* problem.

So far as she could find, Roar Thorirsson had been liked in his career as a wrestler, but he never quite made it to the same level of popularity as the household name guys that even *she* recognized. Even though he was a Seattle native, and had resettled after his attempt to break into Hollywood fell through, she still hadn't heard of him before. There were a few interviews about his interest in his cultural heritage. She watched those, noticing that in the more recent interviews he talked more and more about how life was meaningless and how there had to be more to life than money and fame. She thought that was ironic for a guy in the entertainment industry. After his one mediocre film, he had become friends with the guy who wrote and performed the song in Old Norse which played during the credits. But that friend had been killed about a year ago in a bar fight that got out of hand. Roar had been there with some other friends, including the wolf guy Malcolm had showed her in the video. Maybe those were the friends who became the werewolves? She found at least one article commenting on how Roar had been spotted with a necklace of Mjolnir a few months before the bar fight.

Malcolm had said that things aligned based on energy. Maybe Roar had been getting serious about his roots, and somehow that was enough to turn him into a draugr? That seemed like a weak explanation to her.

Then there was the fact that he had murdered his wife and killed himself. Even if his wife was having an affair, that was no excuse to murder her. Cammy glared at the photo of Roar on the gossip article speculating about his marital issues. One of Roar's friends—someone who always seemed to be in his entourage—had been interviewed afterward, and had unsavory things to say about Roar's wife, Laura, who had kept her maiden name, Amor. He said she had been going to leave Roar. Cammy wondered if the marriage had been one of those "celebrity" matches that had limped along longer than most. They'd both been in wrestling, and in the 2000s had gotten married after some sort of staged romantic rival drama involving Lance Bryant. Apparently there had been some sort of grudge thing going on between them. And then Lance had made it big and Roar hadn't. Cammy didn't get most of the context, but she watched the video. They had a great big cake brought out, and Lance was there to try to break the whole thing up. Roar fought with him, tearing his suit like The Hulk bursting out of his clothes, and eventually Lance ended up in the cake. The audience seemed to love it.

Dracula's Match

Cammy looked at the pictures of Laura from back in the day. Bleached blonde hair, well very defined muscles. She was really pretty. They looked like a perfect couple in the photos of them together. Now they were both dead. And maybe it wasn't vampires this time, but it was still something supernatural. Like with Heather. Cammy felt ill.

She set down her phone. Why was she even doing this? She couldn't possibly help with the problem. Heck, it looked like even *Boese*, with the might of the US government behind him, was struggling. There was nothing she could do. Just like Dracula and Malcolm kept telling her.

She slammed her forehead down on the kitchen table. The only thing she was apparently good at was getting people killed. She wanted to run away, but to where? To do what? Hide from whom? She wished she could never talk to anyone ever again.

For want of any relief, she checked Twitter and some of her other feeds. Kenzie and Lindsey had posted about the incident at Pike Place and the Selfie Museum. Lindsey lamented that the Selfie Museum had been attacked, as she had taken some great photos there. Kenzie had also messaged her about Andrew. She hadn't heard from him—which wasn't unusual, Andrew was painfully shy—but Cammy couldn't help worrying something might have happened to him if he was down there when Roar went on his rampage. Aslan hadn't responded either, but he might be busy with school assignments. She hoped she'd bump into him on campus today.

Cammy's throat tightened, choking her. She texted Andrew again. Maybe he'd answer. She *needed* him to answer, but he didn't. Even a few days with no reply wasn't out of the ordinary for him, but of all the times for him to go quiet...

The news wasn't reporting much on Pike Place. Just that a dangerous individual—reports differed whether he had been armed or not—had rampaged through the area, killing about seven people and hospitalizing several more. The Space Needle attack was much harder to figure out. Very little information had been released, but the conclusion was that there had been an act of vandalism with injuries.

Why would he attack these places? Cammy wondered. She hadn't come across anything that indicated draugrs liked to kill people. Guard treasure, sure, but that couldn't be what he was doing: he was destroying locations that had nothing to do with where he lived or presumably kept his stuff. She wondered if he was killing certain people for some reason. That didn't seem likely. He couldn't possibly know who was going to be where, could he? He'd killed his wife and himself; was there someone else he was looking for, maybe? That was a sobering and terrifying thought: an undead rage-zombie on the warpath for someone in particular, who would kill anyone who got in his way. Even—though she *really* hoped not—Andrew.

Have the humility to know your own limitations.

It seemed she was *quite* limited here. Vampires, even the modern type with all their movie trope limitations, had proved too strong for her. This monster might too strong for Dracula, meaning she *definitely* couldn't do anything about it.

Was that it? She was totally helpless? There wasn't anything she could do to help her friends? Could she warn them? Maybe. She felt pretty sure Boese wouldn't like it. He'd incarcerated her before for less. He might do it again. He didn't want anyone finding out about the supernatural. If he found out she'd told someone, would he disappear that person into his lab?

She felt ice running down her back at the thought. But what *could* she do, then? Nothing? She couldn't do *nothing*. But it looked like she might have to. She gripped her hair.

A knock at the door snapped her out of her ruminations. She stuffed her phone in her purse. It occurred to her she didn't have a key for the door, but Dracula often left it unlocked. Hopefully he wouldn't be angry at her for leaving his house unattended, but she couldn't do much about that.

"Thanks, B," she greeted him when she came to the door. Brian was glowering at the eaves, and she had the impression he was thinking something unpleasant about her host. Even her appearing at the door didn't yank him into the present. When he gave his attention, he still looked distracted.

"Did something happen? You don't usually have free time," she said.

"I have PTO right now," he explained.

"What happened?"

"Got injured. Not on duty. Don't worry about it."

She *was* worried, though. Brian needed money, just like everyone, but there was a dangerous monster running the city; so maybe it was for the best if Brian wasn't on duty. He might end up getting sent into its path.

"Is it serious?" she asked. He looked at her, and she felt like there was some kind of accusation in his eyes.

"Cracked ribs. I'll be fine." He sounded tense, unfriendly.

She looked at the ground. Something was really wrong. Even Brian was grumpy. She watched him walk. No limp or anything. Once they were in the car and on their way, Cammy decided to press.

"How did it happen?"

Brian turned on the radio.

Apparently everyone was in a bad mood.

"How's Melissa?"

"She's fine," he said shortly.

"Ok. You sure you're—"

"Why are you living up here?" he interrupted.

Oh. He was still upset about that.

"Vlad had extra space," she mumbled, and gestured the way they'd come. "And I told him I had no home."

"Right. K." Brian said. "You notice anything… weird about him?"

"Weird like what?"

Brian shrugged, shook his head a little. "Anything? Like his *garlic allergy*?"

"Yeah, he told me about that." Oh, Brian was suspicious of a whole *different* situation. Should she tell him? *Could* she tell him? Dracula wasn't all that concerned about keeping himself or his real identity a secret, so far as she could tell. He'd been pretty open about it, in fact. Presumably the only reason the whole world didn't know he was here was because he barely spoke to anyone he didn't already know. But could Brian handle it? Especially now that there was a super monster on the loose? He was suspicious about her living with Dracula. What would he do if he found out Boese and his agents had dragged her down into a secret lab without reading her her rights or allowing her a phone call? He was a cop because he wanted to help and protect people. Wouldn't he want to stop Boese, too?

Dracula's Match

No, bad idea to tell him. He'd get himself into trouble.

She shrugged in answer. "He's old-fashioned. I guess that's how people behave in Eastern Europe."

"Right. *Old-fashioned*. Sure."

She couldn't think of what else to say, and he didn't try to fill the empty air with anything but the radio. They made their way into the city in the same, horrible, awkward silence as before. He dropped her off at campus.

"Do you think you could give me a ride back here after my shift?" she asked. Usually she didn't work shifts between classes, but she had volunteered to help cover Billie's shift at least partially, about a week ago.

"When?"

"In a few hours. I'll text you."

Brian glanced at the Cascades.

"Don't go up there," Cammy blurted.

"What?"

"Don't go up there," she repeated.

"I wasn't—"

"Okay. I'll see you later. Thank you, B." She darted across the parking lot.

Classes were not the sweet contrast to all the supernatural terror she had hoped they would be. Sitting in a room with strangers who didn't know what was going on made her feel terribly alone, and as if she were somehow not where she was supposed to be. The general air of complacency grated on her.

The walk to the bus stop took nearly half an hour, but today that might be nice. She couldn't get her mind to stop racing in class, but walking usually helped. Just be alone for a while, not worrying about Brian or Andrew or anyone. She'd be late, though, so she texted ahead to let Kenzie know.

The fog and light drizzle hid the blocks ahead from view. It was like she was walking into the unknown. As she came to an intersection, the next block came slowly into view, buildings and people materializing as if from smoke. Near the bus stop, she could hear sea gulls cawing up above, but could barely see them. Like ghosts swooping above her.

One bus ride later, she walked up to the Mindful Bean, with its logo of a coffee bean sitting in a lotus position, meditating on a lotus flower. The owner, Luna, had designed the logo. It looked pretty good for something a local person had come up with, though Cammy thought it was a little funny-looking. It seemed to welcome her as she opened the door.

"Hey," she greeted Kenzie.

"Hey!" Kenzie answered. She was cleaning the nozzle on the steamer. "Welcome!" she called to someone behind Cammy. Cammy turned, to see Siri behind her. She let out a little squeak of surprise.

"Whoa, Cam, you ok?" Kenzie asked.

"What are you doing here?" Cammy demanded in a whisper.

Siri was wearing the same skirt as before, and Cammy wondered if these were the only clothes the huldra had. Her hair and clothes looked damp; the misting drizzle outside couldn't have done that quickly. The huldra must have been outside for some time.

"I followed you," Siri answered, as though that was perfectly normal and not the sort of thing a stalker would do. The huldra looked around the shop, taking in the sights with a sort of sparkling wonder.

"Why did you follow me here?"

"I vanted to see vhat you do," Siri said.

"This a friend of yours, Cam?" Kenzie asked, walking up to them both.

"No," Cammy said. "No, but she... she goes to the same college. I've bumped into her a few times."

"Huh," Kenzie said. She offered a hand. "Nice to meet you."

"Siri," the huldra provided. Kenzie's phone beeped.

"Whoops," Kenzie pulled her phone from her apron. "That's gotta suck. You've got the same name as the phone lady."

"The phone lady?" Siri asked.

"Yeah, the digital assistant program on phones," Kenzie said.

"Get back to work, this isn't a sleepover, you know," Luna called from the back. "Cammy, what are you doing? You can't hang out by the door like that. If your friend isn't going to order anything, she needs to go."

"She's not my friend," Cammy protested weakly.

"Order something?" Siri's lightning eyes swept over the display case of quiches, salads, muffins, and other goods. She strode up to the display and leaned close to study them more closely.

"Don't bother anyone," Cammy hissed at her and hurried to the back to put her things in her tiny locker as quickly as she could. She came out to clock in on the POS. Siri was talking to Kenzie. Placing an order.

"Just milk? This is a coffee shop, you know," Kenzie laughed.

"Hmm, you are correct," Siri said, and touched her chin daintily. "Do you have coffee vith milk?"

"A latte? Yeah," Kenzie said. "Sure." She gave the total. Siri reached into a pocket in her skirt and produced a series of wadded up bills. Kenzie exchanged a look with Cammy. Gingerly, she took the damp bills and tried to flatten them so they'd fit in the register, then passed back change. Siri looked confused.

"If you don't want it, I can put it in the tip jar," Kenzie told her.

"Certainly."

Siri watched with no hint of understanding as Kenzie dropped the change into the tip jar. Cammy decided to let Kenzie handle the order. She checked that Luna was back in her office, then scooted around the counter to the customer side to confront Siri.

"What are you doing here?"

"I told you: I vished to see vhere you vent."

"Why, though?"

Siri shrugged. "To see how a human he likes spends her time."

Cammy herded Siri away from the counter.

"Don't talk about supernatural stuff where people can hear!" she whispered.

"Vhy not?"

"Because!" Cammy realized she didn't really have a follow-up. Then she remembered what Dracula and Malcolm always said. "It's dangerous. People don't know about that stuff anymore. They'll get hurt."

Siri looked perplexed, then wounded.

"Hey, um..."

Dracula's Match

Cammy and Siri turned to see Kenzie waving the latte and a mini quiche in her hands. "Can't say your name or everyone's phones will wake up."

"Thank you." Siri accepted the order. She looked around the coffee shop, then decided on an empty table under the big front window. She slid gracefully into the seat.

Cammy didn't want to risk Luna getting mad again, so she grabbed the broom and dustpan and went to the trash near the door and pretended to sweep. She saw Kenzie eying her odd behavior.

Cammy swept imaginary crumbs as Siri took a sip of the coffee. Her beautiful face twisted in disgust, and she looked at the brown liquid through the clear plastic.

"You don't like coffee?"

"Vhat is wrong vith the milk you people use?" Siri demanded. "The only good milk I have had since coming here vas at his Majesty's estate."

"Huh? You mean the milk from Vlad's place? I think it's fresher. Raw, perhaps?"

Siri's shoulders shivered.

"Why do you like milk so much?" Cammy asked. Dracula seemed to as well.

"It is not only milk. Food must be natural. Full of goodness. How else could something like me—or him—survive?"

Cammy hadn't really thought about it, but Dracula didn't seem to eat out very much. The vegetables up at his place were all fresh, fresher and sweeter than anything Cammy could buy from shops. She had started to feel a bit more energetic over the months since staying there. And the milk he had in the ceramic jar in the fridge *did* taste different—better—than the store-bought variety, though she couldn't say why. It just *did*.

"Maybe it's the processing," Cammy mumbled. "But you can't avoid it. That's how all food is made."

Siri looked at her, then picked up the quiche and nibbled it. Her forehead wrinkled with distress, but she kept eating.

"What do you think you're going to accomplish here anyway?" Cammy asked her.

Siri looked down and traced a meaningless shape on the wood with one finger.

"My homeland is not as it vas," she said in a low voice. "Vhen I set out, I hoped I might find a new home for us all. But having seen this place, I do not think it vould suit us. Perhaps the voods near vhere his Majesty lives, if he vill have us. I vill tell the others about it. But no vun remembers us. Not as ve vere, nor as ve vish to be now. Even if they did, their offerings of food vould be…" she gestured at the quiche and the cup of coffee. "There are still voods in my homeland. But the people…" She looked out the window. "The *people* are not the same. They do not understand."

"And that's the reason you chose Vlad?"

"He understands. How people vere. How things vere. This land vas vunce known for opportunities. For fresh starts." Siri shrugged.

"Yeah, I think that was a while ago," Cammy said. "And it wasn't for everyone anyway."

Siri traced more lines on the table.

"Men are not vhat they vere. They have gone mad."

"What do you mean?"

"Vhen ve helped them vith their charcoal, they understood the vorld, the nature of things. That they lived by vork-ing vith the natural order, vithin it. They did not take vithout giving back, they knew they did not exist independent of the voods and the vorld. They vere not separate, as they believe now; they ver... *more*. Men had humility, vere grateful, had respect, knew their place in the world and their relationship vith it. They vere not... devouring, aloof tyrants and strangers, as they are now." She frowned at her cup. "That vas vhy I thought..."

"You can't convince him to love you, you know," Cammy told her.

"Vhy not?" Siri demanded, her eyes flashing like lightning. Cammy felt her chest tighten.

"You just can't."

"I can offer magic. Many things. Things he might like."

"That's not how love works. Giving things might help, but love isn't... it can't be bought."

"Then how does vun get it?" Siri demanded.

Cammy had no idea. It wasn't something she'd ever thought about. Love—at least the "true love" variety in movies—wasn't really what it was cracked up to be, right? She'd never seen it in real life. Couples got divorced, parents didn't care about their kids. Everyone was single and relationships didn't last.

"I don't know," Cammy confessed. "I've never... been in love. I've never had it."

Siri looked at her, her bright eyes unlike anything human. Beautiful, but eerie. Cammy glanced at the counter. Kenzie was looking at them both while making a drink. Had she heard? Cammy hoped not. They had kept their voices down.

Cammy put the broom back on the hook on the wall, and took up position behind the counter and started serving new customers. Siri people-watched out the window for about an hour, then got up and sauntered out the door without a glance back.

Cammy could barely keep her mind on drinks or cleaning, especially when Kenzie shared with her that she had seen videos posted online that showed some guy throwing a car with his bare hands at Pike Place, and people's posts about loved ones sighting someone on a rampage. But these and similar videos about the Space Needle had all disappeared. Cammy supposed Boese's people must be working overtime to keep the whole thing under wraps, but could they really stop every single person from talking or tweeting? There must be a lot of witnesses by now. Kenzie asked Cammy what she thought of the videos.

"They have to be fake, right?" Cammy said. "No one can do that."

Kenzie eyed her, then didn't talk to her for the rest of her shift.

Cammy wanted to ask Dracula or Malcolm about what had happened, but she doubted they would talk to her. Boese would know, but she did *not* want to talk to *him*. Kenzie had no word from Andrew, and Cammy had no replies on her phone either. She felt sick.

After her shift, Brian picked her up and drove her sullenly to the university.

"You know, you can talk to me," he said as they pulled into the parking lot.

"What?"

"You can. We've been friends since middle school. If something's going on."

He looked at her. She fidgeted. But what could she tell him?

"You can also live with us. Or..." He looked at the campus. "I could get my own place. If you wanted, we could..."

"Thanks, B," she said. "I have to go. Let's talk about that later?"

Brian nodded stiffly. "Ok."

She took out her phone and searched for those posts Kenzie had talked about, but couldn't find them. Kenzie forwarded some screenshots she had taken. Reading those confirmed that at least a few people had recorded video, taken pictures of, or just plain *seen* the draugr. One post was *very* insistent that it was Roar Thorirsson specifically. She wondered what Boese would do about that. Then she realized she didn't want to wonder.

As she left the class, she scanned the campus with the adder stone. Just in case. Instead of anything supernatural, she spotted Aslan taking photographs of a nearby tree. It was full of crows cawing. She hurried over to him.

"Hey," she greeted. Aslan lowered the camera and waved to her.

"Hey, Cammy. How are you?"

"Have you heard from Andrew?" she blurted. Aslan frowned.

"No. You texted about that, right? He wasn't online last night. I guess he must be busy with the farm or something."

"You haven't heard from him at all?" Cammy felt her stomach twisting. Aslan shook his head.

"No. He hasn't been online. Did something happen? You look pale."

Cammy shook her head. "I'm fine. If you… hear from him, will you let me know?"

"Sure," Aslan answered.

As she turned to leave, she spotted Siri standing near a building, across the brick walkway. Cammy tensed. The huldra had come back here? Then she noticed Aslan had spotted Siri, too. The "bohemian look" did stand out a bit. Aslan raised the camera to snap a photo.

"What are you doing?" Cammy asked him. The shutter clicked. Aslan looked to her.

"Taking a picture."

"You can't just take people's pictures without permission," Cammy told him. "That's rude."

Aslan's light brown eyes studied hers for a moment, then he lowered the camera. Siri hadn't approached, but she was looking right at the both of them.

"Don't talk to that girl, ok?" Cammy said.

"What? Why?" Aslan asked.

"Just don't. She's… she's really mean. Just don't, ok?"

Aslan looked at her funny. "Ok," he said.

"See you later." Cammy walked away. She snuck a look at Siri. The huldra slunk around the corner of the building she had been standing against and disappeared. Cammy didn't spot her around the next building she walked past, so she pulled out the adder stone to see if there was anything else amiss.

There was the boy from the other day, clearly watching her. He wasn't bothering to hide, just standing on a bench between two trees, with his arms crossed, his eyes on her. The moment she spotted him, he jumped down and ran. He did weave through people, so despite the fact that he was invisible, it must be that he was still tangible. So probably not a ghost.

Should she follow him? If Malcolm was correct and the invisible boy was dangerous, then obviously she shouldn't. But now he was clearly spying on her. She decided to text Malcolm to let him know. If he was supposed to keep an eye out on her, he'd want to know about this development.

"Is something the matter?"

Cammy jumped. Siri stood looking over Cammy's shoulder at her phone. She was a tall woman, so this wasn't very hard for her to do. Siri scanned the campus grounds for what had arrested Cammy's attention, but it seemed she could not see the boy. However, Siri obviously knew about the adder stone, because she snatched it the moment she spotted it in Cammy's hand. She held it to her own eye, dragging Cammy up against her face. The cord wasn't very long.

"Ah," Siri said, and dropped the stone. "That looks like *huldufólk* to me."

"Hulduh..?" Wasn't that something Malcolm had said before?

"Hidden People," Siri said. "Cousins of mine, if you vill. Vhat are they doing here, silly little creatures?"

Couldn't someone say the same of you? Cammy thought. If those kids *were* some kind of hidden people—now she remembered what Malcolm had said; the word sounded different when Siri spoke—they didn't resemble Siri at all. They wore specific costumes, were always invisible, and clearly didn't have tails. Siri hooked her arm around Cammy's.

"Let us see vhat these little children are up to, shall ve?"

"No," Cammy tried to wriggle free. "I need to go home."

"Home?" Siri straightened up, and looked down at Cammy. "Vhere he lives?" Her other hand gripped Cammy's arm, preventing her from easily escaping. "Vhat does he see in you that I cannot give instead?"

"We aren't a thing," Cammy protested. "Really. We're not."

"Then you do not care if I should try to vin his heart?"

"You can do whatever you want. But let go—"

Siri pulled her along.

This might get bad. If huldras were bad news, she shouldn't go along with this. She was also discovering that Siri was *strong*. Much stronger than she looked. Siri hurried on, dragging Cammy with her, around the corner of the nearest building. She snatched the adder stone again, and laughed "Ah *ha!*" then addressed the air in her own language. Cammy saw nothing, but Siri must have gotten a response, because she said, "Ah, this vun is no trouble. Vhy vere you spying, little mouse?"

All of a sudden, the boy simply *appeared* right in front of Cammy and Siri. His bright eyes bounced back and forth between them.

"Why are you spying on us?" he demanded in yet another accent Cammy didn't recognize.

"Yes, vhy vere you?" Siri asked of Cammy, releasing her. Cammy hid the adder stone under her shirt.

"Sorry, I wasn't—I didn't mean to," Cammy said. "I was borrowing this, and I was just curious if I'd ever see anything with it. I wasn't looking for anyone."

"But you chased my sister!" the boy accused.

"I saw her almost get hit by a car, so I was worried she might get hurt."

The boy made a face.

"She shouldn't hurry like that," he grumbled, almost apologetically. His bright eyes studied Cammy. "Thank you for watching for her safety."

"Sure," Cammy said. "Are you guys… are you guys homeless? Do you have parents?"

"That is not your concern!" the boy snapped. "We were just…" He played with his fingers. "We were trying to find food."

"You guys don't have any?"

"We came to this city to make a new start. But it was a mistake."

So Siri was not the only one with that goal. But perhaps Cammy knew why they'd come *here. Something I can help with!* Cammy realized. "I know a guy who runs a sanctuary for supernatural beings," she said. "Have you asked him?"

"His Majesty, Wlad Dracula?" the boy guessed.

Wow. The supernatural world really *did* know he was here.

"Have you tried asking him?"

"We met with obstacles," the boy said. "No one we know has ever found a way past them."

Huh. Apparently Cammy had just lucked her way up there, if this boy and Siri were both wary of Dracula's guardians. "Well, I could introduce you sometime," Cammy offered. The boy looked confused. "I live up there," she explained.

This set him aback, as he studied her up and down closely, scrutinizing her for something. "But you are human?" he asked.

"Yes."

The boy looked to Siri, who shrugged and played with a lock of hair. The boy frowned with concentration.

"You could make introductions?"

Cammy nodded. Then she realized she had no idea when Dracula would be home. Brian was going to pick her up.

"Oh, Brian!" she realized. She checked her phone. He had texted to ask where she was. "I gotta run. Do you guys live here, on campus?"

The boy crossed his arms and looked away. He eyed Siri. "No," he admitted at last. "We were looking for food. We didn't think..." he gritted his teeth, "we should get it near where we are hiding."

"Where are you hiding?"

"Near the troll."

"The Fremont Troll?" Cammy checked.

"The troll turned to stone," the boy said.

She was about to inform him the Fremont troll had been made out of concrete, when she suddenly realized that it might be a *real* troll that Boese's people had turned to stone. Who could say? She texted Brian that she would be right there.

"I might be able to get there later," Cammy said. "If I can get a ride."

"Perhaps we will see you there," said the boy.

Cammy turned to go.

"Oh! What was your name again?"

The boy stiffened. Now that she was standing close enough to make out his very fair skin, she thought he was actually older than she had thought, but he was small for his age. He looked like he might be twelve, but he was the size of a much younger boy. But maybe she was wrong, and of course, no kid should talk to strangers.

"Well, I'm Cammy," she said. "Nice to meet you. Stay safe, ok? There's a bad monster on the loose right now."

The little bit of color he had drained out of the boy's pale face. He almost hugged himself. Then he vanished. Cammy turned to Siri.

"You know that guy I was talking to earlier when you spotted me?"

"The young man with the long hair and the camera?" Siri checked.

"Yes. Leave him alone, ok? Don't bother him or talk to him."

Siri arched an elegant eyebrow. "Do you love *him*, then?"

"No. He's a friend. Just… don't hurt him. He doesn't know about all the supernatural things, ok? Leave him alone."

Siri shrugged with one shoulder and played with a long lock of her wild hair.

"I vill not. I vill leave him be."

"Thank you," Cammy said. "Thanks."

Siri nodded.

Cammy walked towards Brian's car while Siri trailed very openly behind her. She didn't know what to say to Brian about a possibly murderous hidden-person-nymph-with-a-tail, so she pulled her phone to text Malcolm about the situation. Fortunately, she reached the parking lot alone, Siri having parted ways near one of the university buildings. Cammy set down her bag on the sidewalk to open the passenger side door.

"Hi, sorry," she apologized. "I was talking to someone."

"Someone," Brian grumbled. Cammy scrutinized him. His jaw was tight.

It was just like Brian these days to be suspicious of everyone. Stupid cop training. He almost actually glared at her out of the corner of his eye. "I was talking to Aslan, actually. You met him at my birthday, remember?"

"Yeah," he conceded.

"Why is everyone in such a bad mood?" Cammy grumped. Malcolm, and now Brian. Maybe Dracula, too, but he always had an edge to him—it always felt a little like being near a blade just waiting to be unsheathed at the slightest provocation.

"Probably," Brian grumbled, "it has to do with that thing massacring people all over town."

Cammy was stooping to pick up her bag; she froze and stared at him. Did he suspect it was supernatural? But he couldn't know it was a *draugr*, right?

Something rough slipped over her head, blinding her, and she felt hands on her arms and wrapping around her. They yanked her backwards, and she hit the asphalt. She screamed and kicked her feet, but could feel she was being dragged away from Brian's vehicle. He shouted her name, and she thought she heard his car door open. The asphalt gave way to a curb her hip discovered, then she was dragged over grass, then *down*, and everything got darker. She could just hear Brian shouting, but his voice faded halfway through her name.

"Brian!" she screamed, but heard nothing in response. The hands on her were wrestling to keep her from kicking or punching at whatever owned them. She couldn't see anything—there seemed to be a sack over her head. *Boese's peo-*

ple! It had to be. They'd kidnapped her before, thrown a sack over her, and dumped her down in that creepy lab, wherever it was. Suddenly she was back there, shivering in a metal chair, blinding white lights glaring hatefully down. Boese's pale, sallow face with the scars notching into his ear, his fixed smile mocking her.

"Let me go!" she shouted. "Let me go! I didn't do anything!"

She received no reply, just more bruises as she was dragged across a semi-flat, stony surface.

"Tell Boese I don't know anything! I didn't tell anyone anything!"

Still no reply. She had the feeling she was partly wrapped up in a bag or a blanket. She couldn't wriggle out of it, and was still held fast. If these were Boese's people stealing her, Brian had just witnessed it. They'd go after him next, maybe.

"Brian doesn't know anything!" she shouted next. "Leave him alone!"

This outburst was answered by someone—a man, by the voice—speaking in some foreign language to someone else. It sounded like a question to her. The answer was half-grunted out by the person who had her left arm and pulled the hardest.

Wait, **not** *Boese's people?*

That was far worse. If they were speaking a foreign language, were they supernatural? All the monsters she'd met recently didn't speak English as a first language. Where were they taking her? Where was she? The ground was damp—it was seeping through the sack and into her clothes now. She could smell moisture, maybe even some mildew. Everything was dark and all she could hear was fabric rustling and small grunts of exertion and feet on stone. Who had her? Where were they taking her? What would they *do* with her?

"Let me go! I know Dracula! I'm his guest!"

Whoever was dragging her slowed. She heard several voices now. It sounded like a hushed debate. They understood English, at least.

"I mean it! He's going to find you guys! You're going to be real sorry!"

More debating. Her heart rattled around inside her. She had no idea where she was, and no idea if Dracula *could* find her if he ever got out of Boese's lab. Nor did she have any idea where these people were taking her. She didn't even know who or what had grabbed her. Trolls? Goblins? Ghosts? Werewolves? Something she'd never heard of before?

She couldn't get out of the sack. Or their hands. But she had to do something. No one was going to be able to find her, despite her threats. It was like before. When those vampires had grabbed her and dragged her screaming from a vehicle. She hurt all over. She was suffocating. She had to do something. Anything. She had to get free.

Think! she screamed inside her mind. *Think! Don't panic!*

Only one person might be able to find her. Malcolm. But she didn't know where she was to text him. Or where they were taking her. Could Malcolm track her by scent? Maybe. He had implied he had an animal-like sense of smell. She guessed she was underground somehow. Who could say if he could track her that way?

But she had his number. And her phone was still in her right hand. If she craned her neck just so, she could peek past some of the cloth and see her phone screen, especially if she turned it on. She unlocked it with her thumb while the debate continued. She could just barely see what she was doing. She shared her location, and then texted out "help."

*Please, **please** come,* she thought. *Please find me!*

The debate was over. Her kidnappers hoisted her into the air and jogged along. She tried struggling, which slowed them down, but didn't stop them.

She clutched her phone tight. It was her only hope right now. Every sound thundered in her ears as her captors carried her along. It sounded like they were underground, in a tunnel of some sort. But the voices were muffled; they didn't echo. Where *were* they?

They carried her for what felt like half an hour, with her kicking periodically to see if they'd gotten tired. On her last kick, they dropped her hard on the stone floor and she yelped in pain. The first dragging session had left her more hurt than she had realized. Still no sign of Malcolm. She hoped he was on his way, but it was looking pretty grim. If he knew how to get underground, surely he would have done it by now. They had to be underground. She hadn't heard a car or any other noise than her kidnappers' feet, breath, and occasional grunting.

Suddenly she heard the buzz of conversation. Snippets of English, and other languages she didn't know. She smelled meat cooking somewhere, some spices that tickled her nose, and some very inexplicable sense of *wrong* all around her. Nothing she could put her finger on. Just a sense of "awry"-ness that set her teeth on edge and gooseflesh rising all over her arms. Like the sense of being watched, like watching a horror movie and just *knowing* that something uncanny was about to jump out and kill someone.

Amaya Tenshi

Where *was* this place? What did these monsters want with her? Where was Malcolm?

"... you got there, lovelies?" came a voice. It sounded male, but she couldn't be sure.

"Nehwer mind us," one of her captors replied, with one of those odd accents she couldn't identify.

"Passing through," said another.

"This one's wery light," said a third.

"Human?" the first voice demanded.

"A nosy one," the third captor supplied. She heard the others grumble at him.

"How much for her?" the first voice asked.

Cammy's stomach turned to a rock.

No, no nononono!

"Don't you dare!" she screamed. "I told you, I'm Dracula's guest! He's going to be *so* mad when he finds out you guys kidnapped me!"

"*Him?*" the first voice gasped.

Her captors lifted her again and ran. She heard whoever it was who had come to talk to them shouting behind them, but couldn't understand what he was saying. Her captors grunted urgent messages to each other and hurried on. She heard the shouting recede as they went, and the sense of "wrong" growing weaker. It was like a blanket being pulled slowly off. It had felt wrong to her bones, and she was grateful it was gone. Assuming where she was going was any better.

They carried her for another ten minutes or so, and she could hear her captors breathing heavily from exertion. Whoever or whatever they were, they obviously got tired. So, probably not vampires.

Dracula's Match

They slowed to crawling speed, dropped her again and switched to dragging. Her hip and leg were sore from all the dragging and dropping, and she yelped again. Whoever that other person—or monster—had been who asked about her had been spooked hearing Dracula's name. These guys weren't, though. Did they not care? Or maybe they simply didn't know about him.

She was dragged painfully over more rough stone, or maybe concrete. The cloth kept catching in it, wrinkling and bunching, then stretching back into shape. She whimpered.

Panting, they suddenly hoisted her up, and did their best rolling her onto what felt like sod. She had a sense she was above ground again. The air felt clearer, crisper. Her captors dragged her a ways and finally came to a stop, panting.

Another male voice called to them, asking a question. The first of her captors answered between gasps for air. She couldn't understand what was said, except one word: "Dracula."

So they *did* know about him. Maybe her name-dropping would save her skin. She hoped so. Now that they had let go of her, she checked her phone. Malcolm hadn't replied. Tears welled up in her eyes. No, she couldn't lose it yet. She had to do something. Desperate, she dialed Dracula. She listened as best she could to the ringing. She thought she heard someone pick up, but couldn't hear who. It didn't matter if it was Boese on the line, though. She put it on speaker.

"You guys better let me go! You're going to be sorry when Dracula finds out you kidnapped me! Let me go right now!"

Whoever had picked up had the sense not to speak, but the call was still connected.

Amaya Tenshi

It turned out a blanket had been thrown over her, because someone ripped it off her, to reveal—empty air. Cammy sat bolt upright and looked around. No one in sight.

She was near the Fremont Troll, of all places. There was a small fire someone had lit and she could see what looked like a seagull being roasted on a spit between the troll's hands.

Not a person in sight, no matter how she whipped her head in every direction. She crab-walk-scooted away from the troll, got to her feet, stared at her surroundings in the pale glow of the dying day, then grabbed the adder stone. She checked the troll.

A crowd of people stood clustered around the troll, arguing with one another. They were wearing some kind of folk costumes with embroidered jackets, skirts, and aprons. The men wore knee-high tights. One woman wore a tall, white hat shaped almost like a cone. One of the men noticed Cammy had the adder stone, and pointed at her while calling for the others' attention. Cammy dropped the stone. They were invisible. She raised the stone again. There they all were. Then she realized her phone was still on speaker.

"What are you all doing at the Fremont Troll?" she demanded as loudly as she could. Whoever was on the line ought to be able to hear that and figure out where she was. Maybe she could stall for time and someone, even Boese's people, would come.

Then she recognized the costumes. They were dressed like the invisible girl and boy from campus. He had told her they were hiding near the Fremont Troll. And here they were.

One of the older men came towards her, one hand held out in a gesture of non-aggression.

Dracula's Match

"My apologies," he offered. "My grandsons were too impetuous. They heard you were spying on Fjola and Trausti and feared you meant us harm. They thought to bring you here so we could see what sort of danger you posed."

"I just talked to him! You didn't have to kidnap me! You could have just talked to me!"

As if on cue, the boy she had spoken to on campus came darting into view, panting. He waved his arms at Cammy and shouted in his language at the others. The older man gestured for him to calm down, and reassured him, Cammy guessed. The boy turned to her.

"Are you all right?"

"No! I am *not* all right!" Cammy shouted. "They dragged me..."—She was at the troll. She had been in Capitol Hill with Brian–"like, *miles!*" she concluded. Though how they'd managed to get here underground when the only routes would have been *bridges* to cross waterways she didn't understand. "What is *wrong* with all of you?" She lowered the stone; only the boy was visible. "This is really annoying," she told them, raising the stone again. "Can you just be visible?"

She lowered the stone and the older man and a few others were still there. She accepted that.

"Ok, so who are you guys, and what are you doing here?"

"My apologies," the older man repeated. "We have left our homeland and come here, as we heard it was a good place for folk like us."

"Yeah, well..." Cammy looked to the boy. "I'm sorry that's not working out."

"Your stone," the older man said, and gestured at it. "We thought you were a witch or some sort of hunter, or that you worked for Ophois."

"No, I'm a barista," Cammy said. "I'm borrowing this stone. From Dracula."

"Again, I sincerely apologize," the man said, and bowed respectfully to her. "Please, accept our apologies. Please, will you pass our sincerest apologies to him?"

"To… him? Wait. You're not even apologizing to *me*, then. You just don't want Vlad to hunt you all down." She almost added, 'He's not really a forgiving type' when she spotted one of the women in the back with a baby in her arms, and thought of Vlad's casual 'I might have impaled someone for making a shirt badly' and shut her mouth. Right. She had to talk him out of coming after them. *And* she had already told the boy she was going to talk to Dracula about their staying at his estate.

"So ok, you guys came here for some reason. And you're sorry for kidnapping me. Fine. But what's *not* fine is now my friend from middle school saw me get kidnapped."

Three of the young men exchanged a look.

"He doesn't know about this stuff!" Cammy snapped. "He's going to freak out! What do I tell him?"

The whole group eyed each other uncomfortably.

Great, Cammy thought. Now what was she going to tell Brian when she saw him again? She'd have to tell him something, and *fast*. He might have called his cop buddies by now. She raised her phone, to see the call was still connected. *Oh no.*

"Vlad?" she asked.

"What is happening?" he responded. Well, at least he had picked up, and not Boese.

"Are you all right? What happened to you?"

Dracula's Match

"Never mind about me. Where are you? What is going on?"

He was still on speaker, and Cammy looked to the hidden people to see how they reacted. The ones she could see tried to be subtle about craning their necks to watch her. She didn't know if they recognized Dracula's voice.

"There was a misunderstanding," Cammy said.

"A misunderstanding that led to you being kidnapped?"

"Yeah…" She looked to the hidden people again. "I was watching two of them with the adder stone you gave me. They thought I was some kind of hunter for Ophois."

"I see. You are still at the Fremont Troll?"

"Yeah."

"I am on my way."

"Wait," she said. "What am I going to tell Brian? Did you hear?"

"That he saw what happened? Yes, I did. I would advise you simply tell your friend the truth."

"But… he… he's a cop—"

"All the more reason to tell him. It would be safer for him in the long run, surely."

Cammy thought about it. Maybe. Maybe she should. She didn't know how Brian was going to take it, though. Wouldn't he try to do something heroic? Go off and try to protect people from monsters? She thought about how Dracula had pretended to get staked to death to save her. Brian didn't have options like that.

The image of Heather's wide, seeing, but dead eyes flashed in her mind and froze her skin. She shook her head. She couldn't take the risk he'd do something and get himself killed—or much *worse*.

"I can't," she whispered. Somehow, he must have heard her anyway.

"Very well. You are staying there for the moment?"

"Yeah, I think so. And, just FYI, these people were hoping to set up at your monster sanctuary."

A pause followed.

"Really."

"Yeah, so..." Cammy had no idea what to follow up with. "I'm ok. You don't need to worry."

"I shall see you shortly," he replied, and hung up. Cammy realized he probably didn't know what "FYI" meant, and pictured him ruminating on it as he drove. She almost giggled at the thought. Nerves were getting to her again, it seemed. Her leg and hip throbbed from all the dragging and hitting snags and being dropped. She winced and gingerly put a hand to one of the injuries. It had hurt before, but not like now. Why were injuries like that? They always hurt more later, for some reason.

She turned to the hidden people.

"Ok, when he gets here, I'm going to have to talk to him and make sure—" she was interrupted by a voice that drawled and growled simultaneously.

"Ok, I just had to crawl my way through the Underground, through a goblin market, and I am in *no mood* for fun and games!"

Cammy turned to see a man dressed in what looked like biker gear, armed with a shotgun, and she could see a long-handled axe and what might be a shield strapped to his back. He was wearing a motorcycle helmet, so his voice was a bit muffled, but she could still recognize him as Malcolm. He

Dracula's Match

raised the shotgun, and Cammy realized one of the hidden people had moved.

"Turn invisible, I double dog dare you. Cammy, you all right?" She started towards him, then considered the shotgun.

"Wait, are you gonna hurt any of them?" she asked.

"Cammy, I have *just* been through the worst several days of my life, and I am *this close*"—he held up his fore finger about an eighth of an inch from his thumb—"from going berserk here. Me and my boomstick are *very* happy to cause some mayhem. Now get over here so I can get you somewhere safe before nightfall."

"Why? What happens at nightfall?"

"At nightfall, the *draugr* is probably going to come back. I don't know where he's been going to ground during the day, but he seems to like to play at night, and I *don't* want to be outside when he does his little rampage, all right? Also, you're welcome."

"For what?"

He squared off to her, and she hopped backwards a bit. He stared at the hidden people, then took off the helmet.

"For coming to rescue you, *obviously*," he snarled. She could only stare at his face. He looked totally different, but she could still recognize him, even though she shouldn't be able to. Like before when he had killed all those vampires at Dracula's place, he seemed *bigger* somehow. But also, his forehead and jaw were heavier, almost ape-like. When he snarled, she could see he had gross-looking, freakish canine teeth that weren't really fangs, just human teeth that were bigger than they had any right to be. So much so they didn't fit right in his mouth. His hairline was lower, and he almost had a unibrow. Not remotely the incredibly handsome potential model he normally looked like. She hadn't gotten a good look at him when he'd gone berserk before. Was this what he looked like when he did?

He noticed her staring, and grimaced. He looked aside, seemingly embarrassed or ashamed, and gritted his teeth. He angrily waved her to his side again. She didn't want to get near him when his yellow eyes looked like that. Angry, malicious.

"Cammy, I am *not* playing around here," Malcolm snarled. "Get over here, *now*."

"Vlad's on his way."

"*Great!*" Malcolm seethed. "So get over here so he doesn't skin me alive when he gets here, huh?"

Are you going to skin me alive? she wondered. From the murderous look in his eyes, she had serious misgivings. He'd told her before that when he went berserk he was "liable to kill anything that moves." She didn't want to test that.

Headlights shone across both of them, and Cammy shielded her eyes. Malcolm glared right into the lights. The car stopped just before the freeway overhead, and she heard the car doors pop open.

"Cammy?"

Brian's voice! What was *he* doing here? She squinted past the lights, seeing two silhouettes, one on each side of Melissa's Honda. Two?

"Are you vell?"

Siri's voice? Siri had come with Brian? Well, the cat was out of the bag now. She tried to walk around the direct beams of headlights, and cast a glance over her shoulder at the troll. Only the boy remained visible. The other people had disappeared. The boy looked nervous and unsure. His eyes bounced back and forth between her, Malcolm, Brian and Siri. Cammy realized he might be staying put to placate her so his people would have a chance when Dracula arrived.

"Cammy? Are you ok? Come here." Brian waved her over. She started for him.

"Don't you do it. No huldra's going to get you while I'm around," Malcolm growled.

"Hang on," Brian said. "Weren't you at that bar in Pike Place a few nights ago? What happened to your face?"

"Who is that?" Malcolm demanded of Cammy.

"My friend, Brian," she explained. She turned to Brian. "How did you find me?"

"Your tablet. It was in the car. I didn't know what else to do."

My tablet? Then she realized he'd tracked her phone using the same technique she'd used to track Dracula before. There was some serious irony there. If that was how the word was used correctly.

"Cammy, you know that guy?" Brian checked.

"Cammy, do not take one more step," Malcolm warned.

"Just what is going on here?" Brian demanded.

Cammy gulped. This might get *really* ugly. Mostly because she didn't know what Malcolm was going to do. He seemed very on edge. Not himself. She didn't know why.

"Ok, everyone stop," she said. Then she realized she didn't know what else to say. She just didn't want things to escalate. Now that she looked, she could see Brian had pulled a nine millimeter. It was hidden from Malcolm's sight by the Honda, but that meant they both had guns at the ready.

She couldn't get air for a few seconds. She pressed her fingers to her temples as painfully as she could and forced a few deep breaths.

"Ok, everyone. Everything is ok. There was just a misunderstanding," she said. "Why don't we all just calm down—"

"Calm down?!" Brian repeated. "You want to tell me how you know that guy?"

"Maybe you want to explain why you're so keen on following me," Malcolm growled. He turned a bit so he could keep one eye on the boy and another on Brian.

"How about you tell me what your tattoo means?" Brian demanded.

Tattoo? The one Malcolm had on his wrist? How did he know about it?

"Cammy, who is this clown?" Malcolm snarled.

"Cammy, who is that guy, and why do you know him?"

"Look!" Cammy held up her hands. "This would be a lot easier if everyone could just cool it for a second, ok? I... ok. Malcolm, this is Brian. Brian, this is Malcolm. Brian is my friend from middle school. Malcolm works for Vlad."

"Wait," Brian stared her down. "That guy. Works for. The guy whose house you're staying at?"

"Yeah. It's kind of complicated." She looked to Siri, who had carefully moved away from Brian's car and was eying Malcolm and his arsenal of weapons. It didn't seem like either Malcolm or Brian had noticed her slinking to safety.

"Hey, did you bring him here?" Cammy asked her. That drew attention to Siri. The huldra considered Brian and Malcolm, and Cammy. She tossed her hair.

"I saw you taken. I thought I should speak to your friend. He did not know vhat vas happening, nor vhere to find you.

Dracula's Match

ve spoke for a time, until he thought of the method to find you."

"Gee, Cammy, you keep making all kinds of great new friends," Malcolm snarked.

"I could say the same," Brian echoed sourly.

Another car rolled up behind Brian's. Malcolm growled—it sounded like it came from a literal wolf—and grumble-swore at the newcomer. Brian turned, a bit slowly, perhaps because of his injury. He still kept his gun at the ready.

The new car came to a stop behind Brian's and parked. The engine did not turn off. The door opened, and Dracula stepped out. It took her a moment to recognize him. He wasn't dressed in his customary suit. Instead, he was wearing jeans and a flannel shirt that didn't fit him at all. He stood behind the door of his black vehicle and took in the scene.

"Cammy, are you all right?" he asked.

"Yeah, I'm fine. But hey, there's a situation here—"

"Ok, everyone's got about ten seconds to tell me what is going on here," Brian said.

"Good evening, Officer Warren. I was not expecting to see you here," Dracula said. Cammy could see he had spotted Brian's gun; he curled a pair of fingers at her to come to him.

"Cammy, let's get out of here. You can tell me in the car," Brian said.

Cammy had no idea who to go to. Malcolm probably didn't want her now that Dracula was here. But she didn't know who she should go to instead. Brian would freak out if she didn't go with him—then she'd have to answer a billion questions about everything and she had no idea where to begin. And she had no idea if Dracula would be mad at her for choosing Brian if she did.

"Cammy," Dracula repeated, in that tone that sent shivers down her spine. The tone that broached no dissent. "Come here."

She scooted for him as quick as she dared.

"Yo, Vlad, you got this?" Malcolm called.

"I'm not yet certain," he answered. Once Cammy had come around the door to his vehicle, she saw he had his magnum out of its holster, but like Brian's weapon, it was hidden from view by his car door. She shuddered. He looked her over, and noticed the stains on her leggings. A lot of it was moisture from wherever she had been dragged through, but some of it might be blood. She hoped she wasn't bleeding. "Are you well?" he asked her. She nodded vigorously.

"Yeah. It was a misunderstanding. No big deal."

"Get in the car," he told her.

"Wait, we gotta tell Brian—"

She could see a look of disbelief and hurt on Brian's face in Dracula's headlights. A twinge of guilt twisted in her stomach. A dog started barking in the distance.

"Officer Warren, it is a pleasure to see you again. I believe you still have my effects."

Brian looked at him. Looked at Cammy. Wounded and confused.

"Look, if this is all about to get wrapped up, I'm heading out," Malcolm said. He strode past Brian's car to approach Dracula's vehicle. "I'm getting real twitchy here." He shook himself all over, like he was cold. "Can't think straight."

"What else is here?" Dracula asked. Malcolm gestured to Siri with his empty hand, then waved at the troll.

"Huldra there. Buncha elves over there unless they bolted. Haven't noticed anything else. Just this guy," he waved at

Brian. "Apparently you guys know each other." Two more dogs started barking. They sounded a bit closer than the first.

"Officer Warren and I are acquainted, yes. If you surmise the situation is not currently dangerous, then go," Dracula told him. Malcolm let his breath out between his bared, oversized teeth, and nodded. He turned as though to walk out into the neighborhoods and stiffened so straight, so fast, Cammy jumped. His movement didn't seem natural.

"You ok?" she called to him.

A strange, weird, croaking, groaning, growling noise rumbled out of his mouth, sounding nothing like any human could make. The sound startled Brian, who turned, then clutched his side. Malcolm jerked backwards, but it was almost like it wasn't him moving, more like he was *being* moved somehow. Dracula held out an arm between her and Malcolm.

"Get in the car," he repeated. *"Now."*

Malcolm dropped his shotgun, and it seemed like something *threw* him down on the ground, rather than him dropping to it. He bark-snarled like an angry dog. Then, and Cammy struggled to understand what her eyes were telling her, he turned into a black wolf. Only it wasn't like in movies. There wasn't a big, drawn-out transformation, no screaming, no contortions, no body horror. He just suddenly was one. Only it was like somehow, a wolf form had covered over him. In a flash, so she couldn't quite make it out. Just blink once, Malcolm, blink twice, wolf. The eyes were the same yellow, but they were nothing human at all. They looked evil. Demonic might be the right word, even. She wouldn't have recognized the animal as Malcolm if she hadn't seen him *turn into it*.

"What the... !" Brian gasped.

The wolf's head snapped towards him, bared its very long fangs and snarled.

"Cammy, get in the car!" Dracula pushed her with his free hand, keeping his eyes on the black wolf foaming at the mouth and snarling at Brian. A whole bunch of dogs were barking in the neighborhood nearby.

She lost her balance and fell up against the car. *Brian!* she thought. Then, *Are they going to shoot Malcolm?* She fumbled for the handle for the backseat, couldn't find it, and turned to look. Behind her were two more wolves trotting very fast up the street towards them all. One tawny, the other huge and gray. The tawny one started running.

"Vlad! Behind us!" she warned.

The charging wolf howled and snarled in a weird, eerie sort of way. Not like a real wolf. But if *felt* the way that wolf howls felt in stories. Dangerous, alien, frightening. She sensed Dracula turning around behind her. He wrapped an arm around her to pull her behind him and raised his gun. She plugged her ears—she'd already heard a gun fire near her before. She didn't want to hear it again. The magnum roared and stabbed into her ears despite her best attempt to keep out the sound. Something thumped against Dracula's shoes, and Cammy recoiled when she saw it was a blond man —lying dead on the dusty street.

While she tried to understand this, the big, gray wolf charged past them, its long white teeth bared, and leaped at the black one that had been Malcolm. They fell to the street in a flurry of snarling, growling, and snapping teeth that were rapidly turning red.

Dracula's Match

Dracula pushed her into the vehicle, and she found herself in the driver's seat. He leaned down to shove her to the passenger side.

"Brian—!"

"Move!" Dracula hissed at her. She tried to scoot, only to see something yank Dracula straight off the ground, out of the car, and out of her vision. A stench like she'd never experienced hit her like a blast of air. Her eyes burned, her throat burned. Someone was looming beside the car. His skin was pale and bluish. Dracula hit a truss holding up the freeway above them, but landed on his feet on the other side of the road. The pale man let out a scream that was almost a roar and ripped the car door free, the car lurching as he did so. She felt ill, waves of something that churned her stomach washing over her. She pulled her legs up to her chest, as far out of reach of the pale guy as she could get.

Cammy watched, gripped with a panic that held her like a vice, as the pale guy threw the car door at the Fremont Troll. She didn't spot any of the hidden-people-elves. Either they had gone invisible or they had run away.

Brian stood beside the Honda, eyes glued to the stranger who had thrown the car door. He hesitantly raised his gun. She could see terror in his eyes. But he aimed the gun all the same.

No! Cammy thought. That idiot. The gun wasn't going to do any good. He couldn't afford to draw attention to himself like that! She scrambled to get out of the car.

She could see the pale guy was some kind of giant of a man. This must be the draugr. And if it was, she couldn't let Brian get involved. The draugr was able to toss Dracula around like a toy. It would kill Brian in a heartbeat. Brian fired his gun at the draugr, and the world slowed down.

The draugr turned towards Brian, its muscles rippling as it moved. Brian's eyes swelled at the sight, but he aimed again to fire another shot. Cammy knew that wasn't going to work. The draugr was going to charge him, and that would be that.

"Brian!" she screamed. "Get out of here!"

The draugr turned slightly back towards her, slowly. Brian fired again. The draugr spun back, and charged for him.

"No!" But she'd never get out of the car in time, and even if she did, she couldn't possibly stop that thing.

Helplessly, she watched the draugr grab Brian by the front of his hoodie and hurl him towards the troll. Brian landed badly, and didn't move.

Somehow, she was out of the car and running past the draugr towards Brian. The monster turned slowly, hearing her coming. She somehow dodged its cumbersome swinging clutch, and kept going. She skidded to a stop near Brian, dropped down, and touched his shoulder. She had no idea if he was alive. He certainly wasn't moving. She looked up, and the draugr was storming right for her. She grabbed Brian's wrist and tried to pull him out of its path, but she couldn't. He was way heavier than she had expected.

"Come *on!*" she screamed in frustration. Somehow, she got him moving, dragging across the dusty street towards a sidewalk. But she was never going to get them out of the way in time. The draugr was covering a *lot* of ground with each stride.

Dracula came up behind it and swept its leg out from under it. The draugr toppled to the ground, and Dracula threw himself down on the giant. They wrestled with each other,

Dracula's Match

and Cammy saw the draugr take a giant bite out of one of Dracula's arms, until all of a sudden Dracula had the draugr seemingly pinned in a complicated-looking hold of some sort. He pinned the draugr's two arms by using his arms for one and his legs for the other.

"Flee!" he shouted at her. Cammy looked down at Brian. It might be possible to drag him to Dracula's car, though that wouldn't be fast. But even if she did, she couldn't possibly lift him into it. But she had to try. She started dragging Brian towards the car. "Leave him!" Dracula shouted at her.

"I can't! He's hurt bad, I can't—"

"I said *leave* him!" he snarled.

"But I can't!"

The draugr bucked, taking itself and Dracula off the ground. Dracula kept his grip, but it was clear his hold wasn't going to stop it forever. Maybe not very long at all. Brian still wasn't moving. She felt tears in her eyes and shook her head. The image of Heather dropping dead across her knees kept flashing before her. She couldn't leave him here. She couldn't let the last memory of Brian be him lying motionless on the street while she drove away. Her head shook all on its own at the thought.

"Cammy, leave him there, and *go!*"

That was the authoritative tone, mixed with anger. Rage, even. She had to, but she couldn't. But she had to. But she *couldn't*.

The invisible boy appeared beside her and grabbed Brian's other wrist and started to pull. Cammy blinked at him, bewildered, before some instinct surged in her to do *something* and she tugged. Together, they got him moving. Two more of the hidden-people-elves appeared, and they stooped to lift

Brian off the ground. Then a few more came, and soon they were all able to rush Brian to Dracula's car. Cammy opened the back seat and the elves helped load him in. When she turned to get into the driver's seat, there was the black wolf staring at her.

Malcolm—she couldn't believe that was Malcolm—was covered in scratches and blood. Behind him a large, dead man covered in bites lay in a pool of blood. She recognized the salt and pepper goatee. The other wrestler that was friends with Roar. All of a sudden, she also recognized the blond man on the ground too. The musician's brother. Both of them. Dead. Her stomach twisted on itself, so very painfully.

Malcolm bared his fangs, stained red. They seemed longer than any real wolf would have. His tongue was red, like in a story, not like real life.

She didn't have any weapons. She'd passed by his shotgun on the way over here. But if she shot him, he'd die. Just like Heather. She'd see Malcolm's dead body lying on the street, not an animal. Dracula was busy with the draugr, and she worried for a moment that if he wasn't, he'd just shoot Malcolm. If she fell backwards into the driver's seat, Malcolm could still kill her since the car door was gone. She'd have to sprint. But to where?

Somewhere. Anywhere. Or should she not move? Would he not kill her if she didn't move? He said he'd kill anything that did. Maybe she should stay put?

Malcolm's head jerked to one side, and she saw he had spotted Siri. The huldra stood further off, at the corner of Trolls' Knoll Park, under a streetlight. She folded her arms elegantly across each other, her electric eyes clear even in the dark. Her skirt seemed to flutter in the breeze or maybe that

Dracula's Match

was her tail moving. Malcolm snarled at her. Siri considered him, and Cammy. Then she beckoned to the wolf. His yellow eyes stared with all the hunger in the world, sizing up his target.

Malcolm charged her, and the huldra darted up over Troll's Knoll Park, disappearing from the street lights, with the black wolf behind her.

Shaking, Cammy dropped down into Dracula's car. She had to adjust the driver's seat and strap herself in and not think about the missing door. The elves still stood beside the vehicle. The sounds of angry and frightened dogs echoed through the night.

"I can drive you somewhere," she offered. The elves shook their heads, and disappeared. She put the car in reverse, and caught a glimpse of Dracula and the draugr still fighting on the ground in the Honda's headlights. Then she turned around and sped away.

CHAPTER 8
RETREAT

    Cammy looked up the nearest hospital on her phone and drove straight there, parking in the patient drop-off and running inside to demand help. After she spurted several sentences of near gibberish in her panic, an attendant at last came out to the car to see what she was talking about. Then —*finally*—a team of EMTs were called and they managed to carefully get Brian on a stretcher and wheel him inside.

    "What happened?" asked one of the nurses who had come out to help her. Cammy blanked. She couldn't tell this guy that Brian had been thrown by a draugr. But she hadn't even thought up a lie.

    "I-I don't know," she sputtered. The nurse frowned.

    "How did you know he was hurt?"

    "I... saw him," she said.

    "Why didn't you call 911?"

    "I-I don't know. I panicked," she said.

    "And you are... ?"

Dracula's Match

"Why?"

The nurse frowned more at her.

"Are you family, or a witness?"

"Oh, uh, no. I just found him. Is he going to be ok?"

"If you're not family, I can't tell you that." The nurse looked her over. "Did you get hurt?"

"Huh?" Cammy looked down at her legs. Now that the moisture had dried, she could definitely see she'd bled down the one leg that she'd been dragged on the most.

"Oh, uh… no. I… that's a stain."

"Were you in an accident or something? Are you feeling all right? You might be in shock…" the nurse said. He held out a hand to lead her inside.

"No, I'm ok, thank you!" Cammy hopped into Dracula's car and sped away.

She had no idea where to go or what to do. She couldn't go back to help Dracula, couldn't stay and see if Brian was ok. Who knew where Malcolm was now. And Boese? No way. She'd never risk that again.

She typed in Dracula's address, but found her phone wouldn't direct her there. Maybe the gps-satellite stuff wasn't supposed to tell people how to find him.

She did her best to find the mansion from memory, though it was different when she was driving than when she was a passenger. She knew how to drive—more or less—but had never driven herself there before. At last, she got off the freeway onto that long drive to the mansion, turned up the gravel driveway, and saw the building standing dark against the night gloom.

She parked, ran inside, slammed the big front door shut, and slid down it to the floor. And started to cry. She hugged her knees and pressed her forehead to them. This was too much. She hadn't wanted Brian to be a cop in the first place. Now he might be dying because he came to rescue her. Was he going to be all right? She couldn't even find out. She couldn't take it if Brian died, too. Heather had always been there. Brian had always been there. She'd tried to keep him out of all this. Telling him what was really going on had always seemed like a bad idea. He'd throw himself into danger beyond anything any normal person could handle. Dracula and Malcolm couldn't deal with the draugr, but Brian had gone and tried to fight it. He'd have done it even if he knew what it was, she was certain. She didn't want anyone to die. Especially not because of her. She had wanted to save Heather, not kill her. She hadn't meant for Robert to get killed, she was trying to stop the vampire mastermind from causing more mayhem. She hadn't meant for Brian to be involved in any of this, she had just *needed a ride.*

"Melissa!" she realized. Brian had been borrowing his sister's car. It was still sitting at the Fremont Troll, for all she knew. Plus, Cammy had taken Brian to a hospital that was nowhere near Shoreline, where Melissa worked.

I should call her. Cammy pulled her phone, already down to less than 30%. *And tell her what?* Cammy had no idea. She couldn't just lie to Melissa like that nurse. Melissa was like a real mom—well, ok, maybe a cool, young aunt, but she knew Cammy. She'd be able to tell a lie *immediately.* Plus, Brian was her brother.

In her mind, she could see Melissa calling and calling and texting and texting and getting no response. What would she think? She wouldn't know Brian was all alone in a hospital somewhere. And Brian *was* all alone in a hospital somewhere.

Dracula's Match

Cammy had been totally useless. Maybe no one had died because of her, but they'd gotten close. She couldn't even pick Brian up to put him in a car by herself.

Dracula had told her to mind her limitations. But she hadn't gone looking for trouble; she'd just wanted to get a ride to work and school. She hadn't wanted to talk to Siri, and talking to that elf boy had seemed to be going well. Surely it wasn't too much to offer to talk to Dracula on their behalf, was it? Was it too much to ask for a ride to work or class?

And then there was the problem of Malcolm. What had happened to him? There was nothing in that raging animal that resembled his playful smiles, his over-styled hair, even the warmth of his honey-colored eyes was gone. The yellow animal eyes had seemed to glow with a cold, hungry energy. A little like Siri's, but far more intense. It made her shiver to think of those bottomless portals to nothing but hunger and cold rage. They had stared straight through her.

She cried until she couldn't anymore and her hip and leg were throbbing so much she couldn't ignore the pain. She hobbled her way upstairs to the bathroom she used and took a look. Her leg was badly bruised, scraped, and yes, had been bleeding from a few of the really, *really* bad scrapes. The blotches were all brilliant red and dark mottles. The open wounds were swollen, ringed by dots of black scabs. Her leggings were ruined. They had ripped in patches, and in the light she could see the stains from moisture, dirt, and blood. She started the bath running, still sniffling, and found the rubbing alcohol Dracula had given her for her hands. She didn't want to use it, but it wasn't like she could afford a hospital or a doctor. The liquid burned like a dull, red hot knife ripping into the wounds on her leg, and she had to bite her knuckles to keep from crying out. When she took a bath, the water turned just a little reddish-pink.

She wondered if Malcolm was going to be all right. Or Siri. Or Vlad. Or Brian. Were any of them ok? She wiped the tears from her eyes. The bath water was warm on her face.

She had just gingerly laid down in bed when her phone started to ring and ring and ring. Cammy checked it. Melissa was calling. Cammy stared at the name. What could she say? The phone stopped ringing, and a new voicemail appeared. Then, Melissa texted.

Where are u??

U ok?

Brians in the hospital!

What happened?

He was going to drive u?

Call me!!

Somehow, Melissa had found out where he was. But Cammy couldn't tell her. She couldn't lie, and couldn't tell the truth. She should never have called Brian. She couldn't even call someone to do something *normal* for her without them getting hurt.

She shoved her phone to the other side of her nightstand. Dracula had told her ages ago that she didn't want to be involved in all this. Malcolm had told her as well. She should have listened. Should have just stayed the night and then gone back to her normal life and lived somewhere, somehow. Dracula or Boese would have found Heather eventually. And Cammy would never have known. Brian would never have gotten hurt.

Stupid! she thought to herself. And cried some more.

Dracula's Match

Malcolm came to slowly. Came in and out a few times, actually. He figured that out once he realized the harsh, white light wasn't just more weird dream-state.

Never in his life had he wanted to die more. He hurt absolutely everywhere, and couldn't move. Part of that was complete exhaustion. Berserking took a lot out of him, and so did turning into a wolf. Just another reason he didn't like to do it. That, and because he'd do horrendous things. He did remember killing that other guy—other werewolf. He remembered what the guy's blood tasted like. He remembered turning on Cammy next.

After chasing the huldra, things got very fuzzy. Lots of running around in the dark after her. Some people here and there, barking dogs—one of which he had killed. Hating absolutely everyone and everything and being so *glad* to finally not have to bottle all that up. Just go to town and murder every single thing he saw.

He hated himself. He hated that he was like that. He'd rather be charming all the time, not have all that darkness bottled up in him. Nasty little genie in a bottle, his demon. But he couldn't be. Never. He'd be stuck being him, having all of that raging inside him until he died. And given the track record for most of Ophois' werewolves, that wasn't going to take too long.

A buffed metal door he'd scarcely noticed popped open, and a middle-aged man with shaven, shiny head and watery blue eyes stepped into the room, flanked by two of his agents. And Malcolm realized where he was.

"Whoa, buddy! I'm not one of your lab rats!" he shouted, though his throat was raw and protested the sudden use and force.

Director Boese looked up from the manila folder in his hands, and his eyes hardened. He smelled sick. Something was very wrong with him. The oiliness might be a symptom of some sort. The paleness too. But he smelled sick as a proverbial dog. The agents were dhampirs, but healthy.

Boese came up to him, and Malcolm realized he was strapped to a gurney. Strapped very *thoroughly* to a gurney. Not that it mattered. He had no strength left. He couldn't have sat up if his life depended on it. He was in a small room with buffed metal walls, the harsh, bright lights, a one-way mirror on one wall, some machines for monitoring his condition, like a demented sort of hospital. Malcom supposed Special Services might have these sort of rooms in their lab to deal with injured agents that couldn't or shouldn't be taken to hospitals. Boese tapped on Malcolm's shin with his manila folder, sending a blast of pain shooting through him.

"No, but you've got me extremely upset, Ophois boy," Boese told him. "You could say you spooks got my underwear in a wad."

"I didn't make that dragur or his buddies," Malcolm protested.

"Maybe you didn't. Maybe you did. Or it was your pals. Doesn't matter to me. What *does* matter is I have a bit of a crisis on my hands. Way beyond TARFU and into FUBAR territory. And whoever did the actual transaction, your little outfit"—pointed at Malcolm—"is responsible."

"Well, *I'm* not. I don't deal with any of that stuff. If some celebrity wants to sell their soul, that's not my department."

Dracula's Match

"But your department *is* contributing to the things which people in *my* outfit have a hard time with. What you call gods or spirits and all that crap."

"Still not me," Malcolm retorted. "I have nothing to do with summoning or recruiting. If it bleeds, I can kill it. Maybe. And all I remember of yesterday is that I should probably go to a hospital before something turns septic—"

"We already got that taken care of, don't you worry, buddy," Boese told him. He tapped on Malcolm's forearm with the manila folder, sending another bullet of pain firing off. Malcolm realized he was tapping injuries specifically. Now that he took a look at himself, there were bandages all across his arms and one leg. When he moved his head, he could feel bandages around his throat. The other werewolf had certainly tried his best. But his best hadn't been good enough. Malcolm had recognized the scent; the guy had been Roar's retired wrestling buddy. Big guy. But not used to wolfing out, like Malcolm was. If he had been, things might have gone *very* south for Malcolm. But he'd been a fan of "Wild Wolf" Shaw when he was a kid watching the wresting matches on TV. To think, one day he'd rip the guy's throat open with his own teeth. He grimaced. He'd never met his dad. He wondered if killing Shaw was a little like killing his own father. Someone you looked up to and admired.

"So here's the deal. I need this undead joke out of the picture, and I need him gone yesterday," Boese said.

"Don't know what to tell you. You need to subdue him—wrestling him into his grave is the method we have on record, good luck with that—then burn him to ash, then cross your fingers and hope that does the trick."

"Well, that's proving a bit difficult to do, and I still need him gone."

"For starters, get him back in his grave."

Boese slammed his hand down on the gurney, and Malcolm relished the wave of relief that it wasn't on one of his injuries instead.

"Why do all these freaks have such *stupid* rules that never make any *sense?*" Boese demanded of the air.

"All the rules do make sense. Maybe not to you, but they make sense," Malcolm told him. "You're just thinking of them the wrong way. I mean, I'm sure you can imagine having some sort of grudge or hate that's so strong that even death couldn't stop that bad juju. Like a demon that lingers on. And ground, Earth, dirt—or salt in a pinch—can neutralize undead stuff. Especially ground that *contained* the guy before he monstered."

"I'm not here for a lesson in mumbo-jumbo," Boese snapped. "I want your little escaped science experiment out of the picture and out of my hair."

"I called my people. All they did was teach him and his buddies how to turn into wolves. That's it. And it wasn't even our branch. It was the one in Hollywood."

"Hollywood's got *all* the loons," Boese muttered. He addressed Malcolm, "So then why'd he get back up?"

"Probably he was really mad about something. And because he was already leaning all 'Norse', boom, he came back that way. Who knows, maybe he *wanted* to come back that way."

"But *why?*"

"Do I look like I've got a two-dollar crystal ball? I don't know, man. You'd have to ask him."

Dracula's Match

Watery as they were, Boese's pale blue eyes managed to burn with cold disdain.

"I've been on the line with your people for the last few days trying to fix this mess. They've been giving me quite the run around, spinning all sorts of stories, and I don't like how they charge by the hour. Since I've got you down here, I think I'll keep you as leverage to make your people a bit more co-operative."

Malcolm squinted at him.

"Friend, you don't know how we work. That is a *real* bad idea."

"You might have all those 'spells' all over you, but from what I've heard, you front liners die like regular people. So don't kid me about your spooky 'magic.' I think you'll find that raw manpower, money, and science does a pretty fine job most days."

"Until days like the last couple in a row," Malcolm pointed out.

"Well, I know they need you. Not for much longer I bet, but they need you all the same. So you're staying down here." Boese tapped Malcolm's leg wound again. "Free of charge, even. See if that doesn't inspire some actual help from you clowns and witch doctors."

"I wouldn't do that. I really wouldn't—"

"And you're going to keep your mouth shut because I ran your DNA sample against some of the cold cases the cops have been wondering about and I know you've been a pretty busy boy. So in the future I'll know which cases need to get disappeared, and I think I'll be having your people pay *me* for that. Sit tight. You're on vacation as of now."

Amaya Tenshi

"You're going to regret this," Malcolm snarled. Boese smiled, and let himself out.

Cammy lay in bed and couldn't get up. It wasn't just that she was exhausted. It wasn't just that her leg throbbed. She just couldn't get up. Pale gray light illumined the room through the pulled curtains. It had been light for hours. Cammy didn't remember if she worked today. Her phone was on the far side of the nightstand and she hadn't checked it for anything. There wasn't any point.

A knock at her door caused her to jump, then grimace from pain.

"Are you within?"

"Yeah," Cammy grumbled.

"May I come in?"

"Yeah."

She flopped back down in bed. The door opened and she heard her host striding across the floor until he stood beside her, taking in her state.

"How was Officer Warren?" he asked.

Cammy shrugged. "Dunno. Hospital won't tell me."

"Has his sister been informed?"

Cammy nodded.

"Can't she tell you?"

"I can't talk to her. What do I tell her? I can't tell her what happened."

Dracula didn't respond.

"Are you well?"

"I can't do anything," she said. "I only get in the way."

Dracula's Match

"It sounded to me as though this particular incident wasn't your doing. You said you were kidnapped?"

"Yeah. But I don't think they were going to hurt me." She saw the look in his eyes. "Really. I don't. They were just scared."

"I shall address that later. Would you like anything? Tea, or broth, perhaps?"

"Broth?" she repeated, wrinkling her nose at the absurdity of the offer.

"To warm you, and it should be easier to stomach than solid food."

"I just…" Cammy twisted her fingers. "I want things to go back to the way they were. I can't take this. I can't deal with people dying all the time, or… or… getting hurt." She could feel tears coming on. He pulled a handkerchief from his breast pocket—he was dressed in his usual style: immaculate black suit, not an attempt at looking like a hipster. He handed her his handkerchief and left the room while she emptied her tear ducts again.

She had totally used up the handkerchief; it was thoroughly soggy. It was sort of nice, not having to use up half a box of Kleenex on one crying jag. Maybe she should start carrying one. But what would she do with one once she used it? Add it to the laundry pile, she guessed.

There was another knock at her door.

"Yeah?" she called. She sounded hoarse from all the crying. The door opened, revealing Aki in her human form. The kitsune entered the room and set a tray on the nightstand. On the tray was what looked like a cup of tea, a teapot, an extra cup, a little bowl of what Cammy guessed must be broth, plus a sugar bowl, cream, and utensils.

"What would you like?" Aki asked. Cammy forced herself to sit up, wincing as she did.

"You don't have to do that," she said. "I can get it." Aki bowed her head, but shot a look at Dracula, who stood in the doorway, for confirmation. He nodded, and Aki brushed past him to deposit the tray on the table. He bowed before leaving the room. Cammy reached for a cup, but Dracula stayed her hand.

"Cream or sugar?" he asked. She looked at him.

"*You're* get me something?"

"I worked as a doctor for a long time. I am used to ministering to people in bed."

"I just don't get you," she sighed. He exhaled angrily, poured cream into the cup of tea, dropped two lumps of sugar in, then passed it to her. He drew up the chair from the corner of the room and sat in it. Then he poured himself his own cup of tea with a generous portion of cream.

"Sorry," she said.

"I gather you don't understand that I'm neither in the habit of nor desirous of talking about myself," he said. "It seems to me the obsession with interrogating other people about themselves is some sort of modern habit, and not one I wish to acquire."

"I'm... not trying to say that in a judge-y way," she semi-lied. Hard not to get judge-y at a guy who casually killed people for the weirdest of reasons. "But I mean, I just *don't*."

Her host stirred a lump of sugar into his cup. He gritted his teeth, and cleared his throat.

"We come from wildly different backgrounds," he admitted. "So it is fair that you struggle to understand."

"But, I mean, surely it's hard for you to understand *me*, then, right?" she asked.

He sipped from his cup. "Yes. I find most modern people incomprehensible."

"Then why'd you let me stay?"

He sipped more tea, then set down his cup.

"Because you were… sent to me."

"Sent to you? What are you talking about?"

"In all my years since being released, I had yet to make any sort of helpful contact in the wider, modern world."

"You said you have friends."

"I have friends. Of a sort. But they are people with a background somewhat similar to my own."

"What about Malcolm?"

"I don't understand Malcolm," Dracula said. "We have worked together, but he is… like an overgrown boy. All the people I meet seem to be."

"I'm not a…"

"You also seem immature for your age. You are… twenty-one, correct?"

"Yeah."

"And going to university for seemingly no reason whatever, with no occupation in mind, no husband, no place to live, no plans at all."

"But I have to go to college!"

"Why?"

"To… get a job…"

"What job?"

"Well, it doesn't really matter, because you can't get a job most of the time with a degree anyway," she grumbled. He raised his eyebrows in a simultaneously commiserating and condescending expression. He was still alarmingly good at that sort of thing. She glared at her cup of tea and slurped it. "I didn't make the rules," she said.

"In any case, you are dealing with death for the first time in your life," he said. "And dealing with it as a... as an atheist."

"I don't know. There might be a God, but I don't know."

He shrugged. "I imagine that makes it more difficult," was all he said.

"So does death just not bother you? I mean, with how long you've been around... do you..." She hated to ask, but she worried it was true. "Do you just get used to it?"

"No," he said. She started, not expecting that answer. "You simply become... better at moving on."

"But you've been seeing death since you were a kid?"

"I am talking about the deaths of people you know and care about. Not those you don't know. You can easily grow accustomed to that."

That might explain the cavalier impaling, then. She guessed he might have been messed up as a kid. Maybe he had undealt-with trauma. It wasn't normal to watch people die from childhood. He didn't sound too upset when describing how his family had basically all died, but maybe it had left scars, or something.

"So... you never had a wife who committed suicide."

"That's right."

Cammy thought about it.

"But you had *somebody*."

He looked into his teacup.

"I did."

Dracula's Match

Cammy let that sit. Given what he'd told her, she assumed that was someone he *did* care about. And maybe he didn't want to talk about it because of that. But if this was back when he was in the 1400s, or whatever, maybe he'd moved on?

"May I... ask?"

"She was my *leman*, if you must know."

"What's a layman?"

He sighed and frowned, his eyes jumping from the cup to the wall and back as he searched for the right word. "A... paramour. A... courtesan, a... *demimondaine*... a... lover."

She tried to picture the sort of guy who impaled a woman for making a shirt wrong but who also was the kind of guy who'd have a 'lover' of some sort. She couldn't do it. Obviously, here he sat, but it didn't make sense to her.

"You..." she didn't want a repeat of the other night. Best to be as diplomatic as possible. "You were close?"

"She and I had a son together," he said. "That was a poor decision on both our parts, but it couldn't be undone."

"So you... you loved her, right?"

He looked up from his cup. "What if I did?"

She was taken aback by the defensiveness of the reply.

"I fail to see what the point of interrogating me about this is," he said. "It was a very long time ago. She shouldn't have done it. She should never have done it."

"But, she was heartbroken... right?"

"Clearly. But she shouldn't have done it. If I had been killed, she should have looked after our son."

"But, didn't you feel *anything* when—"

"Is my talking about this going to accomplish something?" he demanded. "Will it bring her back to life again? I was trying not to lose my country at that time. I couldn't spare a moment to worry or grieve over her. She was dead and gone. Nothing I could do would change that." He set his cup down in its saucer. "What is your asking about this meant to accomplish?"

"Because I want to know if you're just a monster like everyone says, or if you're not. And I want to know how you dealt with losing someone important to you!"

He looked at her. She'd gone and done it now. Nothing set him off like accusing him of being a psychopath. He looked at her for a long time, and she thought he looked angry, but it was sometimes hard to tell. He didn't exactly have a pleasant "resting" expression.

"The way I dealt with her death was to carry on," he said. "I was in the middle of a war, with absolutely everything on the line. What do you think I should have done?"

Cammy certainly had no answer to that. "What about after the war?"

"After the war I had a great deal of time on my hands to reflect on what had happened. But ruminating on it is not helpful. I evaluated what I could have done differently."

"Did you pray for her soul?"

He took a deep breath. "Yes."

"Did it help?"

"Did my prayers help her soul? I'm not a holy man, so I cannot say. I certainly hope so."

"Do you still?"

He frowned, but it wasn't quite a frown of anger.

"My prayers no longer do anyone any good," he said. Wait, it wasn't anger on his face. It was something else. Frustration? No. Grief? Something like that. Despair of some kind? She felt unsure.

He drained his cup and set it and the saucer down on the silver tray.

"Your broth is getting cold," he informed her.

How can you be so cold all the time? she thought at him. *How can you be so cold and still get so offended?* How could he think to bring her tea and... not quite soup, and still be so brutally uncaring? He had come to her rescue, but told her to leave Brian behind. He didn't make any sense.

"You should rest," he told her. He gestured to the small bowl of broth. "Drink that. I've had soup made as well." He actually went so far as to check her wrist pulse. His fingers were warm. It took Cammy a moment to register this, and that he ought not to be, right?

From holding that tea cup? she wondered. Maybe. He stood and made for the door. When he had nearly pulled it shut behind him, she forced herself to speak around the lump in her throat.

"Thanks."

He hesitated in the doorway, frowned at her, turned and pulled the door shut.

Amaya Tenshi

CHAPTER 9
NO REST FOR THE WEARY

The broth helped, though Cammy didn't want to admit it. Glumly, she limped downstairs. She could smell something cooking, and followed her nose to the kitchen. She found a large covered pot simmering on the cast-iron stove. A peek inside revealed what looked like some kind of mushroom stew—exotic mushrooms, too—with lots of onions and other goodies. It looked vegetarian, at least. She found some cold, hard-boiled eggs in the fridge near the mayo she'd bought, so she decided to get only a small bowl of the soup plus an egg. She didn't feel *too* hungry.

She forced herself to take a bite, when the sound of voices drew her attention. She rose from her seat and followed the noise until she came to Dracula's study. The door was partly open, so she peered inside to see Dracula seated at his desk with his laptop open in front of him, while a pudgy, middle-aged Asian man stood beside him nodding at whatever was on the screen.

Dracula's Match

Dracula spotted her almost immediately. He held up a hand to pause his conversation and gave her his full attention.

"Are you feeling better?" he asked. Cammy looked the stranger up and down. "This is the tanuki, Komamaki," Dracula explained.

"You can change into a person too?" Cammy asked. The middle-aged man nodded and smiled eagerly.

"I was teaching him how to handle some of my finances," Dracula said. "He is not familiar with modern technology or the internet."

Then don't let him handle your finances! Cammy thought. She would have to tell him later when Komamaki wasn't around. She still got tongue-tied trying to pronounce that name, but Dracula had managed it effortlessly.

Dracula turned to Komamaki. "We shall continue this at a later time."

The tanuki nodded enthusiastically, bowed a few times, and scooted past Cammy out the door. Cammy watched him get to the front door, open it, and drop to the ground in his usual badger-raccoon form.

"I guess you've got your new tenants hard at work," she tried not to snipe.

"Most of my tenants and servants are not well adapted to helping inside the manor," Dracula explained. "Since these seem capable of doing indoor work, I have been testing them. The fox is more competent, but I will see whether this creature is as good at handling money as his wife claimed."

"What if he loses your money?" Cammy asked. Dracula looked at her, and she felt sick in the pit of her stomach.

"… You'd… kill him?"

"He said he could. If he didn't think he could do it, he should have declined," Dracula told her. "He knows the price of failure. If he's willing to risk that, then it is on his head. In any case, you are up and about." His eyes fell to her leg. "How are you?"

"Dunno," she repeated. "What happened last night?"

"The draugr is very strong, but not as skilled as I had feared he might be. It seems that perhaps more than twenty years ago Mr. Thorirsson did engage in real fighting of various types, but he has grown rusty over the years. However, his immense strength cannot be overestimated, so I was unable to overcome him for very long. After he broke my hold he defaced the hideous troll statue, then the Lenin one you people have erected not far away."

He didn't sound upset about the Lenin monument. Cammy pulled out her phone. There were some news reports of vandalism. The Lenin Statue was absolutely covered in blood, rather than just having his hand painted red, which was the usual Seattle vandalism-commentary. She looked to Dracula. Was that *his* blood on the thing? If so, how could anyone *stop* this monster?

"Why is he going after all our tourist spots?"

"That is an excellent question, and one I haven't been able to answer," Dracula said. "It puzzles me. From what I have heard from Malcolm, these monsters usually guard treasure, but Mr. Thorirsson seems to have no interest in hoarding anything. Moreover, Special Services has put a watch on his grave since he emerged, and he has not returned, so far as they can determine."

"Can he be out during the day? He only seems to attack at night."

Dracula's Match

"Malcolm informed me that draugrs can go out in daylight."

"Well, why doesn't he attack anything by day?"

"That is another good question."

Cammy chewed her lip. Probably it was a waste of time thinking about all this. But she had to do something. Andrew still hadn't gotten back in touch with anyone. Dracula must have seen something in her expression, because he asked, "Is there something in particular which troubles you?"

"I'm worried about Andrew," she said.

"Your friend: the young man who is shy?"

"Yeah. He hasn't responded to anyone."

He considered her.

"Shall we call on him?" he asked.

"I tried calling him—"

"I mean to ask if you would like to visit his home?"

Cammy hadn't expected him to offer. *Why don't you make sense?* she thought at him. "You know where he lives?"

"I spoke with him just a few days past. Yes."

Cammy squinted at him. Was he… stalking her friends, or… ? She didn't know what "or" there could be.

"Why did you let me stay here?" she asked. He'd said something weird about that earlier.

"Because you were sent to me."

"*Sent* to you? What are you talking about?"

He didn't reply right away. Then he said, "… I feared I would at long last be utterly adrift in society. But you simply *appeared* on my doorstep—"

"I didn't *appear*, I tracked my phone and rode a bike like, *miles*—"

He held up a hand to stop her.

"You appeared. You had nowhere to go, and needed my help. You got past all this estate's protections, which I warrant a miracle. You are able to use," he gestured at her phone, lying on the table, "modern technologies that were inaccessible and incomprehensible to me, and moreover, gave me a reason to *try* to use them. I could not but see that as Providence."

"Huh?"

He shook his head.

"Never mind. I had thought… but never mind that, either. That is why."

Cammy couldn't even begin to understand what he meant.

"Do you wish to call on your friend?"

"Can we?"

He nodded.

When they reached the garage, Dracula went to a less-fancy vehicle on the far side.

"If it should happen again that you require transportation and I cannot take you, this is the vehicle you may use."

She looked it over. It was black, immaculate, and pretty sleek-looking. Then she thought of Komamaki. And shirts. She shook her head.

"Something the matter?"

"Are you going to kill me if anything happens to this car?"

"Are you planning for something to happen to it?"

"No, but you can't always avoid crashes. Even if you're careful. Everyone messes up."

Dracula's Match

He stared into her soul, and she fidgeted.

"Have no fear," he said. "I will not hold you accountable for anything which isn't your fault."

"Yeah, but, I can't say I'm perfect. No one is a perfect driver. I mean, that's why everyone has insurance."

He nodded. "Have no fear. I am giving you permission to use this vehicle if you have need of it, and you are my guest."

"But Koma… Koma…"

"The tanuki is a tenant, not a guest. He is held to a different standard. I'll have a spare key made for you."

Nervously, she slid into the passenger seat. She desperately wanted to check on Andrew, and yet was terrified. What if, when they got to his place, they found out the worst? She didn't want to lose another friend.

"Why is this draugr guy attacking Seattle?" she hissed as they made their way down the driveway. It wasn't fair that some undead monster guy had smashed through where her friends were. First Andrew, then Brian…

"That, as I've said, is something no one seems to know."

"There's gotta be a reason."

"Almost undoubtedly."

Cammy looked at his face. He was just watching the road. If he was thinking something, it sure didn't show. Frustrated, she pulled out her phone. Another look for draugr information didn't tell her anything, so she pulled up articles on Roar. She skimmed the Wikipedia article, not seeing anything helpful, just the same stuff. He had never been badly injured, hadn't ever quite made it big, had started expressing dissatisfaction with life and searching for his roots, and was in the process of divorcing his wife when the whole murder-suicide thing happened instead.

Amaya Tenshi

She scanned through fan sites. They went into more detail. There had been an interview Roar had given where he explained his draw to the gods of his ancestors. "Modern life is an empty shell. Buy this, watch this, take this pill. No one talks to anyone. No one has real friends. We're all just here, going through the motions, pretending to be happy for the camera and the world. You're born, you try to make something of yourself, you realize everything you did was meaningless, then you die."

That hit Cammy right in the gut. Why was *she* doing anything? Why was she majoring in Communications, trying to graduate? What was she going to *do* with the rest of her life? She hadn't had any idea *before* finding out about vampires and monsters, but she *really* didn't know now. She couldn't picture herself at an office job for the rest of her life. Decades. She shivered at the sudden realization. Was that all there was? Decades of an office job, then retirement and playing bingo before she ended up in a box? Was that all there was? Everyone did it, but *why?* Because there was no other choice?

She couldn't follow this thought. It led to somewhere she couldn't go. Couldn't. Wouldn't. She bent her mind on the video and the interview.

Roar had been struggling with this thought. And what he said sounded pretty bad. She wasn't sure if it was bad enough to murder-suicide your soon-to-be-ex-wife, though. She found Roar's comments on Seattle the most interesting. He lamented how Seattle had been slowly losing its personality. All the corporations moving in seemed to suck all the individuality out of it. The main thing Roar liked about the city at this point were his fans. Here he had a chance to talk to some of them in person when they bumped into each other while out getting coffee. It was because of them that he'd come to really appreciate his wrestling career. He confessed he hadn't liked it at the start because it was all "fake", but their sincere admiration had him rethinking the whole thing. He'd realized people were so *desperate* for an escape from the brutal soullessness of the modern world that the over-the-top stories that wrestling presented were a welcome escape. So was Hollywood. People needed stories.

Cammy turned that over in her mind. Did they really? She had to confess to herself that "being an adult" and "living in the real world" wasn't the most palatable thing ever. Endless work, endless bills. Lather, rinse, repeat. Andrew and Aslan played video games all the time. Lindsey danced, Kenzie liked horror movies and trivia. Heather had found an escape in drugs, sort of.

Cammy hugged herself. Was that all there was? She hated the idea of getting a job to pay off debt just to find a place to live just so she could... what? She'd never had any clear idea what to do with her life. Was that why she couldn't care about college?

Everyone got married, got divorced, maybe had a kid or a dog. *But why?* Cammy couldn't help wondering.

A sense of loneliness welled up in her so fast she was choking before she even knew what hit her. All the... everything *wrong* with life came crashing down on her. It *hurt*. Exactly like a knife in the heart. It stole her breath for a moment. She couldn't bury it like earlier. It was back, it was *strong*, and it *hurt*.

"Are you all right?"

"What?" Cammy gasped.

"Are you all right?" Dracula repeated. Cammy shook her head and looked out the window. There wasn't any point going into it. She wrestled with it, fought it, and put in a deep, dark place. *Stay there*, she thought angrily at it.

She swallowed all that bitterness and returned her attention to her phone. Some fans were discussing Roar's wife's affair and had pretty ugly things to say about Laura. Especially because the manager she was carrying on with was a balding, overweight guy while Roar was a six-foot-plus mountain with a full head of long, blond hair. Cammy could agree with fans that the manager wasn't much to look at, but she knew that looks weren't everything. For all anyone knew, Roar had been abusive. Or maybe he'd weirded her out because of his Norse obsession. Or ignored her. A guy who actually paid attention to you would probably be a nice change from being ignored by a husband who chose to hang out with guys who wanted to become werewolves.

The manager hadn't been involved in the murder-suicide, but there was speculation that he might have been a target. He'd made a reservation at a restaurant—possibly to meet Laura—but never showed, for unknown reasons. There was security footage showing Roar had stormed inside and looked around before leaving the night when everything went down.

"Do you think he's trying to kill his manager?" Cammy asked.

"Why do you think so?"

"Well, he murdered his wife, maybe because they were having an affair. It looks like he was maybe trying to find his manager, too."

"Do you have any idea where his manager might be?" Dracula asked. Cammy shook her head.

Dracula's Match

"I could look it up."

"Please."

She tried, but couldn't find anything.

"Sorry, no publicized address. Are you planning to go talk to him?"

"It may be worthwhile. At the moment, we have few other options." He glanced at her. "Have you found anything else which you think might tell us anything?"

"Not yet..." She kept scrolling. Then, just for kicks, she checked Roar's Instagram. Might as well scroll through his social media. He had some photos inspiring people to go to the gym, find meaning and purpose in their life, and quite a lot of images of his wife. They'd started dating after some sort of wrestling fight event where Roar's wrestler persona rescue-stole her from Lance Bryant as part of a publicity stunt. Cammy had looked up the video of the event earlier. It looked like some dumb soap opera beefcake-fest. The other guy had been cheating on her and talking down to her and threatening her, then Roar came in, defeated him, and "won the girl" to applause and flashing lights. Big kiss on screen. Big cheesy show.

On Instagram, the couple looked happy together. But she thought about his statement about "looking happy for the camera." He'd said that was something everyone did. All the complaints about the "selfie generation" and so forth.

Selfies?

Hadn't Roar attacked the Selfie Museum first? He'd rampaged through Pike Place, but maybe the museum had been his goal. She scrolled through his Instagram, and found a series of photos he'd taken with his wife at the Selfie Museum. She recognized some of the props from Lindsey's photos.

There they both were, smiling and laughing. Cammy checked his other social media, and confirmed the guy had been a pretty proud Seattleite, not just a native of the city. He had always kept a house in the city, often returned to it, and tweeted about Seattle's character. One tweet called the city "quirky, fun, there's something for everyone here" with a selfie of him and his wife at some coffee shop. He might have been famous, but he had never been *that* famous, so maybe that's why he could still walk around like a normal person. She found some local news interviews with him from a decade or more ago talking about his childhood growing up in Ballard, and his frequent visits back. He'd even donated money to local charities, done some events over the years to support local communities, art projects, that sort of thing.

Then there were a number of photos he'd taken at Pike Place, and the Space Needle—surrounded by fans who recognized him—there was a picture he'd taken in front of the Fremont Troll with his wife. She was doing the stereotypical fifties damsel in distress on the ground recoiling in horror while he stood in the way ready to punch it right in its big nose. The two of them in front of the statue of Lenin...

"Wait, I think I got it," Cammy said.

"What did you find?"

"I think he's destroying places he has fond memories of. Or at least, memories of his wife."

"Why do you think so?"

Cammy told him.

"You mentioned these places in order."

"I'm going backwards through his timeline," she said.

"If he is doing the same, then do you know where he is likely to head next?"

Dracula's Match

"He's got a few in front of the Pink Elephant Car Wash sign."

"And if not there, then where?"

"Museum of Pop Culture."

"Where are you finding this?"

"On his Instagram."

Dracula grunted, but it sounded like a happier grunt than an unhappy one.

"It remains, then, to determine where he hides during the day."

"Will that help you defeat him?"

"At the moment, I cannot say. But that would solve another outstanding mystery."

Cammy wondered about that. The social media stuff was easy. But where would he hide if not his own grave? These things guarded treasure, supposedly? What treasure, and where, if that was what he was doing? More digging only turned up one more video which Roar had uploaded the morning of the day his murdered his wife and killed himself. He had clearly filmed it on his phone in his car.

"Hey, everyone," he said into the camera, eyes ringed red. "Look, I just want to say that I've had it with this town. We lost all our local shows and flavor and it's all corporate now. Conglomerates. Money ruins everything. Turns us all into whores, huh?" He sniffed and stared out the windshield. "We don't need more mega-corporations, we need a reason to get up in the morning. You guys... you've always been there for me. It means a lot to me." He pressed a fist to his mouth. "That, that helped me a lot. You guys, your support. And you, too, Elise. It means a lot." He squeezed his eyes shut and bared his teeth. "I'm sorry, dad. I tried to give your preaching a chance. I can't... look: I appreciate you all. Without your support, I woulda quit ages ago. But now..." His eyes darkened, the light gone out of them. He stared into the camera. "Anyway, I guess I don't have a reason anymore. I'm sorry. I love you all." He ended the video. Cammy felt ice in her stomach. She turned off her phone and watched the gray day slide past her.

She ignored the time, but at last some houses began popping up like little scattered wildflowers along the side of the road, and she gave them attention. They must be getting close now.

A hand-painted sign on the road pointed to "Egger's" at a turn off, which they followed. Blackberry bushes, weeds and cedar trees lined the roadside. Despite the fall gloom, the plants gave a sort of tranquil feeling as they drove past quaint little houses. One of the homes was painted in bright blues and yellows, with lots of other painted objects in the yard. The handiwork matched the sign at the corner of the street. She saw other signs giving the names of people or small businesses. It was funny, the sort of things you could find just out of the city. The houses were spaced wider apart now, because there were fields of various crops, or herb gardens, filling the spaces. She spotted some kids playing in one of the yards.

"Huh!" Dracula grunted.

"What?"

"I haven't seen that for some time. I had begun to wonder where children were being kept."

"Inside. It isn't safe outside," Cammy explained. He did not reply to that.

Dracula's Match

"How did you and Mr. Swindlehurst become friends?" he asked.

"Who?" Cammy had no idea who he was talking about.

"Andrew."

"Oh! Well, that was because of Kenzie. That group formed before I got invited. I think it was that Lindsey moved into town and she liked vampire romance novels, and Kenzie saw her reading them at lunch and they bonded over that."

Something like disappointment and disgust washed over her host's face.

"Anyway, Andrew and Aslan were already friends, and I think they both had a crush on Lindsey and sort of hung around. Then Kenzie latched onto them and dragged them into the group. She does that sort of thing. That's how I ended up in the group. Because I was talking about other nerd stuff with her at work."

"I see," he said, but nothing more.

Andrew's family farm had a cute little fence—white picket and everything!—with a sign reading "Egger's" hanging above a well-worn dirt driveway. There were cars parked around the front and side. Chickens wandered around just behind the house, and a peacock screamed as they parked behind a red SUV.

As they approached the house, a middle-aged woman with red hair, wearing a denim apron and carrying a box, came towards the nearest car.

"Here you are. Sorry we weren't able to drive to the shop."

"Things are crazy right now," said the man who accepted the cardboard crate. "Hard to even get around anymore with all the police tape. They're all inhaling donuts while this insanity goes on. Bad enough the city's gone all corporate."

"Take care," the redhead replied, and sent the man off with a smile. She noticed Dracula and Cammy.

"Hi there," she greeted them, clearly trying to figure out if she should be expecting them or not. "Did you call ahead for an order?"

"No, I'm a friend of Andrew's. I wanted to know if he was ok."

The woman's pale face grew paler, the freckles standing out. Her eyes scrutinized them both with an expression of suspicion and fear.

"He's fine," she said, not even attempting to fake a smile. "Who is asking?"

"I'm Cammy. Like I said, I'm a friend of his. You can ask him."

"And you are... ?" the woman prompted Dracula. Cammy dreaded which introduction he might give. Unless he had some reason to play "FBI" on someone, he liked to use his real name.

"Vlad. I am a friend of Cammy's. Your son and I met earlier this year at Cammy's birthday, and we spoke for some time a few days ago at your stand in Pike Place."

"Well, thank you for coming to check on him. But he's not feeling well today. Maybe you could come back later?"

Cammy was going to say 'sorry' and go, but she wondered about Andrew's mom's sudden and clear anxiety. Surely if Andrew was all right, she'd just say so and wouldn't be so nervous. Unless...

"Did he see something?"

Dracula's Match

"No!" the woman shook her head. "No, of course not! What are you talking about?"

Dracula looked to Cammy. She recognized it as him wondering whether she wished to push to see Andrew, or leave. *Push*, she thought.

"But can't he talk for a second?" Cammy asked.

"Mrs. Swindlehurst," Dracula said, "I'm with Special Services. We need to speak with your son again."

Cammy could *see* the tension gripping Mrs. Swindlehurst's whole body when she heard that. She looked to Cammy, then to Dracula.

"He hasn't told anyone," she whispered.

"We know. We'd just like to speak with him."

A vein stood out on Mrs. Swindlehurst's forehead, and another on her throat. Cammy hoped that wasn't a problem for her companion. Mrs. Swindlehurst turned slowly and led them to the cute home, a not-quite-cottage surrounded by \reclaimed items, like a real fire hydrant with a ceramic dog beside it, a large-scale "dipping-drinking bird" in a straw hat, one of those Japanese bamboo water fountains that goes "thunk" when it fills up, a few gnomes—including one on a miniature Penny Farthing bicycle—and more. Mrs. Swindlehurst shot a dirty look at them over her shoulder as she let herself inside. She stepped out of the galoshes she was wearing, and Cammy noticed a row of shoes kicked up against an inner wall inside the door. She obliged by kicking off her own shoes. For a moment, she thought they looked cleaner than she remembered, which was weird, given the wet weather. Whatever. Meanwhile Dracula had clearly been debating doing the same. She shot him a look, which he did not react to. At last, he untied his dress shoes, but carried them with him.

Mrs. Swindlehurst led them down a narrow, short hall to a small laundry room behind rolling, shuttered doors, with two more on either side. She knocked on one of the doors.

"Andrew, there are… more of those people here to see you."

She got no answer, but opened the door anyway. Inside, the room was a bit untidy, some clothes on the bed which might be dirty laundry or clean laundry needing to be put away but crumpled and ignored instead. Andrew was sitting at a small, reclaimed antique desk with his laptop shut on it, staring at the door in dread.

"Cammy?" he said, sitting straight up when he saw her. He looked to Dracula, clearly recognizing him, but unsure what to say. His mother hesitated.

"You know them?"

"Yeah, Cammy's a friend. What are you guys doing here?" Andrew rose from his desk. Cammy could see he wasn't injured. No limp, no bruises, no favoring some wounded arm. Relief poured through her. She stepped into his room and hugged him.

"I'm glad you're ok!" she said. "I was really worried! You could have said something!"

"No, he couldn't," Dracula told her. She looked back at him. "You heard me introduce us as 'Special Services.' They've been by to tell him not to say anything."

"Boese and the other—"

Dracula glared at her. She shut her mouth.

"Wait, how do you guys know about it, then?" Andrew asked. "I don't understand…"

"Who are the both of you?" Mrs. Swindlehurst demanded.

Dracula's Match

"As I said initially, we are friends," Dracula told her. "And we know what happened."

"Those men said… they said we mustn't tell *anyone*!" Mrs. Swindlehurst gasped, her voice hoarse.

"I also work for those men. After a fashion. There is no trouble if you speak to us."

"What is going on?" Mrs. Swindlehurst demanded. Cammy could see her eyes tearing up, her face contorted, her shoulders tight. "What's been happening? Who was that man who tried to kill my son?!"

"He didn't try to kill me, Mom. He didn't see me," Andrew told her. "He only went for…" his jaw tightened.

"He targeted someone in particular?" Dracula asked.

"Maybe. Some middle-aged bald guy."

Middle-aged bald guy? Cammy thought. She pulled her phone. "Did he look like this?"

"Yeah, kind of," Andrew agreed. She had shown him a picture of Roar's manager. She shared the photo with Dracula, and was about to tell him who it was.

"He certainly killed another man who looks like that," Dracula interrupted. "It's fair to say he may have certain people in mind, not just structures with passersby as incidental casualties."

"Who *are* you people?" Mrs. Swindlehurst demanded again.

"I am Vladislav Dracula. As I told you, I am well-acquainted with Cammy and have met your son before. As you know, there is some terror running rampant through the city, which you have been instructed to keep silent about. I am trying to find some method by which it can be stopped." He returned his attention to Cammy. "How are you?"

She nodded. "Better. I'm glad you're ok," she told Andrew.

Andrew nodded back, a bit confused. "So... you know about all this?" he asked.

"Yeah. I found out earlier this year."

Andrew considered Dracula anew, and Cammy realized he was now reevaluating the name, given this new information. The realization that the name probably wasn't just because he was *related* to a certain famous someone from the 1400s, like Kenzie had been guessing, washed over his face. Andrew pointed at him, looking at Cammy for confirmation. She nodded.

"I'll tell you about it later." She suddenly felt relieved. She'd be able to tell someone she knew. Maybe she *could* tell Brian after all. But he was in the hospital. And she didn't know how he was. The only way to find out would be to call Melissa. But then she'd have to tell *her* something.

*For that matter, if Brian is ok, what has **he** told her?* If she called Melissa and lied, and Brian had told her something else, that would be *bad*. Meaning she couldn't call Melissa at all.

"We can't stay long," Dracula told her. She bid Andrew good bye.

"You guys are going to do something... about that monster?" he checked.

"We're going to try," Cammy assured him, then waved timidly at his mother. "Nice to meet you."

Mrs. Swindlehurst just stared, her mouth agape.

Once they had returned to the car, Dracula pulled his flip phone.

"I may have something," he said into it, "The next location your draugr might appear."

Dracula's Match

He pulled out of the driveway and, once they were on the open road again, explained what Cammy had discovered. He did not reveal that Cammy had discovered it. He also asked about Roar's manager.

"Is that a fact?" he said. "Send me the address." He nodded to Cammy, who pulled her phone to type whatever address this might be into it. Looked like it was in Queen Anne. Dracula confirmed he would head over, and hung up.

"Who was that, and where are we going?"

"I reported what you said to Special Services. They may at least be able to move people out of the way of the next attack. That address is the domicile one Calvin Schlimme, Mr. Thorirsson's manager. He was brought in for questioning after the murder. He's out on bail from a separate altercation, and heading home."

CHAPTER 10
GRAVE MISCONCEPTIONS

It was a pretty nice apartment complex. Sleek, modern, clean lines, crisp angles, the works. Then they found out they needed a code to get in.

"Wonderful," Cammy grumbled. Dracula pulled his flip phone. He explained the situation, and they waited. A few minutes later, he got a call back and punched the code in, and they were able to get inside. The place had its own gym and pool, Cammy noticed. She wondered how much the rent was for a unit. They were heading up to the 9th floor, and stepped into a pristine elevator to get there. The hallways were bright, the floors immaculate. They came to Mr. Schlimme's door, and realized at almost the same moment that there was something funny about the door to the apartment. It was shut, but looking closer at it, the handle was punched into the door somehow.

Dracula held out a hand to stop her from advancing, then motioned she move down the hall. When she had retreated to the elevator, Dracula pushed the door open a little and peered inside. He checked that she was staying put, and slipped in. Cammy waited, expecting any minute he'd come out trailing blood behind—manager guy was probably murdered in there. Roar must have gotten to him. She didn't want to see it.

What felt like twenty minutes later, Dracula emerged, still immaculate, and simply shut the door behind him.

"Is he dead?"

"He's not inside."

"What about the door?"

"Someone definitely broke in and destroyed everything in sight, but there is no sign of Mr. Schlimme."

"Did the draugr kill him and walk away with his body or something?"

"Mr. Thorirsson hasn't killed a single person cleanly that I have seen," Dracula said. "Considering the lack of evidence, I doubt it. We may assume Mr. Thorirsson came by to look for Mr. Schlimme at some point, and did not find him."

"Maybe this was where he was hiding during the day?" Cammy suggested.

"If so, he is not in there now, and neither is Mr. Schlimme." Dracula tapped his mouth to think. "I am not equipped to seek out a single man in a city of this size, and Special Services will be busy clearing the next location."

Cammy waited for an "and" or a "but", but none followed.

"So what now?" she asked.

"At the moment, that is as much as we can do. I would say it would be best for you to check on Officer Warren."

Cammy winced. Dracula's expression didn't change, but she *felt* something like frustration or disappointment lurking behind that stillness.

"Something the matter?" he asked.

"What do I tell him? How do I make him understand everything that's happened? How do I..." She bit back her tears and her words. *How do I say I'm sorry to him?*

"I see," he said. "As there is little else we can do at the moment, let us see about visiting him without his sister's aid."

"How?" Cammy asked.

"A few days ago, I had intended to try an old skill of mine to see if I can still use it effectively. Let's go."

They went to a chain clothing store, of all places. Cammy waited and watched, utterly baffled, as he found a pair of jeans, a dark gray T-shirt, and a faux leather, stylish jacket. She was even more baffled when he came out of a fitting room with all of it on and looked... like a normal person, though he did wear his hair longer than most modern men in their forties. Not enough to draw attention, though. If she'd seen him walking down the street, she wouldn't have looked twice. He still had his dress shoes on, but he didn't stand out like James-Bond-goes-to-a-funeral anymore. He had taken the trouble to hang all his original clothing on the hangers, and pulled all the tags off the new clothes.

There were lines behind the two cashiers, and he stepped into the shorter one.

"There's self-checkouts right over there—"

"No," he said.

So they drove to the hospital with him dressed like a normal person. When they came inside, Dracula spoke first to the woman at reception.

"Hello, I'm here to see Brian Warren. I heard he was admitted?"

Dracula's Match

"Name?" the receptionist asked.

"Brad Delacroix," Dracula said. "His uncle on his mother's side. And this is his cousin."

"Let me check..." She typed on her computer and told Cammy the room number. "They moved him. He's awake now."

Cammy felt her stomach flip with elation and anxiety—a rather unpleasant combo. The receptionist gave them stickers with the room number written in marker, and off they went.

Cammy felt ill. It was absolutely stupid how badly she wanted to make sure Brian was ok, but also not see him. What would he say? He'd seen the whole thing. He'd seen Malcolm, and talked to Siri, and maybe some of the elves.

They came to the door, and Cammy hesitated. Could she look him in the eye?

Dracula gently touched her back and applied some pressure. He opened the door and pushed her slowly through.

Brian was lying there, not moving; he looked like he was barely breathing. There were machines monitoring his heart rate, which seemed high to her, but she wasn't sure what counted as high. She didn't know what all the wires did, but she recognized an IV drip.

"Cammy?" Brian asked, hoarsely. He sounded woozy. Probably pain meds, she supposed. She hurried to his side, forgetting all her worries about what she was going to say. She wanted to hug him, but he didn't even try to sit up. He raised one hand, so she grabbed it.

"Are you going to be ok?" she asked. Brian didn't really move his head, but his eyes trailed past her, and she realized he had spotted Dracula. She motioned he stay back, so he did.

"Yeah," Brian replied, sounding a little hazy. "Cracked my head pretty good. Really broken ribs this time."

Cammy clutched his hand tighter. She felt some tears plop down on both of their hands.

"I'm sorry, I was so worried. I didn't know—"

"S'okay," Brian assured her. He glanced past her again. "I don't remember what happened."

Cammy blinked the tears away so she could look at him. There was bruising and swelling up by his hairline. His eyes weren't totally focused.

"You... you don't?" she said. He sort of blinked-shook-his-head, clearly unwilling to move it very much. "Has Melissa been by?"

"Yeah. She came before. She had to work. The car got towed or something."

Cammy gripped his hand.

"Does she know how you are?"

"Yeah. Told her I don't remember what happened. I don't remember any of it."

What a horrible stroke of luck for her, Cammy supposed. She could just spin something for Melissa then. She felt relieved and sick at the same time. Should she tell Brian now? But *how* could she? Would he blame her for what happened? Would he not believe her?

"When are you going home?"

"Not yet. Need more tests," he said.

"I was really worried about you."

She felt him grip her hand back.

"Thanks for coming to check on me," he said. She nodded enthusiastically.

Dracula's Match

His eyes drifted to Dracula again. Probably she ought to go. Brian still didn't trust him, and Dracula hanging around wasn't going to make him feel better.

"Sorry, I'll... I'll come back by myself next time," she promised. He blink-nodded in answer. She bid him goodbye, and apologized again.

"You don't have to apologize," he said. She squeezed his hand again. For a moment, she leaned forward to hug him, but then remembered his broken ribs and thought better of it. She touched his shoulder, and let herself out.

As they walked down the hallway, Dracula decided to chime in.

"He's lying."

"What?" Cammy demanded, wiping a tear with her thumb.

"He remembers."

"What? How do *you* know? And why would he do that?"

"I know, because he didn't ask *you* how it happened," Dracula said. "As to the why, I have a suspicion."

"Brian wouldn't lie," Cammy insisted. "He's all about telling the truth." Dracula almost rolled his eyes in response. He did a more dignified looking up and away, instead. She squinted at him while he wasn't looking. She wiped gross snot from under her nose and spotted a bathroom.

"Hang on," she said, "I need to..."

Dracula nodded magnanimously, and she let herself in.

About a minute after Cammy and the creep left, said creep came strolling back in through the door to his room. Brian had no idea why he was dressed down today—he'd never seen that look on him before last night—and he assumed it meant the guy was up to no good. Brian especially didn't like how easy it suddenly was to mistake him for a regular person. Nifty trick, just changing outfits.

Creep came up alongside.

"Officer Warren, I regret not expressing my gratitude earlier upon seeing you survived."

Brian decided to stonewall him. He knew this guy was almost *undoubtedly* exactly what he'd suspected. There were magic things running around, and this creep must have used some sort of hypno-mind-control on Cammy. Why else would she have gone to him instead of Brian? That's why Cammy was being so weird and wouldn't talk to him about it. Either she was being controlled, or she was trying to keep secrets from him. If Creep was *the* creep to end all creeps, Brian didn't have a lot of cards to play, except maybe play dumb, which might give him the chance to figure something out once he recovered.

Of course, Creep coming back into the room all silent-like without any witnesses didn't bode well for Brian making any sort of recovery. *'Gratitude seeing you survived,'* he thought, *'sure.'*

"Something I've noticed about you modern people is that all of you are cowards and children," the creep said. "And you come up with very strange, needlessly elaborate excuses to avoid doing anything."

"Listen, don't worry about me. I'll be fine."

The creep leaned on the bed railing, a sort of ingratiating amusement in his eyes.

"I know you will be."

Dracula's Match

Just you wait, I know your deal now, Brian thought. *I got your number, Mr. 'I can't eat garlic.'* "Like I said, don't worry about me. You worry about you."

Creep leaned over, bringing his face closer to Brian's. It was disconcerting.

"I know that you know what happened. I imagine you think that pretending helps you in some way. What you are doing is wasting precious time."

"Listen here, I don't know what you did to Cammy, but I'm not going to lie down and let you get away with it."

Creep looked nonplussed for a moment, then half-smiled. He leaned a little further.

"You know where she is. If you're serious, then *come get her.*"

He patted Brian's hand.

"You still have my effects. I would like them returned. It has been several months, after all."

"Don't you worry, I'll *return* them to you," Brian told him.

The creep smirked at him, then left the room.

Cammy came out of the hospital bathroom to discover Siri standing in the hallway, her arms crossed, looking down the hall in the direction of Brian's room.

"What are you *doing* here?" Cammy demanded.

"Vaiting for you," Siri replied. "You vent to rescue the young man. I thought you vould come, eventually, to see him."

"Yeah, well," Cammy said. "He's in the hospital, so…" Someone tugged on her sleeve, and she turned to see the elf boy from campus, with the little girl he'd scolded for stealing beside him. "What are *you* doing here?" she demanded for the second time. The boy held a finger to his lips.

"We saw that your friend was wounded and thought you might come to see him."

"Oh, you too, huh," Cammy muttered.

"We hoped you would speak to his majesty on our behalf," the boy said. "To tell him we did not mean any harm." The girl nodded emphatically.

"Yeah, I'll talk to him," Cammy assured.

"Please!" the boy insisted.

"And what, precisely, is going on over here?" Dracula asked, coming up beside Cammy. She hadn't thought about why he wasn't nearby before.

"Please don't be angry!" the boy begged, clasping his hands together.

"Is there some reason I ought be angry?" Dracula asked him flatly.

"I told my cousins that your companion was spying on Fjola, so they thought she was a witch or a troll and took her to our elders to deal with."

"Ah, you lot." Dracula nodded to himself. He took Cammy by the elbow and started walking her away.

"Wait!" the boy shouted.

Dracula ignored the boy, and kept walking Cammy out towards the exit.

"Please wait!"

Dracula stopped, and pushed Cammy behind him as he swiveled to face the boy. The girl trailed timidly behind.

"If you think your youth will be some protection against me, you are gravely mistaken," he growled. "Keep your distance."

Dracula's Match

"Please," the boy pleaded. "We were afraid. We are strangers here, with no friends. But we should not have taken your guest."

"No, indeed you should not." Dracula deliberately turned his back again.

"Please, we had planned to ask you for sanctuary."

Dracula pushed Cammy along and ignored the kid. Cammy tried to shoot a glance over her shoulder, but it was hard. The boy was biting back bitter disappointment, and the girl sadly took his hand, though Cammy couldn't tell if it was to give comfort or receive it.

"They're sorry and they didn't mean any harm," Cammy spoke up. Dracula didn't answer. Her leg was throbbing. "Please slow down," she said.

He slowed. She realized that drawing attention to her leg might work against the elves.

"They didn't do anything—"

"Do not tell me how to conduct my affairs," he told her, flatly. Well, flat with an edge. He was always good at somehow straddling two very different tones at the same time.

"But they didn't mean any harm."

"That is both irrelevant and untrue. His people absolutely meant to take you prisoner, since they *did it*. They laid hands on you. You are a guest of mine."

"Please!"

Cammy and Dracula both looked down to see the boy had knelt all the way down on the ground and was gripping him by the cuff of his pants. Dracula kicked the boy off. Before Cammy could protest, he addressed the boy.

"I am not known for my sympathy. And I am a busy man."

"No, y—" Cammy started to protest

Dracula clamped a hand *hard* over her mouth and glared at her.

"You are never to speak for me," he told her.

"We have a gift," the boy said.

"What gift?"

"We have a portrait of yours which went missing."

Dracula was silent a space. "The one formerly kept by that idiot descendant of mine who died in exile after betraying that gypsy woman he took with him?"

"That one."

"That is hardly enough to placate me. It would have been an appreciated gift had you come to my estate *first*."

"I will do anything. It is my fault. I was too hasty," the boy insisted.

"Were you indeed?"

Cammy tried to peel his fingers from her mouth, to find not only that she couldn't, but that he could grip her *harder*. Dracula considered the boy and stopped applying steadily increasing pressure to Cammy's jaw as soon as she stopped resisting.

"Are your people able to build things?"

"We can," the boy said. He hadn't risen from the floor. Dracula considered him for a few moments longer.

"Very well. However, you have harmed my guest. That is not something I will overlook. You said you would do anything?"

"Anything!" the boy agreed. "I would be your slave, if you wished."

"I have no wish for any slave. But as I said, it is my guest you harmed by your carelessness. I would have you and..." he considered the girl, "your companion be her slaves."

Dracula's Match

"Nmmnnn!" Cammy protested, and felt Dracula's fingers grip tighter.

"Agreed," said the boy.

"Very well. Tell your people to come to the border of my estate. We shall discuss the details of your dwelling there at some future time. At the moment, I have other concerns."

"What other concerns?" the boy asked before Dracula could turn away.

"We are looking for a certain man."

"What man?"

Dracula looked to Cammy. After considering her, he slowly removed his hand so she could speak.

"We're looking for the draugr guy's manager," Cammy said. "He's not at his apartment, but we don't know where he is. And I don't need you guys as—"

Dracula covered her mouth again.

"The sooner we are able to locate this man, the better," he told the boy.

"We can ask in the Underground," the boy said.

"I don't wish to know who or what you contact down there," Dracula told him. He then provided a description and the name of the missing manager. "I spied a restaurant around the corner from here. We shall await your report until this afternoon. After that, it shall have to be tomorrow at my estate."

"Thank you!" the boy exclaimed. He turned to the girl, took her hand, glanced at Dracula, and they disappeared.

"Do not speak for me," Dracula repeated to Cammy. "It is both rude and disturbingly presumptuous of you considering our relationship."

"MmMMMmm!" Cammy protested.

"We are not in a romantic relationship. Please free your mind from the narrow modern use of that word. We have a guest-host relationship, which you would do well to study. As your host, and your social better, I do not appreciate your presumption, and my patience is worn past thin. I am weary of repeating myself on this matter. I am going to let you speak, but do not immediately blurt out something stupid."

He released her. She glared at him and took a step out of arm's reach.

"It vould seem that love is nothing to be desired," Siri piped up. Cammy had just about forgotten she was there.

"Love is more complex than you imagine," Dracula told her.

"I see it makes vun miserable," Siri said. She nodded at Cammy. "To vatch you speak to your friend in the hospital bed."

"We're not in love!" Cammy protested. Dracula and Siri both shot her a look.

"I haven't the time to explain this to you at the moment," Dracula told Siri, "but while love wounds you when you see your loved one wounded, you also feel joy when they have joy. You are given the joy of two people at that time."

Siri's forehead creased with confusion, and maybe some sorrow or longing.

"Thank you for distracting the werewolf," Dracula told her.

Siri nodded, and her eyes lit with some expectation. He nodded good bye to her, and waved for Cammy follow him out of the hospital. She cast a parting glance at Siri, who stood, her arms folded over one another, almost scowling with thought.

Dracula's Match

"So where is Malcolm?" she asked.

"She led him back to the troll in the morning. He was badly wounded and exhausted. Special Services picked him up, along with me."

Cammy didn't like hearing that. What would Boese do to Malcolm if he liked chopping Dracula up when he had the chance? She hugged herself.

Dracula led Cammy around the corner to an Italian restaurant and got them a table. She glowered at him, but he ignored her. He offered to buy her lunch, so she grumpily got a salad and a side of mozzarella sticks. He ordered about three meals for himself.

"That's a lot of food," Cammy commented. He shrugged.

"It is what I must do," he said.

"What's the Underground?" Cammy asked.

"The areas of the city where humans by and large do not visit. Parts of the original city, which was buried. Certain creatures have excavated them and made a network of dwelling places."

"Like the Underground tours?" Cammy asked.

"Not the parts which are toured. Additionally, the supernatural creatures have dug out more locations. They have done so in many major cities. Malcolm told me that Cincinnati has a similar network, as they have a long forgotten subway or something to that effect."

"So it's like what Malcolm said? Things attract similar things?"

"After a fashion."

"Could I visit the Underground?"

"Not on your life," Dracula snapped. "It is a dangerous place. There are many unsavory creatures down there, and powers the likes of which you know nothing of."

Cammy thought about what she had experienced when the elves kidnapped her. That weird, sick feeling that was a little like the draugr. Was that what he was talking about? Or that voice. Whoever—or whatever—had asked to buy her. She felt ill.

"Malcolm followed where the elves took me," she said. "He said he went through a Goblin Market?"

"That's what they call some of the larger hubs," Dracula said, "though such places are no longer true 'goblin' markets. If the elves took you down there, I am even more furious with them. You could have been eaten alive, or far worse."

Far worse than being eaten alive?! Cammy gulped. She hadn't liked that voice, offering to buy her. Who—or *what*—had asked about her? She didn't want to know. But she also *really* did. But if she talked about what had happened, he'd be angrier at the elves. She would ask the elves later.

Dracula did actually eat all three plates of food he'd ordered. He did his best to eat in a manner that seemed "dignified" to Cammy, but there was a sort of urgency to how he consumed food, like he was famished.

"You must really like their pasta, huh?" she commented.

"It is vile and I loathe it," he answered.

"But you're eating a lot of it."

"I have to eat something," he grumped.

She played with her fingers.

"Why?"

He eyed her.

"I'm always hungry," he answered.

Dracula's Match

"Always?"

He nodded. Cammy thought about what Siri had said. Maybe processed food wasn't very helpful for him?

Once they had finished, Cammy ordered a coffee and texted Melissa that she didn't know what had happened to Brian. She figured if she called, Melissa would know she was lying. She still felt dirty doing it. Dracula ordered himself a glass of wine and sipped it angrily while they waited.

She checked her classes, and realized she'd left a book she needed for an essay at the Mindful Bean.

"I forgot my book at work," she told him. "Can we get it?"

"Certainly. Let us see whether or not the impetuous creatures who spoke to us can find Mr. Schilmme. If so, we shall go afterwards, and if not, then we shall leave presently."

Around three o'clock, the elf boy appeared beside their table. A woman the next table over actually shouted in surprise. Her friend asked her what the matter was, and Cammy worried for a moment what she would say. The woman looked the boy up and down, looked to Cammy and Dracula, then turned to her friend.

"Sorry I just… I guess I didn't see him walk up…" she said.

That was part of the reason the supernatural could hide in plain sight sometimes, Cammy supposed. No one wanted to sound crazy. She might have done the same thing if someone had just *appeared* next to her.

"We found the man," the boy said.

"Excellent. Where is he?"

The boy gave an address.

"Very good," Dracula said. He pulled his wallet and passed two hundred dollar bills to the boy. "You should find some other clothes to wear. You stand out. What is your name?"

"Trausti," the boy answered.

"Well done, Trausti." Dracula waved him off. The boy disappeared, then reappeared. He looked at the next table, perhaps thinking of the other patrons' earlier surprise.

"Wait," Cammy said, "before you go. You were looking for food before, right? Let me order something for you."

"There is no need for you to do that for me," Trausti assured her. "I wish to pay my debt to you."

Cammy glared at Dracula.

"Here, I haven't touched the tiramisu I ordered yet. Why don't you take that? I'll bring some garlic bread home too, so when you come later, I'll be able to give you that."

Trausti's bright eyes glistened a little and he shook his head adamantly.

"I am already in your debt. I couldn't possibly—"

"Take the food; she is offering it to you," Dracula told him. Trausti studied the tiramisu.

"It is truly all right?"

"Yeah, let me see if they can get you a box."

She rose from the table and went to the servers' station to ask. They gave her a Styrofoam box which she packed the dessert into and passed it to Trausti. He thanked her and bowed deeply. The women at the next table watched the display, confused. Cammy felt self-conscious.

"You don't have to do that," she admonished Trausti. "It's no big deal."

Dracula's Match

"I will never forget your kindness!" Trausti assured her, then walked out of the restaurant. He got looks—his clothes really did stand out.

"You paid him?" Cammy asked pointedly, as Dracula waved for a server.

"He did good work," Dracula said.

"But you said he would be a slave."

"He's your slave, not mine, and that doesn't mean I cannot reward him if I wish," Dracula said.

You're a psycho and you make no sense! Cammy thought angrily at him.

Soon, they were on their way to a motel, some non-chain building dating to the 70s. The old-fashioned white sign stained by moisture, the old brick exterior, the handful of rooms all looked dingy. It didn't look like it could make enough money to stay in business, but here it was. Dracula had called Boese's people to have them look up what room the guy had rented before they left the restaurant. He got a call back just as they arrived that Schlimme had checked in under the name "Jack Smith" and was told the room number.

They parked right outside the room, the orange-painted door warped and scuffed. Dracula indicated that Cammy hang back a bit, and knocked on the door.

"Who's there?" Cammy heard from the other side.

"Mr. Schlimme, I'm with law enforcement. I need to speak with you about Mr. Thorirsson."

"Don't know who that is," was the answer. Dracula grabbed the door handle and broke it open. He stepped inside. Well, apparently he didn't need an invitation. The stories must be wrong about that, too.

"Mr. Schlimme, I have very little time, and no desire to play games," Dracula said into the room. "And I will leave once you speak to me."

Cammy snuck up behind him to see a middle-aged, overweight, bald guy pressed up against the wall, wielding a baseball bat. His eyes were drawn to Cammy's appearance, and he looked a bit confused. Dracula considered her, then returned his attention.

"I mean you no harm at the moment, but I am short on time," he said.

Schlimme squinted at Cammy, but slowly lowered the bat. He kept on the far side of the mustard-colored bed.

"Couldn't have done much with this anyway," he said. "What do you want to know?"

"More about Mr. Thorirsson," Dracula said.

"What about him?"

Dracula stepped into the room, and gestured for Cammy to do the same. She closed the door, but wasn't sure it was going to stay that way with the doorknob broken. Dracula gestured she stay by the door, then made a quick check of the small closet by the door, and then the bathroom, keeping one eye on Schlimme as he did. Schlimme watched him, clearly taking in the action and evaluating it.

"Who are you?" he asked Cammy.

"I'm—"

"You are speaking with me," Dracula told him. "Never mind her."

"Well, she must be the one with the questions," Schlimme chuckled. "You're the bodyguard here."

Bodyguard? "Why do you say that?" Cammy asked.

Dracula's Match

"He's the one barging in here, checking to make sure it's safe for you, standing there to make sure I can't rush you," Schlimme said. "Plus, look at how this guy moves. How'd you get like that? You must have had to train like an Olympian, huh?"

"Something like that," Dracula said.

"Bet you really know how to handle yourself," Schlimme went on. "If you were twenty years younger, I might ask you if you were interested in being famous."

Cammy almost laughed out loud. The idea of her host prancing around in tights and a speedo was hilarious. Besides, it would be hard for Dracula to get more famous than he already was.

"I would not be interested in the vaudeville shows you and Mr. Thorirsson put on. I am not a clown," Dracula said.

Schlimme wiped his bald head.

"Well, don't know who you are, but you *talk* like Roar. He always was a handful." Schlimme caught himself, and scratched his double chin. "Or is he a *was?* I'm not sure anymore.

"Do you think he is the one who visited your apartment?"

"Him or his friends," Schlimme said. "Sure wasn't robbed. Just smashed up my stuff. Seems pretty personal."

"You were having an affair with his wife," Cammy pointed out.

Schlimme put up both his hands, partly to show he didn't want to fight, but it also looked a bit like he was about to lecture her or sell her a car.

"Listen, kid, we're in a business. You make audiences happy, you make people like me happy, you do well. She was tired of the sham relationship, and she wanted to try to bring her own career back from the dead. She figured offering me favors would help. Wanted to take her own stab at movies. Pretty long shot, but whatever, I said I would make some calls."

"You didn't have to accept the favors."

"Right, I'm a scumbag," Schlimme said. "It's not like she didn't know what she was doing. She'd been in the business long enough. And it's not like she didn't know her time was basically up." He shrugged. "It's harder for chicks. They get too old, people pay less attention. But it's also hard for the guys to keep up after a while. Only so much punishment anyone can take. That kind of physicality isn't for most past forty."

"If it was a sham relationship, Mr. Thorirsson seems to have taken the affair very badly," Dracula pointed out.

"He always liked her. Audiences could see that. I was able to use some of that puppy love for publicity. Never had to tell him to take her on dates. Drove me nuts, but I guess that 'authenticity' he liked to go on about stuck with some of the fans. They could feel it. Ridiculous. He was popular here because of his local history. He was always moping about how Seattle was losing its identity."

"He did not like working for you," Dracula said. Cammy wasn't sure how he'd figured that out.

Schlimme shrugged. "It wasn't just me he had a problem with. He was in the wrong career track. Should have done serious fighting. Then I wouldn't have had to hear the endless complaints about how *inauthentic* everything was," he said, rolling his eyes.

"If that was something he preferred, why didn't he pursue real fighting?"

"His mom or his sister was worried about him getting injured, and leaned on him. I don't remember the details."

"It was his sister," Cammy told him. Roar had talked about Elise—his sister—in a number of interviews. They must have had a good relationship. Schlimme made a face.

"Roar always complained about that decision. Should have just done what he wanted. Roar was never happy about anything. Moaned all the time, while gazing into his navel for *meaning*. Shoulda been a philosopher. Couldn't get him to shut up, even if I threw a woman or two at him."

"You don't care about some kind of meaning or purpose to life? More than money?" Cammy asked.

"Look: life is short. But hey, we have nice cars, hot women, money, all kinds of goodies to fill that void dreamers like Roar moan about. All you have to do is grab for it."

"But you don't wonder about, like, our purpose in life, or why we're here, or *anything*?"

"The way I figure it, everyone says they know 'The Truth' ,everyone disagrees, so I'm not going to give myself a migraine figuring it out. I'm going to stick with the stuff I know: money. Because money *can* buy you happiness. The songs lie."

"You do seem like a very happy man," Dracula commented. Schlimme eyed him. "How fortunate that money never runs out, and can buy you lasting loyalty and friendship."

"Hey, you live your life, and I'll live mine. Looks like you could use a little cash yourself." Schlimme waved a hand at Dracula's clothes. "Chicks dig designer clothes. You can get any one you want, so long as you have cash."

Dracula grunted in answer. Cammy wondered if he'd ever gone that route. He always dressed nice and always had cash. Gross. She hoped not.

"With regards to Mr. Thorirsson," Dracula said, "Do you have any idea where he might hide, if he wished?"

"Hide?" Schlimme laughed. "That six-foot-seven mountain of Scandinavian muscle? Have you *seen* him?"

"I have no time for jokes, Mr. Schlimme," Dracula told him. "Anything you can think of would be of help to me."

"Yeah, sure, Mr. 'Law Enforcement,'" Schlimme replied, air quoting with his fingers. "Fact is: I have no idea. If he wasn't hanging out with his new friends, he'd be home with his wife. He couldn't get enough of her. Don't know why. She wasn't that into him. All he could see was her fake boobs and that smile. That's why she never wanted kids: woulda ruined her figure, but he got busted up about it. Him and his endless moaning about authenticity, and he couldn't see she was no different from your average two-dollar hooker."

"You—!"

Dracula held out a hand to stop Cammy from continuing. He shook his head at her when she started to protest.

"If that's all you know, we shall be on our way," Dracula said.

"Thanks for breaking the door, by the way," Schlimme snarked at their backs. Once they were in the car, Dracula pulled his phone.

"I can't believe that guy," Cammy grumped.

"He's out of money," Dracula told her. "Gambling problem. Has some outstanding debts. He was going to be evicted. He was arrested for harassing some women at a restaurant for money. That's why he's out on bail."

Dracula's Match

Cammy huffed. Served him right, she supposed. He didn't care at all about Roar or anybody.

"I believe I know where Roar goes during the day," Dracula said. Cammy stared, but realized he was talking into the phone. Still, he had an idea? How? "Is his wife still at the morgue, or has she been buried?"

Cammy stared harder. Oh, gross. No way.

"I see," he said. "Check there, then."

"You think he's… visiting her during the day?" Cammy asked as he hung up.

"I think it's very possible," Dracula said. "Since he is not at his apartment, and I know of no other possible location."

"Gross!" Cammy said.

"He was very attached to her, it seems," Dracula said. "She was his treasure."

"He killed her!"

He nodded. "That doesn't mean he may not still love her."

Cammy supposed if anyone understood how *that* was possible, it was him. Why would anyone kill someone they loved? That made no sense. She pointed that out to him.

"Unrequited or betrayed love is indescribably painful," Dracula told her. "And a man can lose himself in rage or desperation."

"That doesn't excuse him."

"I gave no excuse. I gave an explanation," Dracula told her.

Cammy turned to the window.

They reached the Mindful Bean without incident, and Cammy darted into the coffee shop while he waited outside with the car. He ruminated on the fight that would come that evening while he leaned against the hood. Even if Special Services located Roar's wife, the trouble remained of how to wrestle the monster into its grave. So far as he had heard, the monster was not likely to visit Lake View Cemetery, and unless it did, he did not see how it was possible to kill it.

"Hey, you."

The voice drew his attention to Kenzie, his least favorite of all of Cammy's acquaintances, standing nearly within arm's reach, holding a plastic cup of iced coffee in her hand.

"Saw you out here," the young woman said, and grinned. He eyed the numerous pieces of metal in her face. When he didn't answer, she held out the coffee. "Here. On the house."

He accepted the coffee, but did not sip it. No sign of Cammy.

"So," Kenzie said. When he still did not reply, she played with some piece of metal with her tongue. "I saw everything that happened the last few days." He still offered her no response, so she tried grinning wider. "And some video. And heard some stuff right here." She gestured at the coffee shop behind her.

"Indeed."

"Yeah." Her grin spread wider, nearly giddy now. "So, at a guess, I'd say I figured out what your garlic allergy is about."

He looked at her. She wiggled her eyebrows excitedly, as if to insinuate some sort of familiarity with him, he supposed. When he made no reply, she continued, "You're him, right? The real guy?"

"And if I am?"

Her mouth dropped open in a gleeful, silent squeal of excitement.

"That is *sick*," she said. "For real? Really?"

Dracula's Match

Dracula looked to the coffee shop for any sign of Cammy. Nothing so far.

"So it's all real. There are vampires?"

"There are."

Kenzie bounced on her toes in her excitement.

"Oh, Cam's in trouble now! For not telling me before," she said. "So you're really you. That's dope. I gotta ask you something."

"Do you indeed."

Kenzie bit her lip and drew close so she could lower her voice. He suspected he wasn't going to like whatever was about to come out of her mouth.

"Can you, you know, turn me, too? That would be so cool. Super powers and immortality—"

He slapped her. Hard. In the nineties, he'd suddenly developed the sort of super strength that Hollywood had portrayed for some time, and he'd struggled to control it, but he'd had practice since then. He was certain he hadn't broken her jaw or her face, but she wasn't likely to ask him something so stupid and self-destructive again.

Her glasses bounced off the concrete and into a patch of grass as she let out a startled whimper and collapsed to the sidewalk. She shuddered on the ground for a few moments before a hand went to her cheek and she stared up at him in uncomprehending shock. He doubted it was the pain so much as the fact that he had struck her at all which had silenced her.

"Never ask for such a thing ever again," he warned her. "Your very soul is imperiled."

Her dark eyes stared up at him, purblind to his meaning. She snatched up her glasses, and with a sneer, replied,

"Not like I'm using it for much anyway." She darted to the coffee shop, bumping into Cammy on the way out the door. Cammy watched her friend go, clearly confused by her behavior.

"What happened?" she asked, coming towards him.

"Your friend is naïve to danger. You must do your best to steer her from her current path," he told her. Cammy's brow contracted and she looked over her shoulder after her friend. "It is time we returned to my estate," he said.

CHAPTER 11
GET TO GRIPS

After leaving Cammy at his mansion—with additional instructions for his guardians to be extraordinarily vigilant—Dracula changed clothes into something more practical, and headed into the city. The Museum of Pop Culture had been shut down, and he assumed Boese's agents had been occupied moving everything of interest or value out of it to a safe place. He drove there to find the area a veritable ghost town, spotting a few vehicles with government plates. When he came to the doors, he found them left open, with a pair of Boese's agents set to prevent anyone who might still wander by from coming inside.

"You going to stop him at long last?" one demanded as he entered. He didn't bother responding.

Dracula took only a minute or so walking around the crazy layout of the bottom floor before he returned to the agents.

"You have removed whatever nonsense must have been in here before," he said, "but have failed to put anything in its place."

"We don't want this freak to cause more destruction," one of the agents—a human, late thirties—told him.

"Of course not, but if you don't give this monster something with which to occupy itself, it is not impossible it will lose interest and then move on to another location. I think the fifty or so field agents your department has in this city will find trying to contain or stop the monster insurmountably difficult if it moves on."

"That's why you're here to stop him. Like you were supposed to do three nights ago."

Dracula seized the man by the collar of his polo shirt and lifted him nearly off his feet. His partner reached for a walkie talkie—a gun would have been next to useless.

"The only way to kill this monster is to wrestle it into its own grave, and unless I am exceedingly mistaken, his grave is in Lake View Cemetery, while we are all the way down here. Perhaps the logistics of such an undertaking have escaped you, but that is a distance of several miles."

"About ten minutes by car," the agent countered.

"And perhaps an hour by foot. And you expect me to wrestle with a monster which can change his size, shape, and even turn into mist for over an hour through your busy city without being spotted or causing some sort of commotion. Who are you calling?"

"I'm reporting you," the other agent said.

"Tell Boese or whoever he may have assigned to this task that this place needs distractions to keep the monster occupied while we find some method of luring it to its grave and

Dracula's Match

killing it," Dracula told the man. The agent declined to pass on that information, and simply reported some sort of warning code into the radio. Dracula strode toward him and relieved him of the device.

"Tell whoever is in charge to install some sort of distractions in here before the sun goes down," Dracula said into the receiver. "Given that you modern people think anything at all is art, why not piles of garbage?"

"Keep your ideas to yourself," the agent snatched for his walkie talkie. Dracula kept it out of his reach. Whoever was on the other side requested clarification so Dracula provided it.

"Who is this?" the voice asked.

"Who do you think?"

"I have to clear that request."

Dracula had never so wanted to kill a group of people as this over-regulated pack of incompetent bureaucrats. He returned the walkie talkie and waited. At last, an order came back to deliver some pallets and objects. Over the next hour, a pair of trucks came by, loaded with said pallets, as well as some broken chairs and other items he guessed might have been pulled from dumpsters. A little after sundown, there were a few piles of trash scattered about inside, and there was nothing further to do but wait. The plan was to let the monster run rampant while Boese's agents set up a method of observing Roar's wife—still at the morgue, as it happened; no family had come to claim her and she had not put together a will—to see if he would return to her.

Dracula suspected they would manage to make that situation worse somehow, but he doubted any concerns he expressed on that front would be heeded.

Amaya Tenshi

This must have been how Hunyadi felt on the Varna campaign. A man trying to give sound advice to a young king who chose not to heed it, to his downfall, and the downfall of others. Had his majesty, the young king Ladislas, only listened to reason, how differently everything might have turned out. Hunyadi, allied with Dracula' father and older brother, could have struck the Ottoman Empire a decisive blow. Perhaps the whole history of Christendom would have gone differently. If the Sultan Murad II had been killed as a result of a successful joint campaign, Dracula himself might have been put to death while still a prisoner, but it would have been an outcome worth dying for. As for his personal history, Dracula had often wondered whether he and his brother had been spared by the victorious sultan only because the campaign had gone so poorly.

Perhaps it would have been better had he been slain as a boy, along with his brother Radu. Perhaps Mircea, had he become voivode in a smooth transition from father to son, would have strengthened Wallachia, and forged better relations with the neighboring countries of Moldavia and Hungary. In actuality, Mircea had raged against their onetime ally Hunyadi, taking him captive after the disastrous failure of the Varna campaign, and threatening him with death. The Draculas only seemed to come in two kinds: proud, passionate warriors, or demure, mild-mannered creatures devoid of ambition. Mircea had been the former, Radu had been the latter. As for himself, Dracula would rather he had died as a boy, even at the hands of the Ottomans, than be as he was now.

The campaign had come to a disastrous end when the young Polish king Ladislas had ignored Hunyadi's counsel and attacked the Sultan's position. Perhaps Ladislas had real-

Dracula's Match

ized his error when his horse was cut down from under him and he lay on the ground, helpless to defend himself. Perhaps, while the twenty-year-old trembled, realizing his very life was at stake, the Sultan had congratulated himself that his enemy had snatched defeat from the jaws of victory. What had gone through that young king's head as the Suntan's order was given to separate it from his neck?

The same things which ran through yours, perhaps? Dracula doubted it. The young king might have entertained hopes of rescue, given that his forces were not far afield. Or else capture and ransom. A king's ransom. It would have cost Poland a fortune, but that was one of the reasons for levying taxes: to ransom kings taken in battle. Dracula had had no such hopes for himself. Instead, a miraculous and horrifying series of thoughts had flashed through his mind at the end. Somehow, they'd all popped in simultaneously, with time to spare, despite the swiftness of his beheading. He'd even had time to wonder—*very briefly*—on the fate of his son and his country before his head rolled. Not time to think much, but to realize that his entire life was about to amount to absolutely nothing at all, whereas every single decision he had ever made was about to matter to his eternal soul.

But that was all very, very long ago, and it was a waste of his time to ruminate on what-ifs. The past was an unchangeable, ineffaceable monument to whatever legacy any man made for himself, and no one had the power to erase it once the thread of his life was cut.

How curious that everyone feared death, yet no one spent much time preparing for that singular, inescapable event; nor reflected that they must all, every one, one day stare Death in the face. He had known all his life, and yet, somehow, it had still snuck up on him.

Despite his disinterest in ruminating, he had gone and done it anyway, and now his attention was drawn to movement coming under the doors, and the distinctly unpleasant stench of death. He and a few agents had chosen to wait by the main entrance, and a mist was insinuating itself into the building. He stepped back, not desiring to come into contact with it. One of the agents moved more slowly, and Dracula grabbed the man by the back of his shirt to haul him out of the way. He clapped his hand over the man's mouth before he could blurt some pointless protest.

The two others retreated as the mist came pouring in. Dracula sequestered himself and the agent behind the registers to observe. He released the man. The agent grimaced at the smell, and gagged despite himself.

"What now?" the agent demanded hoarsely, after wiping the tears from his eyes. Dracula glared at him, then knelt down. He did not know how well Mr. Thorirsson could see while in that form, but it wasn't impossible he might have missed the few people inside.

The mist coalesced, piling atop itself until it took form. Mr. Thorirsson's once elegant funeral garb was torn and ragged now. He looked like a deranged pauper in those tatters. He did not seem to mind that he was nearly naked; he simply scanned the empty space. The agents on the far side had chosen to follow Dracula's example and hide themselves from view. Dracula ducked completely out of sight as the dead, milky eyes swept his way. After a moment, he peered over the counter to see how Mr. Thorirsson was getting on.

Dracula's Match

The draugr had spotted the sign Special Services had put up stating the museum was closed and apologizing for the inconvenience. He seemed to read it, then take in the silent space. In a rage, he snatched the sign and effortlessly twisted the metal stand on which it had been placed into a haphazard circle. He hurled it into the ceiling with a roar of anger and disgust, then stormed off.

Dracula and the other agents pursued at a safe distance. The rooms inside the museum were quite devoid of hiding spaces now that there were no exhibits, so they used doorways. Mr. Thorirsson dashed to the nearest pile of semi-purposefully arranged trash and considered it. To Dracula's eyes, it was no different than any display of modern so-called "art" but the sight of it certainly gave Mr. Thorirsson pause. He began to smash and destroy what was there.

"What's he doing?" the agent beside Dracula's elbow hissed. Dracula glared at him.

Mr. Thorirsson occupied himself in that way for some time, but at last ran out of items to destroy and made his way towards the entrance. There remained the possibility he might hunt for people or another destination, so whether he liked it or not, Dracula now had to delay him as long as he could.

He stepped through the doorway to call attention to himself. The draugr hesitated, seeing someone in an otherwise dark and abandoned building, but the surprise didn't hold him for long. He charged like a raging bull. Dracula waited until the optimal moment to grab the man and trip him down onto the floor to pin him. He had had not turned into mist the last time Dracula had wrestled him; perhaps once he was held that transformation was denied him.

As before, Mr. Thorirsson proved rusty when it came to actually fighting, and soon both his arms were pinned. Dracula had his arms and legs wrapped around the man's two arms. The draugr could still get up and walk around, but if he did not change shape or size, he ought to be far less dangerous. The draugr roared in his rage and rolled over and over—something an ordinary man would have had trouble doing in an attempt to dislodge Dracula. He tried slamming his opponent against the nearest wall, and though his attempt was awkward, the force was considerable. Dracula supposed that rage was the only reason Mr. Thorirsson didn't simply get up and walk away—carrying Dracula along to a better location outside to dislodge him. He had to struggle to keep his grip as the draugr continued to slam him into the floor and the wall.

He hadn't fought an adversary so strong in centuries. He'd nearly forgotten what it was like to struggle to overpower an opponent since the sudden increase of his strength in the 1990s. That testified to the extraordinary power the draugr possessed. The growing danger was that much more prolonged exposure to the monster's evil aura might prove enough to make him just as stupidly driven by rage. If or when that happened, he was likely to release his hold and attempt to fight his opponent. And in the morning the museum would be painted with his blood—a result he did not wish to experience twice. He could not afford to succumb to blind rage against a foe so much stronger than himself *again*. This was not a personal fight, after all. He strained against the draugr's strength. If he pulled hard, maybe he could yank the monster's arms out of their sockets. He'd *love* to hear that satisfying *pop*.

Dracula's Match

Then the agent who had not moved quickly out of the way earlier came out from behind the doorway, holding up his phone to record the situation. In his other hand, he held up his walkie talkie.

"… looks like he's stuck for now. We could try to move him."

"Copy that."

"You got him?" the agent called to Dracula.

"Not for very much longer—*oof!*—but—yes," he growled in answer, between slammed impacts against the wall.

"Ten minute ride, maybe?"

Ah, at last, a *plan* that might help. Dracula thought he could last ten minutes. Only just. Much longer and he would seriously consider killing that idiot the next time he opened his mouth. The inhuman strength that the imaginations of modern men had granted him would make breaking the bones in the idiot's face to splinters all the easier. He so very rarely had the excuse to make use of the unwanted change.

A few moments later, more agents wearing flashlights on their belts or heads came into the room. They had heavy-duty cables in loops to tighten around the monster's limbs. The draugr did not tolerate them near his feet, but one of them managed to get a loop around one of his pinned arms and called out that he was "secure." Dracula wanted to laugh at the idea, and demonstrate how he felt about the currently "secured" monster with a fist to the man's face. Something pulled on the cable and he and the draugr began steadily sliding across the floor. Mr. Thorirsson roared, sat up despite the pull, and dragged his feet on the smooth floor. He could not find good traction, and was dragged towards the entrance despite his continued struggling.

Once they were outside, Dracula could see Mr. Thorirsson was attached to a custom winch inside the back of a large, sturdy-looking transport vehicle of some industrial sort. A fair idea, but he foresaw that the draugr would likely use the car itself for leverage to break free. In fact, Mr. Thorirsson did exactly that. Once he could set a foot against the back of the vehicle, he strained against the winch. The cable pulled taut and sang under the strain.

The agents who spotted this cursed at each other, yelling accusations of lack of foresight. Seeing this was going to end in failure, Dracula took the risk of letting go with one hand and grabbing hold of the top of the vehicle to lift Mr. Thorirsson off his feet. They both tumbled inside the holding cell, with a roar of frustration from Mr. Thorisson. The sudden movement loosened Dracula's grip on the dead man.

Dracula struggled to reposition himself while the gate at the back of the vehicle slammed shut and locked. A command was shouted to "Drive, drive, drive!" and the truck started with a lurch. The winch pulled Roar upright and finally ceased tightening. He struggled against the cable as Dracula regained his hold. At last, Mr. Thorirsson had the inspiration to carefully slip his wrist out of the loop, and freed himself from the winch. The next moment, he slammed Dracula into the wall of the truck.

His movements were awkward, given that he could not make good use of his arms, but he tried again, undaunted. The vehicle wobbled under the strange movements, and the draugr struggled to keep his balance, ultimately falling to his knees. For all his strength, inability to feel pain, and other advantages, there were still laws of physics he could not overcome, it seemed.

Dracula's Match

Dracula assumed that Special Services had taken the time to block traffic and clear the route for them to Lake View, so the ride ought not to take as long as ten minutes. If he could keep unbalancing the draugr, this just might work. Once they got to the cemetery he would have to knock or roll the dead man into his grave, and if fire-starting agents were at hand, the dead man would soon be truly dead. It would be a temptation to kick the headstone to rubble once it was all over. He himself would need a long walk after this to cool down. He could feel that well of rage rising again, an external force becoming internal.

"Who *are* you?"

The dead man could *talk!* That would have been useful to know earlier, though Dracula didn't see much point to conversation now.

"I killed you! Why are you still here?"

"Don't take it to heart. Many men have thought they'd killed me, only to be disappointed afterwards."

Mr. Thorirsson roared in anger, lunged to the front of the container, then launched himself at the doors at the back, smashing them with his head and shoulders. Dracula was not indestructible, but more than that, neither was the truck. No doubt Special Services had armored the vehicle to the best that modern science allowed, but joints, hinges, locks, and so forth would always be weak points in any defense.

The truck rocked from the impact, so Dracula assumed the driver was aware that something was happening back here, but he could not communicate with anyone. If he reached for his phone, he would be dislodged by Mr. Thorirsson. Besides which, the draugr liked to bite, and he did a great deal of damage when he did. Dracula had no desire to be short an arm or leg again.

The draugr repeated the battering ram attack against the back doors, and Dracula realized they were not likely to reach the cemetery.

Under the third assault, the doors banged open, and the both of them flew backwards out of the truck. Dracula could not afford to be ground up under the wheels of a vehicle, so he let go. Not a moment too soon, for he collided with a government vehicle following behind and bounced up over the hood, against the bullet-proof windshield, then up and over. Finally, he hit the road, rolling as best he could to absorb the impact. If there was any hope left of regaining a hold on his enemy, he had to be ready immediately.

The government vehicle careened partly into the air, rolling over Mr. Thorirsson, who had gone under the wheels. The draugr's immunity to physical damage protected him, and he launched the car into the air and sideways into a concrete apron beneath a bridge overhead. But he hadn't regained his footing, so Dracula sprinted for him.

The draugr heard him coming, bared his teeth, and swelled to thirty feet tall. Dracula skidded to a stop, but could not get away before Thorirsson reached down and grabbed him. Dracula wasn't looking forward to another round of being torn apart, but it seemed Thorirsson had learned that doing so did not kill him, and so instead the giant climbed up over the walls, crossed the freeway, through parking lots and past some buildings. Lake Union appeared as a great, black space twinkling at its edges from the city lights, disappearing into the fog.

The draugr hurled Dracula as far out over the water as he

could with a roar of rage and disgust. Dracula plunged deep into the water, but rose to the surface quickly. He craned his neck to see what Mr. Thorirsson would do. The draugr simply melted into the rest of the mist and disappeared.

Brian was awakened by someone tapping on the plastic bar which kept him from rolling out of the hospital bed. As though he could or would. His side felt like he was being ripped open every time he breathed, and he didn't even want to think about moving. He had been trying to sleep through the pain—managing some sort of weird state of semi-conscious unconsciousness within which he didn't dream and sounds seemed louder than ever, but he felt somewhat detached from the throbbing in his head, shoulder, and side. The tapping popped him clean out of that state like a snapping rubber band.

A pair of strangers stood beside his bed. A man and a woman. Male had short hair, premature gray at the temples, a few acne scars. The female had her hair tightly tied back. They were dressed in nondescript T-shirts and jeans; clean, hardly worn clothes. Both of them wore sunglasses; the male wore his behind his head and looked like a school principal turning his cap backwards to make friends with the middle schoolers, while the female wore hers on top of her head.

"Hey, how are you?" the male asked.

"Don't think I know you," Brian answered.

"We're here to check how your memory is."

Brian made a point of looking at the outfits the pair had chosen to wear.

"Visiting consultants," the male said. "We hear you have amnesia?"

"I don't remember what happened, if that's what you mean," Brian lied. He actually didn't remember exactly what happened after the dead guy pulled off the car door to get at Cammy. But he remembered everything leading up to that, and figured it was better to say he didn't remember anything than to explain that a dead man had showed up and ruined Dracula's vehicle while another weirdo turned into a *freaking wolf*. Cammy was ok, which was a relief, but somehow he had to find out what was going on with her.

All that aside, he couldn't plug the two visitors into anything he'd seen or encountered or heard about, and with his head throbbing he was having a hard time coming up with theories.

"About how you got injured?" the male prompted.

"That's right," Brian said.

"What about a few nights ago. You were at Pike Place?"

Brian squinted at them both. Whoever these two were, they weren't cops. Didn't seem to be from any agency he could think of. But they weren't just asking questions. They were asking questions about two places where Brian knew the dead guy had gone. "Yeah," he said.

"You remember what happened there?"

"Some tweaker went on a rampage. I got in the way."

"In your call to 911, you were saying that tweaker flipped a car. Sounds like things were pretty scary down there."

"Yeah, adrenaline can do that. Plus, I'd been at a bar with a friend."

"You didn't mention you were drunk."

Brian squinted at the guy.

"Well, sounds like you already know what happened," he said.

Dracula's Match

"So, you didn't think there was anything… *odd* about what you saw?"

"Big lunatic," Brian said. "Yeah, I got a little rattled."

"You didn't see him flip a car?"

"I don't know what I saw," Brian told him. Whoever this guy was, he figured it was best to keep a low profile. "Maybe the car hit something."

The male glanced at the female. He pulled his wallet and retrieved a card from inside. He held it up to Brian's face.

"Look, if you remember anything, and you feel you'd like to talk about it—or better yet—do something about it, let us know."

Brian's head hurt too much to scrutinize the card, but all it had was a phone number.

"It's always nice to find people who know when to keep their mouth shut," the male said. He laid the business card on the little serving tray beside Brian's head, then he nodded at his female partner and they headed out the door.

About twenty seconds later, Akerman came sneaking furtively into Brian's room, casting a glance over his shoulder at the two inexplicable visitors as he did so.

"Hey, man," Akerman said.

Brian considered him, and the timing of his visit. "You were avoiding those two. You know them. Do they know you?"

Akerman pressed his lips together. He set a get well card on the serving tray. Brian saw it signed by his coworkers, and that they had largely addressed it to "Bratula." That was the nickname that had stuck to him since he arrested Cammy's host earlier in the year and everyone heard what the creep's name was. He didn't have the energy to grimace.

"Do they?" Brian pressed.

"I told you to keep your head down," Akerman said.

"Well, I'm stuck in a hospital right now, and I'll bet it has something to do with that walking dead guy and Cammy's housemate."

Akerman hugged himself and nodded at Brian. "They keep an eye on things. You don't want to mess with them."

"But who are they?"

"No one you should trust."

"*You're* not talking like someone I can trust. And I know you know what's been going on."

"Warren—"

"I bet you know more about the Count up there than you've let on, too."

"Warren—"

"Am I wrong?"

Akerman glanced at the blinds blocking out the gray outside.

"So it was *you* who made that call. *You* called those spooks! You owe me for all the trouble that caused. And now I've got all the gear from his car when I arrested him. His weird, goth, vampire-hunting props, only they're not props. Solid. And he's got Cammy."

"Warren—"

"If you're my friend, I need your help, and I'm calling in your debt."

"Help with what?"

"Like I said, I've got his vampire hunting equipment," Brian told him. "And I need to return it."

CHAPTER 12
RESTING PLACES

By the time Dracula fished himself out of the lake and returned to the truck, Special Services agents were making calls, radio'ing orders, and receiving orders. The rage he'd felt being near the monster had dissipated. Or else the cold swim had cooled him off. They'd allowed traffic to resume, though flares had been set out so no one would hit the ruined government vehicle. The truck was nowhere to be seen; likely it had been driven back to its warehouse.

"Way to fumble the ball," one of the agents snarked at him.

"Where has he gone?" Dracula asked.

"We have no idea," the agent replied.

He was getting tired of incompetence. Fortunately, he had other resources. Cammy, upset as she was by everything that had happened, had nonetheless demonstrated she was capable of useful insights. He approached the disrespectful agent.

"I need your phone," he said.

"Not now, I'm—hey!"

Amaya Tenshi

Dracula pulled the man's phone from his pocket. It was an old-fashioned one, like his, so he dialed Cammy. She didn't answer, so he dialed again. She had told him she didn't pick up calls she didn't recognize. The third time, she picked up.

"Hello?" she asked.

"Cammy, do you know the next location Mr. Thorirsson might visit?"

"What happened? I thought he was going to the Museum of Pop Culture?"

"He already went there. At the moment, he has disappeared."

"Um, let me check…" she said. He waited for her to find what she was looking for. The agent whose phone he had taken glared at him, but did not ask for it back. "Looks like either the Chihuly glass place, or the Ferris wheel."

"I have my doubts about both of those locations. He was at the waterfront a few days ago and did not touch the Great Wheel, and did not go to the glass museum while near the Space Needle."

"Well, maybe he really is going back through his timeline? So he'll go to them now?"

"Hmm." Dracula considered that possibility. "He would have a good memory of the order he visited these places?"

"I dunno about that. But maybe he has his phone?"

Dracula laughed aloud at the idea. Could a draugr use modern phones? In any case, he thanked her for her contribution, slapped the phone shut and pushed it into the agent's chest to return it. The agent glared at him as he relayed the other possible locations.

"We'll send people. Way to cost us the best chance we had of getting this thing. The whole city's going to explode soon if we don't get this solved. We're all working overtime to try to clean up these messes."

"How fortunate for you," Dracula said. "I understand that overtime pays well. Moreover, it means your job security is assured."

The agent scowled.

"I wish to change out of these clothes," Dracula said.

"We need you to be available whenever we locate him again."

"So alert me when you do." He took back the agent's phone, ignoring his renewed protests. "My phone wet. Call this one."

He walked off.

Cammy couldn't sleep. She settled herself in the middle of the bed and returned to scrolling through online chats and videos about Roar. Hours later, she spotted headlights pulling up to the mansion, so she went downstairs.

Dracula's clothes were damp, wrinkled, and torn in places, and his hair was disheveled, but at least he wasn't missing any body parts.

"What happened?" she asked, as he swung the door shut behind him. It was nearly 3 am. The draugr ought to be running around somewhere.

"It escaped, and I haven't received a call yet as to—what are you wearing?"

Cammy looked down at herself.

"My pajamas," she said. He stared at her, eyebrows slowly descending into a furrow.

"You came downstairs to greet me... in a state of undress?" he asked, very flatly. That flat-edge tone from before.

"It's a T-shirt and pants. I'm not *undressed*," she shot back.

"You uncultured harlot," he snarled, and as she opened her mouth to protest, he stormed past her up the stairs, grumbling in some non-English language. Once he had disappeared, she heard an upstairs door swing open, more silence, then the door shut in not quite a *slam*. He came back down the stairs carrying a robe.

"At the *least*," he growled, and shoved it at her. She took the robe.

"This is fancy," she observed, and put it on. It didn't fit at all, and she realized it must be one of his.

"Silk," he said. "If you have nothing of your own, I will purchase something for you."

Or maybe I'll just keep your fancy robe, Mr. 'state of undress,' she thought. How stuffy could someone be? "It's just PJs," she said. He raised a hand, seemingly unwilling to look at her.

"I will overlook this indecency and disrespect on account of the fact that most Americans are uncultured, uneducated peasants. Don't do it again."

"But it's no big deal—"

"Have some self-respect, if only for your own sake!" he snapped at her. "The self-respect to dress yourself before greeting someone at the door! What have you people *come to?!*"

Whatever, she thought. What a dumb thing to get upset over. People wore pajamas outside to go shopping, or to classes. They were comfortable. Dracula's clothes looked nice, but they couldn't be anywhere near as comfortable. She'd never seen *him* wearing a robe. She wasn't brave enough to go looking for him when he disappeared during the day. The robe smelled of mothballs, maybe, and smoke. She didn't smell any body odor at all, for which she was grateful. Maybe he didn't sweat. Which made as much sense as anything else.

"So… draugr escaped?"

"He is very hard to hold," Dracula said. "And once he breaks free, he can change size or turn to mist. Given the lateness of the hour, I expect that—"

An old-fashioned ring tone interrupted him. He pulled a flip phone from his breast pocket. Whoever had called him didn't wait for him to answer, but apparently just opened with some sort of tirade which Dracula listened to patiently. At last he grunted some sort of non-committal reply, shut the phone, and said, "He retrieved his wife's corpse and ran off with it. No one knows where he is now."

Special Services wanted him to see the destruction Mr. Thorirsson had wrought when he came for his wife's body, so he drove over. Perhaps he would learn something useful.

Modern medicine fascinated and repulsed him in equal measure, but the clinical disregard for the subjects of its study invariably troubled him. Perhaps it was sentimentality on his part: a wish for dignity for the dead, whatever his motives for that desire might be.

The place was not utterly in disarray, as he had been led to believe over the phone. Two of the ceiling lights had been smashed, showering the floor with stardust-sized fragments of glass, and some of the adjustable lights overhead had also been pulled down. Some of these had been thrown, but one had been used as a weapon to bludgeon a Special Services' agent to an unrecognizable pulp. Well, not utterly unrecognizable. One side of his head was untouched, and Dracula could recognize the scars marring the short hair. The one who had mocked him a few nights ago and taken a shot at the draugr at the Space Needle.

"Sorry."

Dracula turned to see the other agent, who was likely this one's partner, standing nearby. He seemed unharmed.

"Sorry?" Dracula repeated.

"About him," the dhampir gestured at the dead agent. Dracula had neither the interest, nor the inclination to assuage the man's conscience.

"Be sorry for yourself, instead," he told the dhampir.

Something flickered in the dhampir's eyes. "I'm not like you," he said. "I die just fine, and stay dead." The agent looked down at his fallen comrade. Dracula wasn't interested in excuses for cowardice.

Boese had taken a page from Ophois' book of operations—folk born and bred for one's organization who had no legal standing, who had been raised in a cage, were easier to rely on. That had been the idea behind janissaries, more or less. Except that janissaries might earn their freedom, while Ophois and Special Services offered their experiments no such hope. But it seemed that Boese had not managed to produce brave soldiers, for all his machinations. Perhaps that was why his organization was so full of incompetents.

"Neill, get over here," one of the human agents called to the surviving dhampir. Neill glanced over, cast his eyes on his dead companion, and then looked up to Dracula. Looking for comfort, perhaps? Direction? Guidance? Judgment? Dracula wasn't certain. He gave the man nothing. It was foolish to think of janissaries as though they were still one's own family. Neill slunk off to the others.

Dracula made a quick survey of the rest of the scene, but saw nothing particularly helpful.

"And *this* is what happens when you fumble the ball," said one of the agents. The same one whose phone he still held. That must be a catchphrase of his. Dracula pulled the phone from his pocket and dialed Cammy in full view of the agent.

"What happened?"

"About what I expected," Dracula told her. "This move indicates he can reason."

"What do you mean?" she asked.

"Despite his rage, he must have thought about the situation and come to the conclusion that there were people who were prepared for him at his intended destination, people who had the resources to combat him. He may have reasoned that such people would know what his treasure was, so he abandoned his mission of destroying parts of the city to guard her. He is also able to speak."

"Really!"

"He is capable rational thought," Dracula said. "Which in turn means that finding him will be enormously difficult."

"So we need to figure out where he might go with her body?" Dracula could hear the queasy tone in her voice. Still, she pressed on. An admirable trait. "Did you figure out if he had his phone with him?"

Ah yes, that question. He made another search of the place. He found an outlet near the fridges where the bodies were kept, and spotted a charger plugged into it, but no phone attached. He fingered the cable.

"Who does this belong to?" he asked the agent whose phone he was using. The man was trailing him, studying what he was doing. Probably to make a detailed report to be used in some further psychological profile, but Dracula did not care.

"Not sure. One of the coroners?" the agent suggested.

"Find out. There must be security footage, surely?"

"We're going over that. You think that matters?"

"It might," Dracula told him. To Cammy, "See what you can determine. I will call you back."

He pocketed the agent's phone again, and waved him off.

There was a vending machine outside the morgue, and though he despised the cheap food he needed to take the edge off his hunger. He purchased several bags of horrible-tasting chips and a little plastic bottle of pasteurized milk which tasted vile to him, then he found a bench outside the morgue on which to sit and wait.

The "fumble" agent came to find him at last.

"Draugr was coming here each night as mist," he said. "Hard to see on the footage unless you're looking for it. He poured up into that fridge and only left at night."

"What about that charger?"

"You gotta look really close, but it looks like once he got in the fridge, the door pops open just a little. We checked: Laura's phone was taken out of evidence. Not sure when."

*Not **his** phone*, Dracula realized. The couple's "timeline" ought to be similar, but there may be differences. He dialed Cammy and let her know.

"Oh, *hers?*" Cammy said. "Hang on, let me see…"

He waited patiently. Even if they found where Mr. Thorirsson was now hiding, the trouble would be stopping the drau-

Dracula's Match

gr at all. Flushing him out of his new hiding place would be a terrible idea; it would merely trigger another rampage. And transporting him back to his grave looked like an impossibility. Just that short jaunt in a vehicle intended to contain him had failed before they'd even gone halfway. If Mr. Thorirsson materialized in some location even farther away, they stood no chance.

"Well, if he's going to destroy someplace, then the Japanese Garden might be next," she said. "But I don't know where he might hide."

He wondered that himself.

"That's kind of sad," Cammy said.

"What is?"

"I mean, this all happened because his marriage was falling apart. I guess… even after everything, he still loves her. Like you said."

"I believe you are correct," Dracula said. "His reaction to his wife's infidelity was homicidal madness. He was already disenfranchised from and disenchanted with modern culture"—something he himself understood all too well—"and his sense of betrayal overwhelmed his reason. But yes, he still loves her, and as such, she is his treasure. He will have to take her somewhere remote and secluded."

"So not his apartment?"

"Special Services have their eyes on his residence as well as his grave. Someplace else."

"Lemme see…"

He waited once more for her to look for an answer.

"Oh, I have a crazy idea," she said. "They got married up on Poo Poo Point. Real married, not the staged thing he did on air for wrestling. That place is pretty remote, right?"

It certainly was. There would be hikers to contend with if Mr. Thorirsson craved solitude, but police were unlikely. He could theoretically kill any hapless individual or group of hikers without authorities being alerted.

"Keep looking. If you see anything more likely, call me back. Thank you."

He hung up and relayed this information to "Fumble" waiting nearby.

"We'll send people up there—"

"No." Dracula emphasized that with a slicing motion of his hand. He dialed Boese. "Director, I believe I know where your monster may be. Send agents to redirect hikers away from the place he made his marriage vows."

"What do you think you're doing, calling me and telling me—"

"At this point, it is clear your organization is stretched to the breaking point. If more people die, you will have a more difficult time concealing the matter from the public. All you have been able to accomplish so far is to clean up after this monster's messes, and you have no idea how to actually *stop him*. To that end, I need you to release Malcolm."

"The werewolf? He's in no shape to do anything, and he can't fight that thing any better than you can."

"I need his expertise."

"Call his people."

"I don't talk directly with the warlocks who run that organization," Dracula said.

"I need him for the exact same reason."

Dracula let out a deep sigh of frustration.

"Director, you are meddling with things you don't understand."

"Listen, friend: I've studied this stuff. I know about all their hocus-pocus and—"

"As a man of no faith, you have no idea what you're meddling with. If you will not release my ally *I* need to find a permanent solution to this trouble. As such, I am returning to my estate to see what I can find out. Tell your men not to engage with the monster or antagonize him."

"My men are professional—"

"Your men are useless, so far as I've seen. They underestimate Mr. Thorrisson's strength and resolution, and they have no comprehension of the faith that moves or moved him. Let a man who understands Mr. Thorrisson's longing and mentality take the reins, Director. I will contact you once I have an idea."

"You can't tell me—"

Dracula hung up. He pushed past Fumble without relinquishing his phone, to return to the quiet of his estate—and think.

Cammy scrolled through Laura's social media for clues. Mid-morning, Dracula returned. He found her in the kitchen, where she was making a grilled cheese sandwich. He poured himself a glass of milk.

"Do you know how to fire a gun?" he asked. She blinked at him.

"No."

"We shall have to remedy that," he said. "Did you find anything else?"

"I don't want to use guns," Cammy told him. "And no."

He grunted and drank the milk. He set down the empty glass and tapped his mouth to think.

"No matter what else happens, we must find a way to put him in his grave to kill him," he said. "The only way I can think to do it is to steal his wife's body and make him chase her back to his grave, then set him alight." He grimaced at the idea.

"He has to be set on fire?"

"Yes."

"That's funny."

He frowned at her.

"Well, you know, Vikings wanted to be buried in a boat and set on fire, right?"

Dracula answered with a small shrug.

"Considering how seriously he took his Viking roots, I'm surprised he didn't put it in his will to be burned at sea," Cammy said, showing him an illustration of a small Viking boat on the ocean, visibly laden with gold and a funeral pyre burning brightly she'd pulled up on her phone.

"Malcolm said these monsters could not cross running water, though I have my doubts, given that he has clearly traveled across waterways. Perhaps we could lure him onto a boat and simply set that alight."

"He could have gone underground, under the water," Cammy pointed out. "Or maybe he can cross water if he's transported. He can turn into mist and change his size, right? So he could have misted into someone's car, then shrunk or something so they wouldn't notice? You said he can think at least a little?"

"It would be much more difficult to travel with his wife's body, but he might have managed to sneak atop a larger vehicle that was going in a desired direction. If that is how he travels, then I doubt we can lure him onto a boat. He would have to be carried onto it. But that gives me an idea. You are certain that such an immolation might appeal to him?"

"I dunno. But it was a thing for Vikings, right?"

"Please double-check that." He went out the back door, and Cammy wondered how to double-check. She could look it up, but then she remembered that Andrew might know. She'd heard him and Aslan discussing Viking shows they both watched. And now Andrew knew what the deal was. She could just call him.

"Hello?"

Good, he answered his phone now. "Hey, Andrew, hope you're feeling better. Um, I have some questions about Vikings."

Silence. Then, "What?"

It occurred to her that she really could just talk to Andrew about what was going on. No need to lie, no need to hide anything. The realization hit her so hard tears began to roll down her face.

"Cammy?" he said.

"Sorry, it's just… I haven't been able to tell anyone what was going on," she said. "I haven't been able to tell anyone about Heather. What really happened. Or with my parents, or anything." She started sobbing.

There was a long silence on the other end.

"I'm fine," she said, and wiped her eyes. "I'm fine. Sorry. It just… it's a relief to have someone to talk to. But not now. That's not why I called. You *do* know something about Vikings, right? The real life ones?"

"A little," he confessed. "Why?"

She brought him up to speed on what she and Dracula had found and why she was asking.

When Dracula got back, she was able to tell him that Vikings usually got buried, but occasionally they did the boat thing.

He frowned, then said, "There would be no way to have a boat of size ready by this evening, but I may have a solution regardless." He nodded to her. "Well done."

She stared at him. He seemed not to notice, and went to his office. Once inside, he made a call. She smiled to herself. *Well done. Ha!*

When Dracula finished the call and emerged from the office, he waved to someone behind Cammy, and she turned to see Trausti and Fjola standing hesitantly in the doorway to the kitchen. They were dressed like normal children, and it took her a moment to recognize them. Trausti wore a T-Shirt and jeans, while Fjola wore a knit dress and tights. Cammy shook her head at Dracula.

"Ok, I'm serious. I don't want... I'm *not* going to have slaves. That is so inhumane."

"That was what they agreed to as payment for the failings of their people. They agreed to those terms. Their word is binding. Take them to your room and let them become familiar with you and your needs."

"I don't want that, don't you understand?!" Cammy shouted, slamming her palms on the table and jumping to her feet.

"This is my estate, and you are my guest," he told her. "As master here, I may make decisions as to who or what may stay here, and under what conditions."

"But you can't *force* your decisions on *me!*" she shouted. "That's not ok!"

Dracula's Match

"If you don't wish for their service, then I would be pleased to have them serve me instead," he told her.

She gulped and looked to the two children. He'd impaled a woman for not making a shirt correctly. She couldn't let him have that kind of authority over them. She glared at him, then stormed from the table, taking both the children by the hands and leading them up to her room in a huff.

Once there, she ushered them inside, shut the door, and locked it with her room key. She sat on her heels to speak to them.

"Ok, as far as I'm concerned, you guys aren't slaves, all right? You can live here and just do whatever you want."

"But if we don't do as we are told, we will be in trouble?" the girl asked. Her voice was high and thin, her accent thicker than her brother's.

"Don't worry," Cammy assured the girl.

"But if we do not please his majesty, my people will be in danger," Trausti explained.

Cammy sighed. "Look, you guys *will* be doing what I said, right? Because I told you to do whatever you wanted." She shook her head. "I can't *believe* him."

"He was wery merciful," Trausti said. "In exchange for a little labor from us, he let us stay, even though we wronged him and you."

"Slavery is *not* a little labor," Cammy said, "and it's *not* ok. He wants you both to be my servants with no pay, having to do whatever I say, until you both die."

"Only, until *you* die," Trausti corrected. "Humans do not live long. So it is not so burdensome. You will be dead more quickly than you think."

Well *that* put things in a certain perspective. She stood up, looking down at him. He didn't seem to realize what he'd said, or why it would bother her.

"That still doesn't make it right," she insisted.

"We were already slaves," Trausti said. "Our father died, and so we were sent to live with my uncle. We owe him a debt for raising us and feeding us. If we work for you, it would be better. You would not demand such a debt from us?"

"You… what? Why would your uncle do that?"

"It is the custom. The humans used to do the same in our homeland to any *niðursetningur*."

"Nih… ?"

"Someone sent to live elsewhere. We are fatherless," Trausti explained, "sent to our uncle."

"Are you orphans?" Cammy asked.

"Our mother remains in our homeland. She is with another branch of the family."

"If your mother is alive, then why don't you live with her?"

"That is not the custom. Her belongings were sold to prowide for our care."

"That's *ridiculous!*" Cammy exclaimed.

Trausti shrugged. "It is the custom."

"And your uncle brought you here? He didn't think you'd want to be with your mother?"

"What good would it be to stay with her? She is a laborer now, also. Our grandfather and uncle came here because the ways of our homeland are changing. The humans do not truly believe in us any longer. And now some humans are trying to bring back the pagan practices of the past."

Dracula's Match

"Pagan… but wouldn't that be good for you? You guys are *elves*," Cammy pointed out.

Trausti nodded. "We are. But we accepted the new religion after the humans did. If they return to the old ways, then…" he pursed his lips together, "so will we. Our Queen of would become… less kind." He looked out the window. When he turned back, he straightened up as tall as he could. "So don't feel bad for us. It is better this way. We work wery hard. You seem kind, we are sure you will be a gentle mistress."

"I am *not* your mistress," Cammy told him. "Don't call me that, it's weird. Um, if it's some cultural thing, fine. But I mean it. You guys can do whatever you want."

Fjola looked distressed.

"What we want is to find a good place to settle and build a new home," Trausti said. "That is why we came. His majesty will let us build a church on the grounds."

A church?! Cammy thought. They really were *Christian* elves?! How weird was that? First Dracula, now *elves*. Absolutely ridiculous.

"Ok, well, you both go have fun, ok?"

"Will you give us our food for the week?" Trausti fetched a wooden bowl with a hinged lid from his clothing and held it open.

"What?"

"It is the custom for the mistress—"

"*Please* don't call me that."

"To give out the food to the laborers once a week," Trausti finished. "Most give it more often."

"You can have food whenever you want. You guys hungry? There's some mushroom soup left."

They both nodded. Cammy escorted them both back downstairs. As she passed the big fireplace on the ground floor on her way to the kitchen, she spotted a new portrait hung up above it. It looked like that famous one she'd seen online. She squinted at it. It was obviously the portrait the elves had talked about, but in light of recent events, a thought popped into her mind. *It really is a kind of a selfie.*

Her host wasn't in the kitchen, so she went to the pot. It was still warm, as was the stove. She fetched some china bowls and spoons for them both. Fjola reached to take them, and Cammy almost passed them over before she realized the girl might be trying to act as a "slave", so she told her,

"Just sit at the table, ok? I'll get this."

The little girl fidgeted with her fingers, but slunk to the table.

"She doesn't talk much," Cammy observed to her brother.

"She does not feel confident about your language," Trausti explained. "She is still learning."

"Learning?" Cammy gave that some thought. She set a bowl of soup in front of Fjola, gestured for Trausti to sit, then set one before him. They both bowed their heads and Trausti prayed in his own language before they ate.

"What about school?" she asked them.

"We do not go to school. It would be nice if we become prosperous enough to build our own. In the meanwhile, we are taught to read and write. The pastor checks our progress."

"What about… you know, public school? Here? I mean, so long as you dress like everyone else, no one would know you guys aren't…"

Dracula's Match

Trausti frowned with thought. "There are schools here?" he asked.

"Yeah. I mean, I'd have to get you guys fake IDs and maybe some more stuff, but I think we could manage it. That would be good, right?"

Trausti scratched his temple. "If you think so, we will try it," he agreed.

"*Not* because you're my slaves though, right?"

His bright eyes searched hers for a few moments.

"No," he said. "It would be nice for Fjola."

"Ok, let me see what I can do," she said, though the very next moment she realized she had *no* idea how to get fake IDs and whatever else she might need for them. Then she realized that Siri might know. She was pretending to be a human, right? She must have gotten some sort of documentation for herself. That would be something to ask Siri about the next time she went to class. Since the huldra was basically stalking her to get to Dracula, she might as well turn *something* to her advantage.

Her host came into the kitchen. He observed the children eating but made no comment.

"I will be out for this afternoon and evening," he said. "Do you need any transportation?"

"No." Cammy shook her head, shooting stink-eyes at him. "Nice portrait out there."

He shrugged.

"Selfies go way back, I guess," she said primly.

"If you mean to equate the costly and elite practice of posing for a portrait with your modern narcissistic trivialities, I refuse to agree."

"But that's what you did? Get someone to paint you?"

His eyes looked colder than slush inside her socks.

"Not at all," he said. "I posed for it. The painting itself was commissioned by someone else."

"What? Who?"

"King Matthias Corvinus, king of Hungary and son of the Royal Governor John Hunyadi."

"*Who?*"

He shook his head angrily.

She glanced to the doorway. She couldn't quite see the portrait over the mantle from here.

"It must mean something to you."

He shrugged.

"I mean, the elves brought it as a gift."

"It has been missing for some time."

"You said your… descendant had it?"

"In his possession. After his death, it went missing, because he was a worthless fool."

"What did he do?"

"He abdicated his throne to marry a gypsy girl."

"Aww, that's sweet," Cammy said. "You annoyed that he wasn't letting racism get the better of him?"

"On the contrary, she deserved better. She even had herself baptized for him. He had an affair one year later, and she died of a broken heart." Dracula added, "Then he died of syphilis."

Cammy bit her lip. "So…that's why you hate him?"

"He was an idiot who abandoned his responsibilities and his throne for some ridiculous ephemeral infatuation, which he promptly betrayed, to then die alone, in exile, of the great pox. He would be the greatest disappointment to have sprung from my loins but for the one who apostatized to *Islam*."

Dracula's Match

Cammy considered that. *Now I really don't want to have kids,* she thought. Next thing you knew, your kid or grandkid did something slimy like cheat on someone right after marrying them. Totally lame.

Dracula grunted and shook his head, as though to shake off the memories. "If you need nothing at the moment, then I shall depart. If I do not return, try to contact Malcolm. He may or may not be available. I have done what I can to see that he is."

"What if he isn't?"

Dracula eyed her, then looked out the window.

"If necessary, have one of your friends come up here to the estate. I'll speak to my tenants. But be certain to warn them not to wander, and *don't* invite Miss Quentin."

Cammy took a moment to figure out who he was talking about; referring to her friends by their surnames threw her through a loop.

"You mean Kenzie?"

"Yes. Do not invite her up here at any time, under any circumstances."

Cammy huffed. It was probably for the best that the vampire fan in her group of friends *didn't* come up here, but it was so like him to be rude about it.

Boese's men had done a fair job of redirecting hikers. Dracula encountered none as he made his way up one of the trails. He had already called Special Services to let them know to leave him be. Perhaps Boese would listen to him this time.

Mist and drizzle turned the picturesque walk gray, the woods alive with a muted chorus of gentle plinking droplets.

Blackberry bushes were bare of their fruit—harvest time having passed—and birds were silent. It was proving to be an unusually dry November, so this rainfall was welcome.

He walked to the knoll itself and waited. Beyond the pines and far below, the city and the sea looked gray under the clouds. His rain coat kept out most of the moisture, also the custom boots made to his specifications and needs. The brownies who made their home in his estate always kept the shoes in pristine condition. He suspected they did the same for Cammy, but he was not certain she had noticed.

After perhaps half an hour of nearly blissful solitary quietude, one of the elves appeared at his elbow.

"Did you find him?" he asked. The elf nodded.

He followed the elf through the woods to a cozy little spot just off one of the trails near to some tennis courts. He smelled Mr. Thorirsson before he spotted him. The draugr was sitting on a pine tree which had recently fallen, wedged between two other trees so that much of its trunk remained slightly elevated above the ground, serving as a makeshift bench. In his arms he held a very dead woman. He hadn't spotted his visitors yet—he stared blindly at nothing in particular, his long hair matted against his cheeks and across his shoulders. Dracula was not aware of any requirement that draugrs needed to be destroyed at a particular time of day, so he stepped forward, intentionally drawing attention to himself.

Mr. Thorirsson's milky eyes fixed on his movement instantly, and he jumped up, clutching his wife to his chest as a girl child might hold a doll she feared would be taken from her.

"A word with you, if I may," Dracula addressed him.

Dracula's Match

The milky eyes remained fixed, the lips frozen in a silent, animal-like snarl.

"Mr. Thorirsson. I am not here to fight. We will accomplish nothing if we do, as I think you know." The snarl remained fixed, but the draugr made no move. Dracula walked closer.

"Who are you?" the draugr demanded. His voice was hoarse, strained. He could speak quite plainly, but Dracula could hear that his throat resisted making sounds.

"You wouldn't believe me if I told you," Dracula told him. "For the moment simply trust that you can neither kill nor harm me. Neither can I harm or kill you. We have tested each other more than once."

"What do you want?"

At last, a demand that might lead to results.

"Mr. Thorirsson, I must inform you that you have come to a very bad end," Dracula told him. The draugr clutched his wife closer to himself. "I see you are aware of the situation."

"I didn't mean to," he said.

"No. Yet here we are."

"I was just... *so* angry. I got angrier so much easier after... after the first time. I tried to be careful. To only go with the others out in the woods. So we wouldn't kill anyone."

*Just **one** of the myriad reasons not to sell your soul for the opportunity to become a wolf*, Dracula thought. *Though Ophois may not have phrased the exchange that way. No doubt they had approached him with a proposition to live as the pagans he idolized had. Only for it to lead to this.*

Thorirsson's head dropped down onto his wife's. Dracula let him be for a space.

"Mr. Thorirsson, it's time to go."

The pale head rose again, the milky eyes considering him anew.

"I just... I wanted to... I wanted there to be a point."

"To existence?"

Thorirsson nodded.

"There is a point."

"I was trying to find it."

"I know."

Thorirsson peered through the trees. The drizzle had ended.

"What do I do now?" he asked.

"You know you can't go on like this. Neither of us can change the past."

Thorirsson looked at him.

"You're like me," he observed. "You met a bad end."

"I did."

Thorirsson lifted an errant strand of hair from his wife's face. Dracula could see it was battered. No doubt he had badly abused her in his berserking rage when he murdered her.

"I just wanted to make a difference. Have some point to my life. Do something."

"So do we all. It is more difficult in your times than it was in mine."

This took the draugr by surprise. He squinted at Dracula, no doubt wondering again who this man who had come to confront him might be. He left the fallen tree and made his way down to where Dracula stood, scrutinizing him with milky eyes.

"This is it, isn't it?" he asked.

"It is."

Dracula's Match

Thorirsson cradled his wife's body. She was starting to bloat. The time away from the morgue hadn't done her any good. What a shame that no family had come to claim the body. Only the man who had killed her in a rage of jealous fury had come for her.

"I wanted to go to Valhalla," Thorirsson murmured. "That sounded so much better than this. Too good to be true."

"I cannot say I don't see the appeal," Dracula said.

"What about you?"

"I don't believe in Valhalla. It's too simplistic a hereafter. It appeals too much to the brute in men. And I have known too many brutes to wish to persist in their company in such a place as they would prefer. For eternity that would be a form of Hell."

"Then what do you think will happen?"

Dracula looked to the ground.

"I cannot say. That is in the hands of God. Who is merciful."

Thorirsson squinted at him.

"You don't believe that."

"I want to believe. That even now… in this moment of twilight stretched for hundreds of years, perhaps…"

Thorirsson's laugh was sardonic. "Dad was a minister. He never convinced me."

"I am no minister. And I cannot say that I am now nor have ever been an exemplar of my faith. As for you, the only way you can end your current existence is to be wrestled into your own grave."

"My sister Elise must have picked Lake View. She was my biggest fan. Talked me into my whole career."

"Your sister loved you," Dracula agreed. "It is a blessing to have such siblings."

"Life wrestled me into my grave," Thorirsson said. "I guess it's still going to."

"Just so. To live is to endure suffering. Without hope…" Dracula turned towards the west. The sun was setting, and the clouds were clearing, though a haze lay over the city, obscuring where the buildings ended and the sea began. It would likely be a beautiful view at the knoll. He inclined his head that way in an invitation that Thorirsson come along.

He led the draugr to the knoll itself. The sun had turned the light golden, the sea sparkling with fire, the clouds glowing red and copper, the fog blending the city into it all. The elves had done what they could, and a makeshift boat was the result. It wasn't much, and not remotely seaworthy, but they had been able to port it this far. The fox and the tanukitsune had cast an illusion to make it appear like a real Viking ship.

Thorirsson stood, captivated by the sight, the whole world forgotten, his wife still clutched to his heart. Perhaps it was illusion, but the neck of the dragon head and the hull gleamed with the fire of sunlight, the red sail glowing like a great ember.

"What is that?"

"Your grave, if you wish," Dracula told him. "To spare you the journey back to Lake View."

"Who are you?"

Dracula answered with silence. Thorirsson stood studying him a moment more, but the sight of that red and yellow ship drew his white eyes. He stroked his wife's hair. Slowly, he walked towards it, steadily, nearly gliding, trancelike. He

Dracula's Match

came up beside it and stood, taking in the illusory image it represented. It appeared as a longship with shields lining its sides, a great sail billowing in the breeze. The whole vessel seemed ready to sail across clouds.

Thorirsson leaped aboard the phantom ship. The sunlight caught in his yellow hair and turned it to fire. His wife had bleached her hair blonde during her career, but it was now its natural dark brown. Even so, the sun illuminated strands of gold in it.

Thorirsson turned back. He bowed his head. Dracula inclined his head in a small bow in return. Then he motioned to the ship.

One of the elves came with a torch.

"You could come with me. You said you were like me. You came to a bad end, too," Thorisson called back.

"I don't know if we are for the same port," Dracula said. "But if we are, then I will join you later."

He signaled to the torchbearer, who put it to the wood.

The ship took to the flames with hungry abandon. Licking tongues of red flame devoured the wood as the horizon blazed with blood red sunlight spilling across the sea. Some of the elves came to watch. There might have been more about, but invisibly. They were proving useful, for what that was worth.

When the ship was little more than glowing embers and the sea was dark, with only an orange glow separating the black of the water from the dark blue of the sky, he called Boese's people to gather what remained and transport it. They were waiting for his say-so. A first, and a welcome one. They would come with their hazmat suits, flamethrowers, perhaps even Ophois agents, and do their best: gathering up what ash they could, and sterilizing or containing the area. He left that in their hands.

He turned to go to his vehicle and spotted the huldra standing amidst the trees, her arms crossed, her lightning eyes catching the remaining orange glow. When she saw he had spotted her, she came sauntering forward.

"I heard you vere coming here."

He did not think such a statement deserved a response.

"Ve vould bring charcoal to the men," Siri said. "I vished to bring you some. But you didn't need any." Her flashing eyes took in the dying light. "Vas that vhat you might call love?"

"Giving a dead man the only mercy I could? Yes. Such as it was."

Her eyebrows crinkled with thought. He nodded goodnight to her and went for his vehicle. Once he had reached it, one of the elves appeared near the door.

"May we live on your estate, then?"

"So long as you perform the tasks I put to you," he told the elder. "We will speak more on that after I have returned home." The elf bowed and vanished.

CHAPTER 13
HORIZONS

Several days later, Boese came up to the estate, alone.

Dracula met him at the door to prevent the man from getting up to more mischief, as he had done months earlier when Cammy had started her stay at the estate.

"I haven't an endless supply of teacups for you to throw around, Director. Or is there some other purpose which brings you here today?"

Boese glared at him and eyed the mansion's interior.

"Getting awful crowded up here," Boese commented.

"Is it?"

"You've got a colony of Icelandic elves, so I'm given to understand," Boese said. "How many?"

"I haven't an exact figure," Dracula said. "They don't all appear at once. Something like thirty in all." He observed Boese glancing here and there. "But you didn't come all this way to take a census of my tenants, Director."

Boese pushed inside.

"I should remind you that I did not appreciate your surliness on your last visit, and I am far less willing to be patient with you after this last debacle, especially on my estate," Dracula told him.

"You need to take a minute to think about your position before you go talking to me like that," Boese said. He made his way to the kitchen. Dracula followed him. There was something about his manner which seemed odd. Nervous? But the man was often nervous. Something else.

He watched Boese fetch a cup and then pour himself *țuica*. He glared at Dracula and took a sip.

"Where's your little friend?"

"I am letting my guest borrow one of my vehicles for her transportation needs," Dracula told him. "She is unimaginably immature. I thought the chance to handle her own needs might push her to finally grow up."

Boese nodded to himself. He took his phone out of his breast pocket and set it carefully on the table, then walked out of the kitchen.

Oh ho. Whatever was about to come out of the man's mouth was bound to be fascinating.

Boese made his way to Dracula's study, and once they were both inside, Dracula shut the door.

"Took you long enough to figure out how to kill that thing."

"I seem to recall I took the draugr down singlehandedly once you stopped hounding me. But, Director, you didn't come sneaking up here to snipe privately at me about my supposed ineffectiveness cleaning this city's messes. Shake off your habits for a moment and tell me why you've actually come."

Boese downed the rest of the *țuica* and set the cup on the desk.

"Something stinks," he said.

"Something?"

"I'm not getting info. Or it gets to me too late. Something's gunking up the gears."

"In your ridiculous organization?"

Boese glared at him. "We serve the public at large. Unlike you."

Dracula decided to ignore this jibe. "Why do you think something is wrong in your organization?"

"I've—we've got to try to stomp out all these tweets and videos and so forth. People sharing theories and images. They bring them back as soon as we get them yanked."

"Well, Director, I suppose that is an oversight on your part. The technology you rely so heavily on to make you effective will be the very thing which unmakes you." Boese glowered, but Dracula went on, "You are at war with the very nature of a thing. Your modern culture has stolen away men's sense of wonder, awe, purpose, and community. People crave more than new phones and shoes. Deprived of all purpose, they will turn to anything at all which provides the meagerest 'more.' Think on our friend Mr. Thorirsson. Besides that, as much as your organization can make clandestine use of the cameras in every person's phone to find unusual things, that same technology also makes secrecy impossible. Anyone can talk to anyone, at any time, in any location. They can share images and videos, as you pointed out. You are racing yourself. With increasing tyranny, you might be able to stop some of the news spreading, but until or unless you are willing to kill every single man, woman, and child who lives, you will never stop monsters. Think on your own experience."

Boese glared harder. He did not touch the scars notching into his ear, but Dracula had heard Special Services agents talking about how he had gotten them.

"We'll see about all that," Boese said. "We made quite a lot of stuff extinct. Some of your pets here are the last of their kind."

"You merely exchanged old threats for new ones of your own making," Dracula said. "Yes, many creatures are extinct, but you've infestations of different species which are far more numerous and problematic than their predecessors. And I suspect that there is no monster so extinct that it could not revive if the environment became conducive to it again. Think of Mr. Thorirsson. But this is truly why you've come? To complain that your organization can't stop people from talking?"

"Obviously not," Boese snapped. "Look, when I say there's something gunking up the gears, I'm talking internally. A breakdown in communication, for one. It feels…" Boese rubbed his bald scalp. "It feels like someone's intentionally making my job harder."

"From within your organization?"

"Yep."

That *was* interesting.

"Internal politics?"

"Maybe. Feels more… feels more like deliberate obstruction than just some bureaucrat trying to make someone he doesn't like look bad."

"Any theories as to who might do that, or why?"

Boese shook his head.

Dracula's Match

"And this, perhaps, is why you gave me the chance to take care of your draugr problem my own way?" Dracula said. "It must be a serious problem indeed if you trusted me to have free rein. Have you observed this obstruction for some time?"

"It was subtle before. I chalked it up to politics, or incompetence. But it dialed up with this draugr disaster."

Dracula marveled. This was a revelation indeed. The organization's days were numbered—he had realized that some time ago, but he had not expected there might be intentional interference from the inside. That did beg the question of who, and why?

"Your people never found who was the mastermind behind the outbreak of vampirism in April?" he asked. Boese shook his head.

"That was what got my attention," Boese said. "All our tech guys couldn't come up with anything. Couldn't figure out who that dentist talked to. All we got was his description of that woman."

"And you still have no idea who she was?"

"No report has reached *me*. Ophois has been stonewalling more than usual, too. Something stinks."

"And you came to talk to me about it." Dracula nodded towards the kitchen. "And you wanted to talk to me unheard?"

"Look: I don't like you. You're a dinosaur. In every meaning of that word: a cold-blooded terror lizard from a million years ago who can kill as easy as walking."

"Why, Director, you'll make me blush if you go on like that."

"But I don't have a lot of resources if I can't trust my own people," Boese said. "We can't afford to let something like that draugr rampage again if there's rats in my own attic. I need you…" Boese gritted his teeth, "to step up. I don't like you, but I've seen your record. You can take down some pretty heavyweight beasts."

"Ah, so in exchange for more freedom, you wish me to carry more of your organization's weight?" Dracula nodded. "Very well."

Boese eyed him. "Don't get too comfortable. I'm fine letting you kill things that go bump in the night, but I've got misgivings about your little sanctuary up here."

"Why, Director? What sort of dangers do you think a handful of satyrs poses to the US government?"

"Or a little village of elves? You tell me."

"I shall certainly do my utmost to deal with supernatural threats. I expect I shall be more effective without your organization's… oversight."

"Fine. But you've got to report to me about any crazy ideas you have about dealing with any future bogeymen."

"Of course, Director."

"Fine. Fine." Boese nodded to himself. He pointed at Dracula. "I mean it."

"Of course you do."

Boese let himself out of the study and stalked to the kitchen to retrieve his phone. "You keep in line," he told Dracula as he made his way towards the door. He left without another word.

Quite the development.

The car that Dracula had loaned to Cammy wouldn't start. She had no idea what to do. Ignoring the fact that she'd have to get to work since she was closing today, what would her host do if she'd broken his car?

Out of desperation, she called Malcolm.

"Sorry to bother you, but Vlad let me use one of his cars and I can't get it to work. Are you able to come by and see what the problem is?"

"Yeah, sure," he answered.

Cammy waited by the car and called the Mindful Bean to let them know she'd be late. As soon as she hung up the phone, Siri came sauntering through the parking lot. She looked over the car.

"His Majesty did not come vith you?" Siri noted.

"Not today."

Siri walked to the front of the car and stared at it.

"How do these things vork?" she asked.

"I don't know. I'm not a car person," Cammy said. Siri knelt down and peered under the car, and looked at the wheels. "I don't think you should touch it," Cammy told her. "If anything happens to this car..."

"I see," Siri said. She backed off, to Cammy's relief. Siri didn't leave, though.

"How are you?" Cammy asked.

"Perfectly vell."

"He's not coming to check his car, if that's why you're hanging around for."

Siri looked at her. So that *was* what she was hanging around for.

"Look, it's not my business or anything, but stalking someone isn't a great way to win them over," Cammy told her. Siri kept on looking at her. "I mean, I think he knows you're interested. But I don't think he's interested in you."

"Vhat can I do to make him desire me?"

"I don't think it works like that," Cammy told her. "You can't *make* someone love you."

Siri's lips pressed together angrily. "The more I hear of it, the less glorious love sounds," she said.

"I mean..." Cammy considered her words. It might be that her advice would set Siri on a path that would affect her whole future, "I'm not sure I can speak from experience, but... I mean, love is the one thing everyone wants more than anything. It's *the* dream, right? And that's why people search their whole lives for it." Cammy felt uncomfortable. She didn't put a lot of value on sentiment. She and Heather had joked that they'd never get married or have kids. Their family lives hadn't exactly sold either of them on the idea of how "great" marriage was. Maybe they were lucky because neither of their parents got divorced, like Brian's mom had, but there wasn't any such thing as the perfect family or the perfect relationship. She didn't want to get married or have kids. She just *knew* she'd mess all that up. Somehow, she'd turn into her mother. She couldn't talk all lofty about this, not like her host could. Though she didn't know how he slept at night—or in the day, or whenever or *if* he ever slept—after the things he'd done.

"A relationship has to have a foundation to work," Cammy said. She'd heard that much. "You have to have something in common."

"But that is vhy I prefer him. He knows vhat I am, knows about the vorld. Other men, modern men, they don't know. They cannot understand."

"There's gotta be more than just Vlad in the whole world."

Siri shrugged.

Dracula's Match

Malcolm's cherry red car pulled up alongside, and he stepped out.

"You made a new friend," he observed dryly, nodding at Siri. He wore a bandage around his throat, and there were stitches above one of his eyebrows. He limped a little.

"You ok?" Cammy asked. Malcolm eyed her.

"Yeah. Never better. Especially now that that draugr's gone." He looked Siri up and down. "Thanks for distracting me that time. Things could have gone... badly otherwise."

Siri nodded.

"But..." Cammy gestured at the bandages.

"This isn't even the whole of it," he told her. He was wearing a jacket and jeans, so Cammy couldn't see anything else. "Pop the hood, willya?"

She obliged him, while Siri looked on. The huldra craned her neck to see what Malcolm did.

"Hey," Cammy said to her. "Do you know how to get fake IDs?"

"No," Siri answered.

"But... how do you get... how do you earn money or get around or do anything?"

"Many people vill give money if you only ask," Siri answered with a shrug. Cammy considered her clothes. They *were* a little stained. Maybe people thought she was homeless?

"Why do you ask?" Malcolm demanded, leaning around the hood to look at Cammy.

"For the elf kids Vlad sicced on me. I thought they ought to go to school."

"You'd need more than IDs for that," Malcolm said. "Vaccination records, school records, parental records."

"How do you know?" Cammy asked.

"Ophois provides that sort of thing to monsters who want to make it in the human world."

"Could you get those things for me?"

Malcolm growled something to himself.

"Yeah, maybe. You'd owe me, though. Big time. Turn 'er over."

It took Cammy a moment to figure out Malcolm meant for her to turn the key. She tried, and the car didn't roar to life. She tried twice more before Malcolm signaled she stop.

"Battery, probably," he said. "I bet it's way too old. Vlad has too many cars to keep them all up and running all the time. I don't think I've ever seen him drive this one. I can jump it, but if I do, it'll probably die again. Where are you headed?"

"I have to go to work."

"Well, I can jump start the battery, follow you to your job, then go get a battery to replace it."

"How long would it take you to get a battery?"

"Depends."

"Let me catch the bus then. They already know I'll be late, and it'll be nice to walk. I need to get used to being out and about again. Would you mind getting me when I'm done?"

"Not a problem," he said.

"Thanks. If you want, I can bring you a coffee."

Malcolm snorted. "Sure," he said.

Cammy walked away. It was about a half hour walk to the bus stop, but she wanted some time to think, and her leg had healed pretty well, though some of the deeper bruises still ached occasionally. A few gross-looking scars. She would feel self-conscious about shorts in the future. She heard Siri talking to Malcolm behind her, but couldn't make out what she was saying.

Brian had his own clothes back and was glad to be wearing them instead of a hospital robe. Except for his shirt; that had been too difficult to put on with his injuries. He wore his hoodie zipped up over his bare, bandaged skin, and sat on the hospital bed. He was waiting for the neurologist to come back with a referral to physical therapy and other follow-up appointments he'd need to make. And the prescription for pain killers. The pain in his side never stopped.

He'd texted Melissa and Akerman to let them know he was being discharged. Melissa should be by to pick him up soon. Suze at the station had texted earlier to let Brian know that Sheriff Schulz had resigned suddenly and announced he was moving to Florida. She liked gossip, but who was or wasn't sheriff didn't interest Brian right now, so he hadn't responded.

An elegant, red-haired woman knocked at the door to his room. His head was killing him, and his ribs, and his shoulder, so it took him a moment to recognize her. The smell that suddenly wafted into the room triggered his memory more than the sight of her. That odd, alluring-off-putting perfume she wore. It attracted his attention, but something repellant about her set off his instinct for danger.

"Didn't I bump into you outside that dance studio?"

The immaculate, red lips pulled into a malicious but playful smirk. "May I come in?" she asked.

"Are you going to tell me who you are ?" Brian demanded. After everything that had happened, there was no way this woman wasn't involved in *something*. Maybe the weird T-shirt and sunglasses couple, or else Dr. McCreep. Or some other group he didn't know about. Maybe Akerman would know.

"You may call me Elizabeth, if it puts you at ease."

"Not even a little bit." Brian wondered where her accent was from. Sounded almost like a stereotypical movie vampire accent.

"May I come in?"

"No. You can tell me what you're doing here and what you want. Then you can get lost."

Elizabeth let out a dramatic, very feminine sigh.

"You know a certain individual who lives just outside the city."

"I don't have the patience for games, lady. Be direct or I'm going to call someone right now to escort you away." Brian held up the call button, his thumb ready to push it.

"I apologize. You can't be feeling well, and perhaps you haven't the strength to engage in long conversation. You know the man called Vladislav Dragula?"

She pronounced the name the same way the Creep did. Brian narrowed his eyes at her.

"I would like someone who knows him to report on his movements to me," the obvious vampire woman said.

"Oh, would you."

"I would pay handsomely if you reported back to me. You also have feelings for that young woman he has at his manor? I could help you—"

Brian jumped up off the bed, sending pain firing all through his head and side.

"You get lost, and you never talk about her, *ever*. And I better not see your face again, got it?" he told her.

Obvious Vampire raised her chin a little bit. She was petite, not as small as Cammy, though.

"I can see that I have disturbed you," she said. "But think on it. I can reward you *handsomely—*"

Brian stormed towards her, and she stepped backwards into the hall. He came to the doorway and caught the door as it was swinging shut. His side screamed in protest. The vampire lady was nowhere in sight. He looked both ways. Just nurses, one guy being wheeled back to his room, and a man with a bouquet in his hand. A nurse taking a phone call. No redhead. Brian felt cold. Holding onto all the vampire-killing stuff from Dr. FBI up in the Cascades was looking like the best decision he'd ever made.

THE END

AUTHOR'S NOTES

Hello again, my dear reader. It seems you have purchased the sequel to *Dracula's Guest*, and even made it to the end of this book. I thank you for sticking with me and this silly premise this far. If you'll permit, I wish to leave a few notes about decisions made for this book.

With regards to some of the history, I don't doubt that I might once again have made errors, to my embarrassment. But quite a bit of the history presented here is highly flavored by a character's personal bias, and it serves to establish a sense of narrative. I portrayed John Hunyadi in a somewhat villainous light, given my choice of Vlad the Impaler as a protagonist, and at the most antagonistic part of their relationship. My intention, should I ever move the series into the historical fiction prequel that I hope to write, will give a far more nuanced look at this important historical figure. On that note, I have played up Dracula's anti-Ottoman position in light of modern takes on the man. In reality, it seems to me he took a more balanced view of his antagonistic neighbors than is usually represented. I have also been using the term Sublime Porte, as I thought that might resonate with Western readers, though to my knowledge this synecdoche is peculiar to English references to Turkey and the Ottoman Empire. Something that irks me at the moment is my lack of resources about the feudal political system in Romania at this time. I referenced "freeman" and "errant peasant" but more or less have a very Western version in mind, and one from at least a century before this novel. I fear that with more research I will find the use of those terms completely erroneous.

With regards to Dracula's thoughts about the Varna campaign, its fallout, and what might have been, I have decided that he admired his older brother and father a great deal (something which will be clearer if I write the prequel series). In history, Mircea was not the sole actor in the capture and attempt to kill Hunyadi after the campaign. Dracula's father, Vlad Dracul, having already advised Hunyadi against the campaign, and no doubt angry over how it imperiled his sons, was enraged enough to want the man dead. However, Vlad Dracul had a cool enough head to let Hunyadi go. Dracula was not present for the campaign himself, and must have relied on second-hand information or eye witness reports to know how it went. For the sake of the narrative I have chosen to interpret the events through Dracula's thoughts (and more specifically, according to *my* interpretation and version of the man) and color them accordingly.

Dracula's assertion of the 'two kinds' his family and descendants presented is obviously reductive, but was intended to show his views on the matter. With time, I hope to discuss more of Dracula's family and descendants.

At the start of this book, I implied that Dracula left Hunyadi to go masquerade as a peasant all alone. This is stupendously unlikely. Though his whereabouts are largely unknown (it *is* known that he turned up again about half a year later in Moldavia), I decided to reference a skill that I have found little historical support for, but which seems to be apocryphal—that he was able to disguise himself very well. Given that Sultan Murad II, who took him prisoner as a child, did indeed disguise himself in order to go about in public without being recognized, I decided it was reasonable that Dracula had emulated the skill. It also seems reasonable that he spent time amongst common people, since he apparently had a good working relationship with the men of his army later on. In reality, it is unlikely he ever went anywhere by himself, or dressed down in this way, except for a very specific purpose.

A small note on names: a number of figures in the region and time of the historical Dracula have names which can be and are rendered in different ways. One of these is Ladislas III, King of Poland and Hungary, whose name I chose to render in that way. Other spellings I have seen are Wladislas, Ladislaus and even Władysław, among others. I chose the spelling I hoped would be easiest for readers unfamiliar with names from the region, and to differentiate it from the spelling of Dracula's introduction for himself in the first book: "Wladislav Dragula," which was also chosen to be more readily recognizable to modern readers.

The history of the woman whom Dracula impaled for not finishing her husband's shirt properly will be expanded on, if and when I write the historical fiction part of the series.

With regards to the scene when Siri first addressed Trausti while he was invisible: she addressed him in Norwegian, but he speaks Icelandic. Cammy understands neither language, and she did not hear Trausti's reply. Trausti told Siri he didn't understand all of what Siri was saying. He responded in English, expecting Siri might know that language, given she was in the United States. Siri's Norwegian is older than the modern version, a dialect more readily intelligible to speakers of Faroese and Icelandic. It is not the same language, and was not an ideal choice, but Siri wished to discover what Trasuti's response might be.

In this series, English is one of the *lingua francas* of the supernatural world, given that it is a widely spoken language around the globe. It is especially used in the United States, and those creatures who intend to resettle in the US make efforts to learn it. I also did my best to incorporate small verbal cues to differentiate Siri's and Trausti's accents. Trausti cannot pronounce the "v" sound except at the end of words, for example. But as I am not very familiar with Norwegian or Icelandic, I have probably done a poor job. These cues exist to help make it clear who is talking and to remind readers that they have accents.

I tried not to go "full Stoker" in this regard, if I may gently tease the author who got me started on this whole adventure. If I have pulled a "Stoker" in this book, it is in the altered hair colors of Siri and Roar's wife Laura, though to a certain extent this was an intentional detail to reference Lucy's changing hair color in *Dracula*.

Take care, my dear reader, and perhaps I'll see you again in the next installment.

ABOUT THE AUTHOR

AMAYA TENSHI

Amaya grew up on mythology: Greek, Egyptian, Norse, and of course fairytales from Europe and Japan. She has spent years amassing a nifty little collection of fairytales and legends from as many different cultures around the world as she could find: China, Vietnam, India, Africa, and more. With interest in subjects like history, theology, folklore, philosophy, and humanity itself, she earned two BAs which have been entirely useless since graduating college.

When not reading hard to find history books or trying to decipher a rare tome in yet another language she doesn't speak, she writes, spends time training her two cats to do tricks, and taking them for walks. She also designs illustrations for an indie comic book.

Dracula's Guest

By

Amaya Tenshi

Vlad Dragulya--Vampire Hunter???

When Cammy, Seattle hipster, part-time barista and college student, survives an attack by a pack of vampires, she resolves to learn more about what is going on in the shadows of her city. What she discovers is that none other than Dracula himself is involved in vampire abatement efforts. She asks to join forces, and refuses to take "No! Absolutely not!" for an answer. So Cammy ends up moving in—minds out of the gutter about that, folks, this isn't that kind of story. The unlikely duo bring their disparate skill sets together in an effort to put down a mysterious horde of Hollywood-style vampires, and to find out where the bloodsuckers are coming from. A friendly werewolf-for-hire tags along to help out as little as possible.

Dragon Blood
by
Bruce Woods

Paulette is sent on a mission to China with the words of her mentor ringing in her ears. "A hot wind is now fanning the flames of racism in China, Paulette." Said Lady Ellen Terry. "And, like dust in a drought, it has blown up an army. They call themselves 'the boxers' society of righteous and harmonious fists,' or some variation thereof, and practice rituals that they claim bestow invulnerability and more. They are ill-armed and poorly trained but potentially numberless.

"Recently an auxiliary movement has sprung up. Reportedly consisting of young virgin women, from the ages of 12 to 18 and accounted uncommonly beautiful. They carry the name "Red Lanterns," and claim the powers of flight, fire-starting, and miraculous healing. It is these I wish you to investigate for any sign of Kindred activity.

Assassins of Alamut
by
James Boschert

An Epic Novel of Persia and Palestine in the Time of the Crusades

The Assassins of Alamut is a riveting tale, painted on the vast canvas of life in Palestine and Persia during the 12th century.

On one hand, it's a tale of the crusades—as told from the Islamic side—where Shi'a and Sunni are as intent on killing Ismaili Muslims as crusaders. In self-defense, the Ismailis develop an elite band of highly trained killers called Hashshashin, whose missions are launched from their mountain fortress of Alamut.

But it's also the story of a French boy, Talon, captured and forced into the alien world of the assassins. Forbidden love for a princess is intertwined with sinister plots and self-sacrifice, as the hero and his two companions discover treachery and then attempt to evade the ruthless assassins of Alamut who are sent to hunt them down.

It's a sweeping saga that takes you over vast snow-covered mountains, through the frozen wastes of the winter plateau, and into the fabulous cites of Hamadan, Isfahan, and the Kingdom of Jerusalem.

"A brilliant first novel, worthy of Bernard Cornwell at his best."—Tom Grundner

PENMORE PRESS
www.penmorepress.com

Penmore Press
Challenging, Intriguing, Adventurous, Historical and Imaginative

www.penmorepress.com

www.ingramcontent.com/pod-product-compliance
Lightning Source LLC
LaVergne TN
LVHW040133080526
838202LV00042B/2895